PRAISE FOR WHYTE KNIGHT

"CB Samet is a master of the craft exhibiting a great narrative style and a strong, captivating voice. I enjoyed a lot about this novel, including the well-paced, intriguing plot, the memorable characters, and the wonderful prose."

— READERS' FAVORITE REVIEWER

WHYTE KNIGHT

A DR. WHYTE ADVENTURE

CB SAMET

For Sam and Johnny

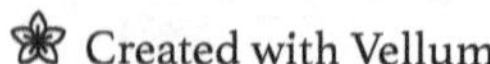 Created with Vellum

CHAPTER 1

L illian sheathed the scalpel and wiped away drops of blood.

"Dr. Whyte, the patient in bed four is in respiratory failure."

She peered up from the sutured laceration on her patient's leg in front of her. A concerned resident physician in navy scrubs stared back at her.

"What's the story, Eric?" she asked.

"She's one of the three fire victims that arrived in the last hour," he began.

A vinyl manufacturing plant had experienced an industrial fire that afternoon, and three firefighters had been transported to the emergency room after a support beam collapsed. Two had traumatic injuries.

"This one's mask was dislodged in the fall, and she suffered smoke inhalation," Eric explained.

After walking to bed 4, Lillian pulled back the curtain and surveyed the stout, young firefighter lying before her. Her pile of clothes reeked of burnt plastic. Second-degree burns peppered her forearm, but her gear appeared to have protected the rest of her. Soot smeared her face. Her breathing was mildly labored, and her oxygen levels were slightly below normal.

Lillian knew smoke inhalation could lead to precarious intubations. Once the fragile mucosal lining inside the mouth and throat was singed, the tissue would swell and obstruct visualization of the airway structures. Furthermore, the tissue would become friable, and normal instrumentation during the procedure could cause rampant, troublesome bleeding.

Although the woman was not currently in severe distress, the airway would continue to swell—putting a breathing tube in place could become a life-threatening event. The resident was right to bring the patient to her attention.

Better to insert the breathing tube now—before swelling makes it hazardous.

"Get the disposable bronchoscope. We'll have to do a videoscope intubation," Lillian explained.

While Eric eagerly gathered equipment, Lillian gave nurses instructions concerning which medication to have ready to give the patient in order to reduce as much discomfort as possible.

"Samantha," Lillian said to her patient, "you have singes on your face, and I think some of your airway may be burned as well.

Samantha nodded, eyes wide with concern.

"Your airway will continue to swell, and it may take a few days for the swelling to go down. The safest thing to do is place a breathing tube down your throat in order to breathe for you until the swelling subsides."

The firefighter gave her another wide-eyed nod, revealing both her state of fear and bravery. Lillian realized that the woman was focusing intently on breathing and controlling her urge to panic. The firefighter was probably close to Lillian's own age, mid thirties, but thicker and more muscular than her.

Placing her stethoscope on the woman's neck, Lillian listened to air moving through her windpipe. She could hear the air, but it was accompanied by a coarse, high-pitched noise.

Stridor.

Stridor was created by turbulent airflow through a narrowing airway. This sound was ominous and only slightly better than events that were sure to follow—no air movement at all.

So much for accomplishing the procedure before it became hazardous.

Eric arrived with the bronchoscope—a thin scope with a camera and light on the end for viewing the airway. A wire connected it to a small, rolling monitor where the video chip projected. He began to set it up; he slid the scope through a hollow breathing tube so it could easily be guided into place when ready. Lillian situated a mask over Samantha's face to deliver 100 percent oxygen while the nurses readied the medications.

Lillian surveyed the scene. Intravenous fluids dripped into the patient's veins. The rate of infusion could be increased in case Samantha's blood pressure dropped during the procedure. Sedation and paralyzing medications stood at the ready in labeled syringes. The respiratory therapists clasped additional equipment if needed. Medical students and other residents gathered around to watch. Eric stood at the head of the bed, ready with the bronchoscope. Lillian instructed the nurses on which medications should be given at various intervals.

Thirty seconds later, a sedated Samantha rested with eyes closed, still breathing on her own. Lillian took a step back and calmly guided everyone through their roles. The respiratory therapist breathed for the patient while Eric prepared to enter Samantha's mouth with the scope. The nurse was ready with more medication.

"As you go in, I want you to describe what you see on the screen." Although Lillian could see the screen herself, it was important her resident know the oral structures through which he was maneuvering.

The respiratory therapist moved the mask off the patient's face. Eric held the bulky end, with a flexing lever and suction button, in his left hand while holding the opposite, slender end with his right. Keeping along the back of Samantha's mouth and throat, Eric advanced the scope.

"I see the uvula," he said. "Everything looks swollen." He wasn't wrong, but Lillian felt his tone was a little too alarmist for her liking.

"Stay midline and flex the scope. You should see the tongue at the top and then the epiglottis." She kept her own voice excessively calm in hopes he would try to mimic her behavior.

She glanced at the patient's oxygen saturation level—95 percent—which was good.

"I see the epiglottis!"

The platypus-bill-shaped structure that protected the vocal cords and airway beneath encompassed most of the screen.

Calmly, she wanted to say. Instead she clasped her gloved hands together and interlaced her fingers. She understood his excitement as he was a young physician in training, but she preferred tranquility in the face of an emergency. He would learn, she knew. If he were going to effectively lead a team through a patient crisis, he would learn to feign calmness.

"Good. Now slide your scope under the epiglottis, and you will see vocal cords. Try not to bump into tissue. It will obstruct your view and cause more swelling."

Eric struggled a little while moving the scope. He readjusted his view.

"Sats are ninety percent," one of the nurses commented anxiously.

"That's okay. Eric, what do you see?" Lillian inquired.

"The epiglottis is really swollen and blocking me from getting to the vocal cords."

"And that's expected," Lillian explained. She connected a syringe to the side port of the scope and administered a diluted dose of adrenaline to coat the swollen tissue. The epinephrine would constrict the blood vessels and reduce the swelling. Samantha, sedated but not unconscious, coughed three times as the liquid spilled over the back of her throat.

"The epiglottis probably took the brunt of the heat exposure and protected the cords and trachea. Stay along the back wall and ease your way under the epiglottis when she takes her next breath."

"I see vocal cords," Eric said excitedly.

The delicate, blanched cords—the gateway to the lungs—looked like two ribbons of a violin bow forming a V on the screen.

Lillian reached up and grasped the endotracheal breathing tube. She slid it over the scope gently. While doing so, she said, "Keep watching, Eric. See the tube pass through the vocal cords."

He nodded. "It's through."

Samantha coughed several times—as anyone would do after having a hollow piece of plastic wedged into one's throat.

"Now confirm the scope is at an appropriate distance from the carina." She pointed to the video screen.

"One centimeter back," he said.

Lillian pulled the endotracheal tube back one centimeter. Watching the screen, she could see that his assessment was correct.

"There!" Eric exclaimed.

Lillian looked down at the tube. "Twenty-three centimeters at the lip."

The respiratory therapist took her cue and inflated a balloon cuff on the endotracheal tube. She began to secure it in place with a Velcro strap. Eric pulled the bronchoscope out of the tube.

Lillian instructed the nurses to give more sedation as the respiratory therapist connected Samantha to the breathing machine.

Lillian took the scope and inspected Samantha's airways. The trachea looked a bit red and inflamed. But there was no charring, so hopefully, recovery would be speedy.

The intubation had been the highlight of Lillian's shift. After the fire victims, she returned to her other patients, most of whom were victims of their own self-abuse—young drug abusers or older chronic smokers with lung disease and heart disease.

———

LILLIAN ARRIVED home at the end of her shift. Home was a three-bedroom apartment in Dunwoody. The best part of home was her wonderful husband waiting for her when she arrived. The second best part was that she was off for the next ten days.

Sean's sandy-brown hair had faint wisps of gray just over the ears. He wore jeans and an Atlanta Falcons T-shirt. He bent down to greet her, as she came through the door, with a kiss and a glass of chardonnay.

With a sparkle in his hazel eyes and a peck on her cheek, he said, "Vacation has officially commenced."

"My hero," she said with a sigh. She took the glass of wine and set down her work satchel on the cabinet in the entryway.

She walked to the balcony, enjoying the view of Atlanta. A gentle breeze ruffled some papers on the patio table. A miniature Eiffel Tower paperweight held them in place. Next to the papers rested Sean's laptop. He must have been writing and enjoying the pleasant weather on the balcony.

"How's the book coming?" she asked.

He shrugged and leaned his tall figure against the open sliding door. "I got a chapter done."

He wrote nonfiction Middle Eastern history. She enjoyed

reading his books as they contained an interlaced passion that could only be achieved by one who had lived there and understood the people and their motivations. He was working on his fourth book, which she thought was monumental given the inordinate amount of research and editing that went in to creating just one of them.

"I cleaned the place up today. Since we're leaving tomorrow, how about we do Chinese takeout tonight?" he offered.

"Sounds marvelous."

She sipped the wine, savoring the crisp flavor and hint of honey. "You remember me telling you about Murtaza?"

"Yes. You said he's really good. You're hoping they'll hire him out of residency."

Lillian nodded. "One of my patients called him a towel head," she said, still utterly disgusted. Murtaza was a Sikh from Pakistan who had trained in the United States.

Sean scowled, a response she knew he would give to people's narrow-minded racism. "What did you do?"

"I told the patient, 'Welcome to the country of mixed cultural history known as the United States of America.' I said, 'Murtaza is at the top of his class and has one of the best bedside manners that I've seen in years, so you can be treated by a phenomenal physician or you can get out of my emergency room.'"

Sean smirked.

"I'm probably going to get written up for that one or at least see a drop in my patient satisfaction scores."

She sipped her wine before changing the topic. "You see the fire on the news?"

He raised his eyebrows. "They came to you?"

Lillian nodded. Owing to patient privacy, she couldn't discuss details of her patients with him except in vague terms. "Saved a firefighter."

"Then you ended your rotation with a win," he observed.

He wrapped his hands around her from behind, and she savored his warmth and smell of spearmint.

"I also learned about a new street drug today," she added. "A drug called gravel."

"Sounds enticing," he said with distaste.

"It's a mixture of prescription pain medications, amphetamines, and who knows whatever else a drug dealer feels like cutting it with. Its users get high, get mean, and don't really care who they hurt, least of all themselves. It can do enough damage overnight to turn a healthy twenty-something into the organ dysfunction of a sixty-year-old two-pack-per-day smoking alcoholic for the rest of his or her now-shortened life."

She shook her head. "As if there aren't enough really bad drugs out there already, let's create a new one. As if life isn't short enough, let's inject something called gravel." She scoffed. "Sounds like a fun time."

Sean squeezed his arms a little tighter around her torso.

With her free hand, she placed her arm over his, still staring out over the city. He didn't say a word, but she knew he was there for support. Sean was a fixer. If there was a problem, he liked to fix it. It worked well for his previous line of work and worked well for writing books, but he couldn't fix what she encountered at work. She had to help him learn that listening and being supportive was all he needed to do to "fix" one of her rough days. He could not directly solve the trials and tribulations she faced. That was her responsibility.

She set her wineglass down on the table and turned around in his arms, feeling them slide around her waist. Smiling at him, she thought of how wonderful the next ten days with him would be.

They embraced.

Her phone chirped. She pulled it out of her back pocket and looked down at the text message from her friend Kelly.

Emailed you the guest list. Pls. review.

Sean peered at her phone. "Wedding planning?"

"Yes. I am discovering that I am woefully lacking the prerequisite skills for this."

"Anything you need to handle right now?"

"Nope." She set her phone down on the table. She was not looking at a guest list after a twelve-hour shift, not even for her best friend.

"Predinner usual?" he asked.

"Yep. Yoga then shower. I'll be done in forty minutes."

He kissed her lips softly and then pulled away. "I'll go pick up dinner."

***

"One milligram epi," Lillian instructed.

The nurse pulled the medication from the crash cart as one of the residents did CPR on a pulseless patient.

Where is her gown?

She should have been wearing a protective gown over her black scrubs so she wouldn't get contaminated while doing chest compression.

"Epi is in," the nurse said after giving the adrenaline injection into the patient's intravenous line. The lifeless body remained unchanged.

Where is my gown?

"Okay, circulate for two minutes, and we'll check a rhythm."

A resident resumed chest compressions.

They would check the rhythm again, though Lillian knew it would still be flatlined. The patient had stopped breathing, likely from his underlying lung disease. Subsequently, his heart had stopped beating. Despite all the "shocking," or defibrillating, that happened on television shows, few patients actually had a rhythm that could or should be shocked. Defibrillating flatline would result in nothing more exciting than more flatline.

The stench of antiseptic and urine filled the room.

She considered giving him a clot-buster.

Thrombolytics.

He had a relatively inactive lifestyle with many medical diseases. Perhaps he had developed a blood clot in his leg that went to his lung. Pulmonary embolism was often a culprit of cardiopulmonary arrest.

Her only hesitation was the laundry list of contraindications to the medication. She was certain he had no recent trauma or head injury. She wondered if he had had any recent surgeries. In addition, the ongoing chest compressions inflicted damage of their own. How much bleeding would he have from chest compression trauma after thrombolytics?

"Paging Dr. Whyte." A voice came through the overhead speaker.

The emergency room seemed to grow dark at the periphery.

"Two minutes," the nurse called.

Lillian felt for a pulse, but there was none. The respiratory therapist continued to breathe for the patient as the room continued to darken.

Did someone forget to pay the electric bill?

"Continue chest compressions. We'll give another epi in one minute. Call the pharmacy for thrombolytics."

"Paging Dr. Whyte."

The edges continued to darken until she was alone with the patient's monitor in flatline beneath a spotlight.

Why had they stopped CPR?

The high-pitched mechanical noise of the monitor hummed steadily.

She looked down at a small white piece of paper in her hand with red lettering on one side and Chinese characters on the other. Her fortune, she recalled, from dinner last night. She read the fortune again.

Forfeit something for the good of another.

Last night, she had taken the words lightly. She playfully promised Sean she would forfeit sleep for his benefit. Fortune fulfilled, she had considered the matter closed.

Now she stared at the words more gravely. Was there something she was supposed to give up? A sacrifice?

She didn't have many possessions—certainly nothing worthy of forfeiting save a modest retirement account. That left Sean and her career. Forfeiting Sean was off the table. Forfeiting her career in medicine wouldn't benefit anyone.

So it's a mystery.

And it's just a fortune cookie.

"Paging—"

Sean's face beside her came into focus, and she realized she had been daydreaming. He had been calling to her quietly—the voice "paging" her. The roar of the plane engine replaced the flatlining whine of the monitor.

"I'm sorry. I was dreaming about work."

"We're on a plane to Canada," he pointed out to her. "You're supposed to be fantasizing about lazy river walks and a four-star hotel."

She smiled and kissed his cheek. Marriage to Sean had exceeded her expectations. Since cutting back her hours at work, they took vacations every few months. Their life together seemed like one long honeymoon. He showed her the world and so many amazing things she had missed in all her years preparing to become, becoming, and then being a physician.

They had hiked a week in the Appalachian Mountains, scaled the heights of the Himalayas, marveled at the palaces and cathedrals of Saint Petersburg, lounged on the beaches of Copacabana, tanned on the islands of Antigua, hiked the Inca Trail to Machu

Picchu, and made passionate love wherever they traveled. Now they were embarking to Canada.

"Did you finish your itinerary?" he asked.

She looked down at the tablet in her hands. A spreadsheet filled with activities for the next five days occupied the screen. "Yes. Museums, shopping, sightseeing. You'll be able to join me for some of it?"

He nodded. "First day is the book signing. After that, I'm all yours."

He took her hand and squeezed it before turning his attention back to his writing.

"Are you going to read that leadership book you packed?" he asked without looking up from his computer.

She assumed he was avoiding the sour look he knew would be coming in his direction. She had reluctantly brought the book on the trip but wasn't sure she would actually open it. Her boss, the chief of emergency medicine, wanted her to read leadership books and take classes on leadership training.

She remained unconvinced that she wanted any leadership roles beyond the teams she orchestrated during emergencies. Sean had tried to be encouraging about expanding her horizons and perhaps mixing patient care with administration to blunt the toll that patient care took on her.

Was it the right move for her? She hadn't figured that out yet. She was certainly not one to ever be coerced into anything.

She picked up her tablet and began to read the news.

CHAPTER 2

"This article is fascinating," Lillian commented, having finished reading a magazine biography on her tablet about Georgia senator Cole Lawson. "He's quite the pacifist. He's given thirty-eight speeches around the world on antiwar politics."

Sean nodded, typing on his laptop.

"Did you know that his mother was a prominent Southern civil rights activist?" she asked.

Another nod.

"Did he really save your life in the Middle East?"

Sean turned and gazed for a moment at the magazine photograph of Cole. A handsome black man with stark-white teeth sat with an arm around his mother, a frail-appearing woman in a wheelchair.

"Well, he wasn't always a pacifist," Sean began. "His mother, who was adamantly against violence, pleaded for him not to enlist. When we were SEALs together, we were on a stealth mission to Egypt, Port Said, but we were not so stealthy. We were raiding a compound with escapees from the Iraq War who were supposed to know the location of alleged weapons of mass destruction. We set off a trip wire, and the entire place lit up with gunfire. Cole and I faced four armed men. We took down three, but one buried a knife in my shin before Cole put a bullet through his chest."

Lillian grimaced, and the scar on her arm tingled with the memory of her own knife injury. She thought back to her escape in Africa. Five years ago, she had embarked on a medical mission to Kenya. Oil thieves slaughtered the entire military camp because they thought the location of their secret stash of black gold had been compromised.

By sheer luck, she and Sean had not been at the camp when the attack occurred. However, during their attempt to flee the country, she had been kidnapped. Her subsequent escape encompassed some of the most terrifying moments of her life. One of the guards had cut her arm with a six-inch blade, causing excruciating pain. She couldn't begin to imagine the agony of a knife buried in a bone.

She remained quiet as Sean reminisced. He didn't often talk about his SEAL days, so she didn't want to interrupt and break his focus.

"Unfortunately, the attacker didn't die right away," Sean continued. "Instead, he reached for an incendiary device. The entire shed was rigged to explode. Cole hoisted me up and out we ran like a three-legged race. He could have run out without me. If he had, he wouldn't have taken tin shrapnel to his back leading to a medical discharge. Of course, he did get a Silver Star for his bravery."

Lillian smiled. "And now he is a pacifist?"

"He had a wild, rebellious youth followed by the shocking reality of war. Combine that with six months of rehabilitation for war wounds and plenty of time to reflect on his mother's poetry, speeches, and life's work, and you have a powerful pacifist."

"He's genuine," Lillian concluded.

Sean nodded. "He's remarkable and, yes, genuine."

"The article here says he's predicted to be an upcoming presidential candidate."

Sean turned his attention back to his computer. "I'd vote for him."

Lillian turned the page with a swipe of her finger on the screen and looked at the politician's family photo. In front of a massive fireplace in a log cabin, his twin girls sat in front of him, and his wife, holding a baby boy in her arms, sat to his right.

She wondered what life would be like with children. The article claimed that violence around the world was declining, yet she couldn't tell from the patients at the doorstep of her emergency room that anything had changed. She still saw gunshot wounds, stabbings, rapes, and unspeakable things done to children. She couldn't imagine having such precious things as children and living in fear of what the world might do to them.

She went on to read one of Cole Lawson's more recent speeches:

> *The Bible tells us that "there is a time for everything,*
> *and a season for every activity" under heaven. And*
> *I say, that time is now. Now "is a time to be born,"*
> *to be born into a world of love and peace. Now is*
> *"a time to die," to dye our beliefs with pastel colors*
> *of tranquility. Now is "a time to plant," to plant the*
> *seeds of faith and forgiveness. Now is "a time to*
> *uproot" the entwined layer of hatred in our souls.*
> *Now is "a time to kill," kill violence, and to heal,*
> *heal soldiers and families. Now is "a time to tear*
> *down" walls of deceit and to build foundations of*

trust. Now we weep tears of joy and laugh at the beauty around us. Now is a "time to mourn" those that have sacrificed for us and "a time to dance" to the present and future that they have created. We will scatter jagged and bitter stones and gather the smooth together. Now is "a time to embrace" peace and "a time to refrain from embracing" disdain. We will search for strength together and give up deceitfulness.

We will keep our beliefs strong and discard our fears. Now is "a time to tear" down walls of oppression and "a time to mend" relationships. Now is a time for our demons to be silent and a time for our hearts to speak—to love one another and to hate violence. Now is "a time for war" against war. Now is a time for peace.

"I'm looking forward to meeting him," Lillian said.

"He's in Montreal this week for the peacekeeping summit. It was nice of him to invite us to dinner when he found out we were going to be in town," Sean replied, typing on his computer.

"So this is a UN meeting? I didn't know they met in Canada."

"It's a subcommittee meeting of the Third Committee. They handle social, humanitarian, and cultural issues."

"How many committees are there?"

Sean thought for a moment. "The General Assembly has six committees, not counting the General Committee and Credentials Committee."

"And this is a dinner before the subcommittee meeting?"

Sean nodded. "Don't get too excited about the dinner," he said. "A room full of politicians is less than an ideal social situation."

"I'm looking forward to meeting a friend of yours," she emphasized. "I don't get to meet many of those, and you've already met all of mine."

"There aren't many to meet."

Lillian nodded. "That makes him all the more valuable. Besides," she added, "you've been to physician gatherings. All we do is commiserate about the decline of health care."

He looked up from his computer, golden flecks sparkling in his hazel eyes. "It will be a lovely dinner," he assured her.

LILLIAN WOKE in a daze with the echo of roaring jet engines and the chatter of overhead announcers ringing in her ears. The sounds faded into tranquil silence. She rolled over and looked around at the posh hotel suite. Sean had ensured they had comfortable accommodations. Sunshine streamed through an open window, casting brilliant light on an overhead chandelier. The bedroom, with its king-size bed and plush pillows, stretched out to meet a small dining room adjacent to the kitchenette. She noted fresh bagels on the table and looked around for Sean.

Stretching, she slid out of bed and grabbed a robe from the bathroom. With her luggage still in transit, she didn't have any nightgowns, so she wore one of Sean's T-shirts to bed.

On the table, she read a handwritten note on the hotel stationary:

Sent your travel clothes to the hotel laundry service. Picking up coffee and clothes for you. Be back soon. Love, Sean.

After their nonstop flight from Atlanta to Montreal, they had landed uneventfully and made their way to baggage claim, a route with which Sean seemed already familiar. Forty-five minutes into their wait at baggage claim, it became evident that Lillian's suitcase did not make it to Montreal with them. After another forty-five minutes at the courtesy counter, it was discovered that the luggage was in LaGuardia. It had evidently hitched a ride on the one-stop flight to Montreal through LaGuardia and would arrive sometime later today.

She walked to the dining table and fixed a bagel with cream cheese. Pulling her tablet from her carry-on travel bag, she scrutinized her list of activities for the day. She planned to see the Montreal Botanical Gardens, an oasis in the middle of the city; the Musee d'art contemporain de Montreal with its contemporary art; and Olympic Park, where the 1976 Olympics had been held. All that was to take place after a morning at the hotel spa, which would give her clothes time to make their arrival.

Sean would be at his book signing today, but they had made plans to meet up for dinner.

She had finished her bagel and had freshened up by the time Sean returned. As she exited the bathroom, she looked at the fruits of his shopping labor displayed on the bed.

"It's a dress," Lillian observed dryly.

Sean nodded.

It was a white summer dress with matching white cotton sandals.

"It's very pretty," she said, hesitatingly.

"Uh-huh."

She knew Sean sensed that she was unhappy with his selection. "It's just that it's a dress. It's hard to see and do everything that I want to see and do if I'm in a dress"—she explained, picking up the shoes and inspecting them—"and heeled sandals."

"Then I suggest you treat this like the vacation that it is and see and do everything at a more leisurely pace. Besides, your suitcase will be here this afternoon."

He pulled her by the knot in her robe closer to him and added,

"I want to see you in that dress at least one night on this trip, looking as amazing as always."

She ran her fingers through his thick sandy-brown hair and looked into his playful copper eyes. They weren't always so playful. When she met him six years ago, he was an undercover CIA agent with a dark past and a determined gaze. She thought he was a Swahili translator at the military camp in Kenya where she was stationed to provide medical care. He was forced to reveal his true identity when a mass murderer and oil profiteer poisoned and shot the soldiers at the camp.

She was captured, but sensing Sean was searching for her helped her summon the strength and courage to escape. She fled to Paris where he soon found her. He stayed by her side and kept her safe until her pursuers were captured or dead. He was her rescuer, lover, and confidant.

She preferred these playful eyes to the more intense ones she had known earlier in their relationship. He made the transition from field operative to teacher and writer, seeming to enjoy the slower pace. He wrote historical nonfiction about areas he had travelled to during his Navy SEAL and CIA tours of duty. Having three published books, his travels now entailed speaking events and book signings.

She recognized that not all his travels were benign, and she had her suspicions that he still did some intelligence gathering for the CIA. They had made a joke of it so that "book signing" was often code for a CIA task. She didn't investigate his travels though and accepted that if he didn't share where he was going, then it was better she not know. She trusted his judgment of the covert.

He kissed her softly, and she savored the moment.

SEAN ADMIRED Lillian's shimmering red hair. He had fallen in love with her while watching her practice the art of healing with

Swahili women and children. Every day, a passion grew within him that he thought had vanished long ago. Clever, cunning, and stubborn, she had summoned the strength to beat all odds and her own execution. Amidst saving herself, she had rescued him from his demons and the obsidian quicksand of isolation into which he had been sinking.

Marriage provided a constant discovery of their interests and the world together. They could just as easily spend three days never leaving a hotel room as they could enjoy excursions or immerse in wilderness through overnight camping. They garnered mutual respect for each other's careers, understanding that sometimes their work ran late and sometimes there were conferences when they would travel alone.

Marriage had also been a constant discovery of each other's sensual desires. Flaming passion became a smoldering, deep-rooted love. Insatiable desire transformed into the ability to perform specific tantalizing motions. He knew every inch of her amazing body and never tired of exploring her curves again and again. He never tired of hearing her breathing grow faster, more ragged. Never tired of the way she groaned or how she moved her hips in response to his touch.

He lifted her up and swung her once in the air, hearing her gasp. Gently he guided her down to the bed and ran his fingers along her neck. Her mouth was open with anticipation as he leaned over her. Passing over the mound of her breast and curve of her hip, his hand reached her thigh. He trailed his fingers up her bare skin. As she moaned with anticipation, he touched his lips to hers and lost himself in her soft skin and lilac scent.

LILLIAN LAY CONTENTEDLY in bed as Sean showered and got dressed.

"I'll be at the book signing probably until eight p.m." He slipped on his shoes.

She looked over at him and arched an eyebrow. "Book signing. Of course."

"I will be *selling and signing* books." He defended himself.

"I'm sure that's not all, but I'm content with blissful ignorance because I will be happily touring museums."

After packing his briefcase, he leaned over and kissed her one last time.

She watched as he left.

Lillian stretched in bed and looked at the time. She had one hour until her scheduled pretourism massage. She decided to spend it reading a book by the room window.

Her phone buzzed.

"Hello, Kelly," Lillian said, answering the phone.

"Hey! How is Montreal?" her bubbling, blonde friend asked.

Lillian stuck out her bottom lip. Her best friend knew she was traveling yesterday, which meant she knew she would not have seen much in Montreal by this morning. Therefore, Kelly must have had an ulterior motive for calling.

Wedding guest list, maybe?

"It's good. How is everything with you?"

Kelly sighed. "I'm ordering the invitations, but I don't know if I can match the tablecloths exactly to the invitation or the bridesmaid dresses."

"I thought everything was teal, white, and gold?"

"I'm sending you a text," she replied. "You'll see what I'm talking about."

Lillian looked down at her phone. There were three pictures of teal squares.

She put the phone on speaker.

"Um, they're all different?"

Another sigh, this one made Lillian feel like she was hardly making an effort. She wanted to be helpful, and Kelly had designated her as maid of honor. Thus far, the honor had involved squinting at various cursive fonts to select one for the invitations, looking at an array of flowers to pick ones that harmonized together, and selecting an overpriced teal dress for the bridesmaids.

Her own wedding had been simple and small. Her bouquet and aisle decorations had been white Easter lilies (naturally) and guests could wear whatever they chose. Kelly, her maid of honor, wore a pink dress, which she had explained to Lillian (in the voice of an adult speaking to a child) that the color was referred to as *French rose.*

"They're different," her friend retorted over the phone.

Lillian began to brush her hair.

"I like the one in the middle," she said. She spoke the truth—she liked all of them since they were practically identical.

"Okay," Kelly said, her tone defeated.

"If you're worried about colors clashing, can you make sure that the bridesmaids are seated at the tables with white tablecloths and the other guests are at the teal tables?"

"Okay. Okay, yes. I like that."

It sounded as though she were taking notes, writing down something.

Lillian relaxed in relief.

Crisis averted. I'll take a level-one trauma over wedding planning any day.

Kelly added, "I've posted a bunch of cake images I want you to look at and use for ideas about what mine should look like."

"Will do," Lillian assured her.

She had some measure of knowledge that the maid of honor was supposed to take the lead on some of the selection process, but Kelly thus far had been a step ahead of her. She had done most of the heavy lifting, and Lillian was relegated to support staff.

Because she was not particularly skilled in the art of decor—and apparently couldn't distinguish one shade of teal from another—she didn't mind the less pivotal role.

They said goodbyes and disconnected the call. Lillian set her phone on the small round table by the window.

She pulled back the curtain. She was excited to be in Canada. Trees peppered between buildings added a splash of fall colors—golden, crimson, and salmon-colored leaves. This was a magnificent city—home to the 1967 World Expo; home of Rufus Wainwright, who sang her favorite version of "Hallelujah"; and birthplace of William Shatner, who boldly went where no man had gone before.

CHAPTER 3

Sean finished signing his fifth book of the day. Being a writer was not a profitable career. With travel expenses, he barely broke even. His supplemental CIA income was helpful though. It was usually some form of uneventful information exchange, which made him an overpaid messenger. However, it balanced nicely against all the more hazardous activities he had done in prior years when he felt grossly underpaid while putting his life in danger.

His current duties included passing along messages from sources to the CIA and vice versa. Despite high-tech encryption, passing notes in person was still a relied-upon, most unhackable means of communication.

He liked book signings in bookstores, even if there was also an information exchange. The smell of the paper and the crinkle of spines bending open for the first time were calming to him.

Another customer set a book down in front of him. He reached for his pen and looked up with a smile. A plump Egyptian with untamed, graying hair looked down at him nervously.

"Please sign it 'To Labaris.' I like chapter eight when you discuss the October War of 1973," Labaris said mechanically.

Sean smiled and nodded casually. He was accustomed to civilians being excessively nervous when transferring classified information. He signed the book and then opened it to the back cover to look for the envelope of information. It was usually a compact disc or a USB drive. To Sean's surprise, it was empty.

The man reached into his coat, and for a moment, Sean thought he was pulling out a gun. Sean tensed. Before the man had a chance to reveal the contents of his pocket and before Sean could leap to stop him, an earthquake seemed to shake the building.

A wave of impact came from the entrance, shattering glass and tossing bookshelves in all directions. Sean dove under the table and pulled his informant with him. He patted the man's jacket down. Feeling a small, tubular structure, he was reassured it wasn't a gun.

When the commotion settled, Sean heard shouts in Arabic. He surveyed the bookstore in ruins around him and a black sports utility vehicle sitting through the front door. Men armed with AK-47s were streaming out of the vehicle. They escorted a captive out with them—a man of fifty dressed stylishly in a suit, though looking dazed. He was holding his left forearm gingerly, as though injured.

Sean swept the room with his eyes. Books, including his books, littered the floor with splinters of wood and glass. Knowing the layout of the building, as he always did with information exchanges, he looked at the northwest corner where he discreetly eyed the back exit. There was no way to make it there without being seen and shot. More importantly, there was no way to get all the innocent shoppers and Labaris to the exit without them getting shot.

The armed men corralled everyone—the store staff and

patrons, including Sean and Labaris—into the lounge of the bookstore, where they were forced to sit in a loose circle. Some of the angry Middle Eastern men loomed over them with their automatic weapons, while others barricaded the front entrance with bookshelves and tables. Sean counted four assailants loyal to a focused leader who barked orders at them. Egyptian syntax and accents.

They placed their captive from the SUV in with the other hostages on the floor. Judging by his suit, Sean guessed he was a politician or lawyer, or both.

The informant, Labaris, sat wide-eyed and panicked. His eyes darted nervously from the assailants to Sean and back to the assailants. Sean realized that Labaris was wondering if he, Sean, had something to do with creating this volatile situation.

He scowled at the nervous man and shook his head slightly, trying to discourage so much eye contact. If this commotion had anything to do with their transfer of information, Labaris staring at Sean would spotlight them both as targets of interest.

Sirens sounded outside and then subsided. The place was certainly surrounded by police. Sean realized he was in the middle of a hostage standoff. Police must have been chasing the vehicle before it crashed into the bookstore in order to have arrived so quickly.

The armed gunmen plucked a hostage from the circle, a young female customer, who screamed as they dragged her into the back office where the leader had taken residence.

Five minutes later, the young woman was returned to the circle, unharmed but shaken. They took the person next to her, a bearded and bespectacled store clerk. Sean realized that the gunmen were questioning and searching each person individually. Sean was next. This was no coincidence, he knew.

Sweat still dripped Labaris's brow.

"We'll get through this. Let me hide the information. What do you have? A flash drive?" They were out of earshot of the gunmen, but Sean kept his voice low so the other hostages would not be able to hear them either.

Labaris shook his head slowly with wide eyes. From his coat pocket, he pulled out a small metal cylinder, slightly larger than a lipstick case. He opened it and flashed a clear liquid vial.

Sean gaped at him in disbelief. "I was told you were delivering information on biomedical warfare, not biomedical warfare itself." His neck flushed with anger.

"I had to make it in the lab to prove my work," Labaris responded in a high-pitched whisper. "This is the only sample," he assured him.

Sean did not find this reassuring. "Sample of what, exactly?"

Labaris closed his jacket and fell silent as the armed guards returned the store clerk and motioned next at Sean. He complied, clutching one of his books.

Showtime.

BEFORE LILLIAN'S planned grand tour of Montreal, she had scheduled a leisurely massage at the hotel spa. She rested comfortably on a warmed table with hot stones sliding across her bare back. Leaving all thoughts of work behind, she sank into relaxation. Here there were no fluorescent lights, no emergencies, no devastated family to deliver bad news to, and no electronic medical record documentation.

She had selected a deep tissue massage with some fragrant lotion that smelled of eucalyptus. She breathed in the soothing scent. She closed her eyes, but peaceful thought was punctuated by vivid images. This was the time when most people might envision waterfalls or ocean waves or starlit skies. Emergency room physicians were not most people.

Images of the patients she had treated flashed before her—terrible traumas and terrible diseases. Head trauma from trampoline falls. Broken limbs from all-terrain vehicle wrecks. Eviscerated intestines from chainsaw accidents. Multidrug-resistant pneumonia. Systemic fungal infections. Outbreaks of meningitis.

Meningitis. That had been rough. A college campus had an outbreak of Neisseria meningitis. It was transmitted by saliva and secretions, so there was no better place to spread its metaphorical wings than a college campus with close quarters and plenty of sneezing, coughing, and kissing.

The bacteria inflamed the lining of the brain and caused confusion, neck stiffness, light sensitivity, and terrible headaches. Twelve students actually had the disease, but the ER physicians had performed a hundred lumbar punctures because every student with a hangover or caffeine-withdrawal headache showed up when word spread of the outbreak.

Lillian did more lumbar punctures that week than she had the entire year prior. It was no easy feat threading a long, narrow needle between an anxious patient's vertebrae.

Hold still, please, while I insert a sharp object into your back and try to not permanently damage any nerves.

The most cooperative patients were usually the truly sick ones. Their symptoms incapacitated them so that they pleaded for anything that would lead to diagnosis and quick recovery.

The little diplococcus bacteria could be identified under the microscope from a sample of the cerebrospinal fluid withdrawn during a lumbar puncture. Treatment was antibiotics, and recovery was usually a week or two. But this outbreak did claim one life. A young freshman suffered a rare complication of meningococcus— meningococcemia—whereby the bacteria disseminated through the bloodstream and into the adrenal glands. As the glands hemorrhaged, they malfunctioned. Malfunctioning adrenal glands in the setting of a fulminant bacterial infection incapacitated the body's ability to maintain adequate blood pressure to perfuse the body. Combined with disseminated intravascular coagulation—a clotting factor mishap where the body simultaneously could not clot in some areas and was over-clotting in others—led to complete organ failure and, finally, death.

Ten minutes ticked by in the massage suite until Lillian finally shook unpleasant images of medical disasters and death from her mind. She practiced deep breathing and meditation to clear her thoughts, something Sean had taught her when she was recovering from the psychological trauma of Kenya. It had taken her a year of daily meditation before she was really effective at it. Initially, she would either reflect on recent patients or her mind would pester her with a to-do list of activities she wasn't getting done because she was sitting and doing nothing. But it wasn't nothing. She was learning to nurture her spirit. Meditation was medicine for the soul.

She envisioned horseback riding on the Arkansas plains. Thunderous hooves stormed the pasture as she fearlessly sat astride her thoroughbred. Life had been simple pleasures then—riding, reading, plucking ripe tomatoes from the garden, eating strawberries while swinging in the hammock. She wished she had savored that childhood more; at least she could still reminisce about it.

Finally, Lillian drifted into a semihypnotic state of relaxation. Her tight muscles loosened, her breathing became more regular, and she melted into the massage table.

This must be what heaven feels like, she thought.

WHEN SEAN REACHED the bookstore's office, his escorts snatched the book from him and patted him down for weapons. They set his book and his smartphone down on the table in front of the leader.

"Sit," said the leader calmly. He had dark skin and black hair pulled back in a ponytail. He was in his midthirties, perhaps ten years younger than Sean. His features were narrow, and his dark eyes shrewd.

Sean sat in the chair across from him. He smiled sheepishly, while calculating the actions and odds of success of an offense.

The leader seemed to be the cleverest and quickest. There were two armed guards, but the space was too tight for wielding an AK-47. Sean surmised they would not have enough confidence to hit him and not their comrades.

His mind automatically began calculating a route to freedom.

Book to lead terrorist's face for distraction.

Three paces back to elbow gunman A in the nose. As he clutches at broken nose, confiscate holstered gun.

Two shots to chest of lead terrorist. Whirl. Two shots to gunman B. Finish with one shot to gunman A before he recovers enough to use his machine gun.

A standard Glock has fifteen rounds. That leaves ten rounds for the other two thugs. Complicating factors—unknown presence of other weapons and the proximity of unarmed civilian hostages.

"I am Khait," the leader said calmly.

Gladiator. Sean recalled the meaning of the name.

"I'm Sean Dean," he offered, pointing to his book on the table. He tried to make himself look small in the office chair.

Khait looked at the book and the author name. He flipped through a few pages as though to confirm the book was indeed a book. He turned it over to the back cover and examined the author picture. He compared its likeness to Sean.

Seemingly convinced, he leaned back in his chair. He was likely contemplating the odds of an American book signing taking place at the same bookstore where his intel had told him a transaction of biomedical warfare was transpiring. He was probably also feeling reluctant to face unwanted repercussions of torturing an American citizen for information. He turned to a laptop on the desk and began typing, then clicking, then scrolling.

"You're an author, and you're in this bookstore today?" he asked calmly.

Sean nodded. "I'm doing a book signing," he explained, making an effort to swallow visibly.

The man was no doubt searching Sean's identity.

Fortunately, the CIA spares no expense on identities.

Khait would likely find Sean Dean's other books, dutifully for sale online with all the major retailers. He also had an author website and about a thousand ratings online. Unless he had access to classified databases, he would not find Sean Jennings, CIA operative.

"Unlucky for you," Khait said.

With a nod of his head, Khait motioned for his men to take Sean out of the office. They returned him to the hostage circle.

If Labaris possessed an ounce of training, if he had not been an inexperienced civilian, the sample in the vial could have been traded without notice as Sean sat and Labaris rose. But no such trade took place, and Sean could do nothing but watch as Labaris and the vial of mysterious substance tucked in his coat disappeared into the office with Khait.

Sean closed his eyes, contemplating a multitude of escape possibilities, none of which fared well for the other hostages. No offensive strategy lacked casualties. For now, he quelled his urge to strike, hoping to soon find a more opportune moment with less risk.

There was shouting, and the inevitable gunshot that Sean had feared.

Chekhov's gun. Combine this axiom with terrorists and a

biochemist, and someone was bound to get shot in a relatively short amount of time.

Labaris was dragged out of the room and dropped back to the circle. Despite hostages screaming, the men resumed taking each person one at a time to the back room.

Sean inched over to the wounded man. Blood soaked through his shirt.

"They took it," Labaris sobbed.

"What was *it*?" Sean demanded in a harsh whisper, applying pressure over the gunshot wound to the man's chest.

Labaris grunted in obvious pain.

"A genetically altered, highly virulent form of Creutzfeldt-Jakob disease encased in a viral exoskeleton."

"What does any of that mean?" He had picked up on the word viral, as in virus, but that was all.

Labaris sighed. "Creutzfeldt-Jakob is a prion disease that crosses the blood-brain barrier and causes severe, rapid encephalopathy and death. There are several different forms, but you have probably heard of it as *mad cow disease.*"

"You thought it was a good idea to bottle *mad cow disease*?"

"I have been under duress, and I asked your country for help."

He winced, causing Sean to ease the pressure he applied to the wound.

"They took your mad cow disease?" Sean shot a glance at the office where Khait was.

Nodding, Labaris said, "Mine is one form of Creutzfeldt-Jakob. It is transmitted by ingestion or injection. It is designed for targeted assassination."

Sean did not find this reassuring. Targeted assassination rather than a widespread epidemic could be almost as devastating.

"Is there an antidote?"

"It is not a *poison*," Labaris fired back with an incredulous tone, followed by another grimace of pain. "It is a prion disease."

Evidently seeing that this not did help Sean's understanding, he attempted to clarify. "A prion is a rogue protein that causes an infinite reproduction of itself. There's no antidote or antiviral or antibiotic."

No cure?

Labaris sighed and added, "There is only one flaw."

"That sounds encouraging."

"One is either susceptible to it or not. We don't know why some people's proteins misform into a deadly disease and others are unaffected. There is no way to predict without genetic testing who will or will not be affected."

"So it is a colorless—no doubt, odorless—protein, gift-wrapped in a viral box and shipped with a bow to the brain where it causes irreversible damage and death?"

"Yes." Labaris seemed pleased that Sean understood the enormity of his work.

"And you brought it here. And now it is in the possession of terrorists."

Labaris's grin faded as he meekly shrugged. With pursed lips, he blew out in a slow huff.

Sean rubbed his face and pinched the bridge of his nose in utter disbelief.

CHAPTER 4

Thirty minutes into her massage, Lillian heard the faint buzz of her phone under her piled-up robe on the chair beside the wall.

Why didn't I leave that thing in my room?

Choosing to ignore it, she didn't budge and continued to enjoy the skilled handiwork of the massage.

It buzzed again. And again. It seemed like three separate calls. Kelly and her cakes could wait.

Moments later, someone burst in carrying a cordless phone. Lillian jolted, and the small woman motioned that the phone call was for her.

Are you kidding me?

Pulling the sheets around her, she sat up and reached for the phone.

"Hello?"

"You don't take my call anymore, Dr. Whyte?" said a man in a distinctive, flat baritone.

Lillian's throat constricted. "What's happened?"

William Austin, assistant deputy director of the CIA, did not casually phone the wives of his operatives. She had met him at her post-Kenya debriefing in the unfriendly offices at Langley. He had no sense of humor, and his attempt at it now was just absurd.

She reached for her robe, keeping the phone to her ear.

"There is a hostage situation at the bookstore where Sean is," he said.

"Meaning Sean is a hostage or the hostage taker?"

It wasn't an unreasonable question. Sean was unwaveringly patriotic. If taking hostages somehow served to protect Americans, then he would do it—for example, hold a room full of people hostage until he identified who the spy was. Yet he was so thorough and meticulous that he was more likely to know everyone in the room before entering it.

Austin answered reluctantly, "He is one of the hostages."

She could hear her heart pounding in her ears.

Sean is a hostage.

It meant he was alive.

Alive is good.

"What's the situation?" She wanted more details.

Who was taking hostages and why? Was anyone injured? What was being done to rescue them? Her greatest fear was that Austin would clam up and claim that she didn't have clearance to know more.

"I will give you details, and we need your help. I can't talk freely over the phone. Be dressed and out front for pickup in five minutes." He hung up the phone.

She finished tying the robe and left for her hotel room.

My help?

Reaching her room, she swiped the key in and out of the key reader and entered. The white dress Sean had bought lay fanned out on the chair—the only clothing currently available to her. The clothes she had worn during travel were still being laundered.

Unbelievable.

She slipped the dress and sandals on, grabbed her purse and phone, and headed to the hotel lobby.

Out front, a black sedan with an American driver dressed in military blues idled. She slid into the back seat, surprised and alarmed to see Austin seated in the car beside her. She strapped her seatbelt on and then drummed her fingers nervously on her purse. The car pulled out of the hotel and headed down Boulevard Dorchester.

She turned and looked at Austin. "What's going on?" she demanded.

The fact that Austin was already in Montreal meant that something was high stakes from the beginning. No simple book signing.

Austin explained, "At 12:23 Eastern Standard Time, Omar Jabal, the Egyptian ambassador to the US was taken hostage by Al Tamsah Alfaraeina, a radical group of nationalists that have been allowed to fester in the current political strife in Egypt. Instead of making it back to one of their hideouts, they were headed off by Canadian police and crashed into the bookstore where Sean is."

She narrowed her eyes. "That can't be a coincidence."

Austin hesitated and seemed annoyed at her interruption.

She sighed. "I am intelligent enough to know that many of Sean's book signings are more than just book signings. I also know you being in Montreal is not a coincidence. Just tell me what's going on."

"We don't have a connection to the hostage taking, but Sean is there to courier confidential information."

"What information?"

"I can't tell you that."

"Dammit, Bill. Then why am I here?"

He rubbed at his elbow, and she knew it was his psoriasis bothering him beneath his sports coat. It always flared under stress.

He sniffed the air slowly. "Eucalyptus?"

"Massage oil," she grumbled.

He nodded.

"We—the CIA—cannot be involved in this incident. Neither Al Tamsah Alfaraeina nor the Canadian government nor the Egyptian government can know that we have classified information within that bookstore. The information was being transferred when the terrorists crashed into it."

He added, "The hostage takers are asking for a physician to treat an injured hostage." He flicked his wrist and held his hand up briefly. "Before you ask, I don't know if it's Sean or not."

Lillian felt a rising frustration. "First of all, how could the Al Tamahaw-something not know about the exchange? Secondly, you want me to be the physician to go in there? I'm not even trained for that kind of thing. Don't you have someone who's not a civilian for that?"

Despite her protests, she desperately wanted to be the one to go in and make sure that Sean was not injured.

"Al Tamsah Alfaraeina—the Crocodile Pharaohs," he corrected her, speaking more deliberately. "We have doctors and field medics, yes. The problem is that this is an intelligent, well-funded organization specifically requesting a civilian doctor. They will have the means to check anyone we send. I don't have time to have my team put together a fake physician identity and pull in somebody outside US soil. They'll know if we're stalling. You're here, your background is easily confirmed, and they cannot connect you to Sean's pen name."

And the CIA moves its pawns as it pleases.

Austin continued, weariness seeping into his voice, "It isn't my preference to send a civilian. It isn't my preference to send you, Dr. Whyte, into danger. Sean will never forgive me for putting you in this situation. You're my only chance to get eyes and ears in there. This is not an order. You can say no."

She studied his face. Time and work had aged him considerably since her last encounter with him at CIA headquarters after her escape from Kenya six years ago. There was a raspy edge to his voice that was new. He was conflicted, she realized. His rational, ambitious side wanted—needed—her to go, but emotionally, part of him was hoping she would say no.

"I'll go."

Of course she would go. Her husband was a hostage, and he could be bleeding and dying this instant. She would go, and Austin knew she would, which was why the car had already been driving her to her doom before she even consented.

Lillian gazed out the car window as Austin dialed a number on his smartphone.

"I have IT updating your profiles on various social media. How do you not have a Facebook account by the way?" He shook his head as he put the phone up to his ear.

She turned to him. "I—" she started to say, but his call was answered, and he began talking into the phone.

Because I actually call the people in my life I care about, she finished in her head.

It certainly was not because she only had a few friends and one living relative.

"We're en route. Prep the bag," he commanded. Then he added, "Yes." Then he pressed the End button on his phone.

"Do you have something more appropriate I can change into?" she asked Austin.

He looked up and down at her white dress and sandals. "No. You're more believable as a civilian doctor dressed as you are."

She glared at him but said nothing.

Then she thought about what he said—Egyptian terrorists. History was not one of her strong suits; however, she had read all of Sean's books, which were based on his most experienced subject—the Middle East.

By 1945, Egypt possessed a pseudoindependence—meaning

British troops still occupied parts of their territory under treaty, and a corrupt monarch, King Farouk, controlled the rest. King Farouk was known for his vast riches and spending sprees. Because of his selfish disregard for his people, his own military plotted a coup. The Society of Free Officers, a group of about one hundred followers led by war hero Colonel Gamal Abdel Nasser, seized control in 1952 and exiled Farouk. It was a perilous exile whereby he took his yacht, his family, and sixty-six trunks of riches with him.

This ended the 140-year-old Turkish dynasty and put Egyptians back in control of Egypt. The Free Officers became the Revolutionary Command Council and proclaimed Egypt a republic and later reclaimed the Suez Canal zone from British control. Though Nasser ended the monarchy, he proceeded to rule as a king.

Three years after the coup, Israeli forces attacked the Gaza Strip. Due to poor Western relations, Nasser struck a deal with the communist Soviet Union under Khrushchev for fighter aircraft. Soon after, he developed political ties with communist China, making him even more hostile in European and American eyes.

Nasser nationalized the Suez Canal Company, which had been owned by British and French shareholders and was functioning as a massive pipeline of oil transport and commodity trading. Britain retaliated with force. The short-lived campaign promptly ended when Nasser sank ships and completely blocked the canal. He was able to reclaim the canal zone from Britain.

However, over the next ten years, Nasser's plans for an Arab socialist revolution had dismal results. Subsequently, in 1967, he lost the Sinai oil fields, and the Suez Canal was closed after the Six-Day War against Israel. In 1970, he died of a heart attack.

Nasser's predecessor, Anwar al-Sadat, opened the door to the Western economy. It was not until after the October War to regain the Sinai Peninsula that he achieved peace with Israel. These actions were heavily criticized within his country, and he reacted with repressive rule. In 1981, he was assassinated by a radical Islamic group.

Egypt only traded one tyrant for another. Hosni Mubarak succeeded Sadat and ruled oppressively under emergency law. The next several decades continued to be fraught with violence. In the 1990s, violence usually emanated from Egypt's Islamic insurgents— veterans from the war in Afghanistan. Bombings were a favored tool, and they often targeted public buildings, banks, theaters, and Western bookstores. Tourists were targets of brutality and murder.

Seemingly annually since 2004, Egypt was battered by terrorist bombings with a dizzying array of factions claiming credit for each—Al-Gama'a al-Islamiyya, Talaa'al al-Fateh Vanguards of Conquest), Mujahideen of Egypt, Abdullah Azzam Brigades, Jama'at al-Tawhid wal-Jihad (Monotheism and Jihadism), and Hezbollah (based in Lebanon).

It was not surprising that another terrorist group, Al Tamsah Alfaraeina, had emerged.

Lillian tried to sound out the words in her head. Although she didn't know what their agenda was, no good could come of kidnapping an ambassador and stealing secrets.

"These Crocodiles have an end game?" she asked.

He looked at her and then out the window. "The less you know, the better."

"Hah." She laughed shortly and bitterly.

He looked back at her incredulously.

She smirked. She guessed Austin was high enough in the agency hierarchy that he was unaccustomed to receiving bitter outbursts as a response to anything he said.

She retorted, "In my experience, the more I know, the better, so I'm not sure if you don't want to tell me or you just plain don't know."

He sighed. "I am not going to tell you, Dr. Whyte, because you need to walk into that bookstore as an ignorant civilian and not as the knowledgeable wife of a former CIA agent."

"Former or part-time?" she asked just to be antagonistic.

Austin shook his head with pursed lips and looked back out the window.

They rode to an abandoned building off of Rue Berri. When the car parked, they walked inside the warehouse.

Lillian gawked at a miniature command center up and running inside the run-down warehouse. Frantic agents anxiously typed on computers, and a large central screen flashed images of suspicious-looking militants, maps of the city of Montreal, and cameras from various viewpoints of the city. In one particularly eye-catching video feed, a tall gray building loomed over a black sports utility vehicle parked through its front entrance. Canadian police were racing around in a nonproductive flurry, reminding her of the zigzagging, clucking hens on the farm where she was raised.

She followed Austin to a nearby table. He opened a box, then pulled out a smaller box, and ultimately withdrew an emerald-cut diamond ring.

Lillian looked at her own wedding ring. Then she stared at Austin with an arched eyebrow.

"You know, you and I are never going to happen," Lillian said.

"Funny," he replied without a trace of amusement.

"This ring contains a beacon," he explained. "Twist the diamond, and we get a distress signal and your location."

"And then?" she asked.

"Then we send in the cavalry."

"My own cavalry?" she questioned with excessive feminine flare.

"Do not cry wolf."

She looked at the ring carefully. "Why my location? I'm going to be in the bookstore, right?"

He looked at her and blinked. Then in a slow, bland tone, as though speaking plainly to a child, he explained, "You will be dropped off at the bookstore and then you will get them to let you leave with the injured person into the ambulance. Since this is a hostage situation, Dr. Whyte, any number of things can go awry. We at the CIA do not take chances. So"—he held up the ring—"distress signal—location—cavalry. Got it?"

She took off her real ring and slipped on the beacon. She put her diamond ring into her purse in a pocket beside her phone and handed the entire contents to Austin.

"If you lose my real wedding and engagement ring, you will have to answer to Sean."

He kept his face flat, but there was no mistaking a slight nervous bob of his Adam's apple, which gave Lillian a glint of satisfaction.

Her phone rang. Austin pulled it out of the side pocket and handed it back to her.

Kelly.

I haven't looked at the cakes.

Reluctantly, she sent it to voicemail. Lillian didn't have time to discuss Kelly's wedding plans. She would have to call her back later.

If I'm alive to call her back later.

Austin turned and led her to a different table to a young man in blue jeans with a buzz cut. The young man stood before a table with a military medic bag.

He introduced himself in a thick Southern accent. "Sixty-Eight Whiskey, ma'am. US Army health-care specialist, also known as a combat medic."

"How'd they find you in Montreal?" Lillian asked.

"I was on leave," the young man explained.

"You and me both."

He pointed to the black bag on the table in front of her. For someone on vacation, his brown hair stood at attention, an impeccable military cut that accentuated his clean-shaven jaw.

"This is our standard Unit One pack." He pointed to different compartments as he spoke rapidly. "Standard IV bags, tubing, and catheters—IV and IO. Tourniquets, trauma bandages, bulky dressings. Airway kit including combitube, crich kit, and chest seal. Shears, tape, gauze, gloves, and cleaning swabs. Stethoscope, blood pressure cuff, and pulse ox. For meds, we carry morphine, naloxone, EpiPen, and some snivel OTC meds. I was requested to add a tranquilizer. So in with your medications is a tranquilizer. It is labeled 'penicillin.'" He leaned forward. "It is not penicillin."

"Got it. Tranquilizer." She nodded.

She finished familiarizing herself with the bag.

"All set?" Austin asked.

Lillian nodded.

"I have spoken with Canadian Intelligence and informed them I have someone to send in so they can spare their people. I've arranged for you to be on the ambulance that's going."

"They allowed that?"

Wishing she had thought to restrain her hair in a ponytail, Lillian brushed an unruly strand of red hair out of her face.

Austin escorted her to an agency car in a row of four agency cars. Sixty-Eight Whiskey followed them, carrying the medic bag for her.

"It took some convincing, but I explained that Omar Jabal is an Egyptian ambassador to the United States. He is our responsibility. I also reminded them of the upcoming UN subcommittee meeting," Austin explained.

Lillian stared at him, not understanding the connection.

Austin bared his teeth in a somewhat sinister smile. "The

United States foots 22 percent of the bill for the United Nations—more than any other country."

"Oh. What percent of the UN budget does Canada fund?"

"Three."

Now she understood. The US held more political and financial leverage in this situation.

He added, "The car will take you to a meeting spot with the ambulance. The ambulance will drop you in front of the bookstore."

"One last thing, Dr. Whyte," Austin said, his voice oddly softer. "As best as you can under the circumstances into which you have agreed to help, please be alert to any details you can absorb—the perpetrators, the hostages, the weapons, et cetera."

She took a deep breath, nodded once briskly, and entered the car.

CHAPTER 5

Lillian rode in the passenger side of the ambulance en route to the bookstore. The emergency truck jostled down bumpy, narrow roads. She neither had Austin to harass as a distraction nor Sean to reassure her. She had only silence and the memories stirred by the noxious diesel fumes of the ambulance.

She hadn't ridden in an ambulance in over ten years. As part of an emergency medicine rotation during medical school, she had been assigned to two days in the field with a paramedic and a basic emergency medical technician. They were a lively pair. One was fat and balding and in his late forties, Herb. The other was scrawny and in his twenties, Ken. They both swore like sailors and the oldest one dipped snuff.

By the end of her second day, she wondered where the real emergencies were. Although they had driven with lights and sirens to many different calls, few of them were actual emergencies. They had responded to several fender benders, but no gruesome traumas. Many of the sick calls seemed more like just simple transports. People felt ill and didn't have a ride to the emergency room, so they hitched one with the ambulance. Ken even described himself as a glorified taxi driver, explaining how it was an expensive ride, but it wasn't like the patient was footing the bill. Few patients could afford that kind of ride, and so the company didn't really expect them to pay. Instead, they relied on county funds.

The last call of the day came—a domestic abuse case. Lillian cringed at the thought of going to a home with active violence. The police were already on the scene by the time the ambulance arrived. They approached slowly, without lights and sirens to announce their presence. Lillian nervously sat in the back, waiting until they came to a halt. She could hear Ken blaring Maroon 5 on his radio in the front of the ambulance.

After they parked, she exited out the back of the ambulance as Ken and Herb unloaded the stretcher. She carried a large blue medic bag.

"F—— me," Herb pseudoswore as he looked at the three-story tall apartment complex. "Tell me it's not on the third floor."

It wasn't. They rolled the stretcher to apartment 48A on the bottom floor of the complex. The door was already open, and just outside was a policeman speaking with a man sitting on the outdoor stairs. Looking destitute, he held his head in his hands. Dried blood was streaked down the side of his face and his arm. As they walked past the injured man in ragged blue jeans, she caught the scent of beer mixed with body odor.

"Inside," the policeman said to Herb.

Once inside, a policewoman nodded a greeting as Herb, Ken, and Lillian entered. She stood with her hands on a robust amount of equipment about her hips and looked at the odd threesome: Herb, sweating profusely even though they hadn't had to climb stairs; Ken, scrawny and pushing the stretcher; and Lillian, a young, wide-eyed medical student with fiery red hair.

The smell of tobacco smoke filled the room.

Menthols, Lillian thought.

"She's over there," said the policewoman, nodding her head in the direction of a lounge chair in the living room.

Although the small apartment was dimly lit, it revealed evidence of a struggle. Vases and picture frames were knocked askew. A thin woman reclined in a lounge chair with a quilt over her lap. Her pale face twisted in discomfort. Lillian quickly scanned her visible face, arms, and hands without seeing obvious bruises, cuts, or scrapes.

"This love has taken its toll . . ." The Maroon 5 song still played in Lillian's head.

"You're up," Herb said to Lillian.

She approached the woman in the chair and asked permission to take her vital signs. The disheveled brunette consented through mascara-smeared eyes. Her pulse and blood pressure were a little high, as expected with a domestic dispute. Lillian proceeded to ask a series of standard questions about pain and discomfort from head to toe. The woman's main complaint was abdominal pain.

"How long have you been having stomach pain?" Lillian asked.

The woman snorted. "Nine months."

Lillian hesitated and looked carefully at the woman. As she slowly pulled down the quilt from on top of the woman's lap, she swallowed almost audibly. A gravid abdomen protruded.

"Here comes another one," she said with a grimace, then began breathing in and out in short, shallow breaths.

"Herb," Lillian called, her voice a little bit too high-pitched and a little too stressed to be considered professional.

Herb had been distractedly chatting with the police and said, "Uh-huh?"

"Herb, she's pregnant. I think she's in labor."

"Shit!" he exclaimed, spitting a wad of snuff into a paper cup he was holding. "Ken, grab the stretcher!" he barked.

With an uncanny mixture of delicacy and haste, they hoisted the pregnant woman onto the stretcher and buckled the straps. Lillian extended her stethoscope, still trying to finish her physical exam. They started rolling the stretcher outside of the apartment toward the ambulance before Lillian had a chance to listen to her heart. With the practiced perfection of working together for years, the men silently loaded her in the ambulance. Herb popped into the front seat to drive.

Lillian hopped in the back and closed the doors behind her. Before she was seated, Herb was strapped in and backing the ambulance out of the apartment building parking lot.

With lights and sirens ablaze, they sped to the nearest hospital. Another contraction hit, and the woman began moaning loudly. Between the smell of Herb's sweat and snuff, the hot back of the ambulance, and the woman's moans, Lillian was beginning to feel nauseated.

"What if she delivers?" she asked.

"Not in the back of my ambulance," Herb declared from the driver's seat.

Lillian looked at him appalled.

"Don't listen to him," Ken assured. "He just doesn't want to clean up amniotic fluid from the back of his bus."

Then he leaned in closer to the woman and whispered, "But if you are able to wait till we get to the emergency room, they can give you some pain medicine."

Ken set to work starting an intravenous line in her left arm. It was quite impressive to watch him start an IV in the back of a jerky ambulance with lights and sirens blaring and a woman screaming in pain. As a medical student, Lillian had wondered if someday she would be able to keep her calm like that during an emergency with so many distracting elements.

By the time they reached the bay and parked, Lillian felt light-headed from taking blood pressures every five minutes while bumping around in the back of the ambulance. She stepped out of the confined space expecting a nice cool breeze to alleviate her symptoms. Instead, she was surrounded by the concrete walls of the ambulance bay, and she choked on a cloud of diesel fumes.

The two men hurried the patient inside the emergency room.

Lillian dismissed herself to go find a cold soda and much-desired fresh air.

Now, some twenty years later, she sat in a Canadian ambulance, once again with a sickening, nauseating feeling, albeit for a different reason. The wheels crunched over glass and debris as they pulled up to the bookstore.

The scene was strewn with police cars, onlookers, and television crews. A TV crew from a local news station squatted about three hundred feet from the scene of the accident and were hastily setting up cameras. The bookstore-turned-parking-garage had a large black SUV hanging halfway through what presumably used to be the front door. Papers and books littered the sidewalk along Rue Saint-Paul.

This was not the image of the Old Montreal she had envisioned. She was supposed to be strolling down the sidewalk along the cobblestone while admiring shops as a gentle breeze blew across the briskly moving, deep-blue St. Lawrence River. She would saunter down Rue Saint-Paul Est to Rue Saint-Paul Ouest, then cut east to Rue de la Commune Ouest and down further south to the birthplace of Montreal. She would amble through a park, under silver maple and white birch trees, and across green grass to a modern, concrete building, the Pointe-à-Callière Museum.

Instead, she stepped over fallen timbers and shredded concrete with protruding steel rebar, carrying the medic bag over one shoulder, as she approached what used to be a bookstore.

You're a doctor, Lillian told herself. *You're going to go in there, and you're going to treat a patient. That is what you know how to do.*

She had dealt with hostile situations and hostile people as an emergency room physician but always with a police officer on either side of her. This time she would be waltzing into danger alone, and her only weapon was her experience.

As Lillian entered the building, two armed men with raised guns shouted at her in Arabic. She recognized the AK-47s but only because her husband was a former operative.

Not former, she reminded herself.

He couldn't be a former CIA operative if he was neck-deep in a hostage crisis.

She raised her hands above her head.

"I am the doctor you requested," she said, shakily.

A cold sweat shook her, and she remembered the last time a gun was held to her. She had escaped Kenya and thought she was safe back near her brother in Arkansas, but her stalker had crossed the ocean for his revenge. His team tried to kill her brother at his home. She visited him in the hospital after the attack. She remembered the barrel of Vanier's gun in her spine, the icy breath of her assassin, and the walk down the long corridor to her awaiting death.

"Stop," Vanier's hostile French voice had commanded, immediately sending the hair on her neck on end and a shockwave of fear spiraling down her spine. By some miracle, her rage and his narcissism had distracted him long enough for her to wound him with a stab to the leg and then to escape.

The terrorists yanked the medic bag from her shoulder, bringing her awareness fully back to the ransacked bookstore. Prodding her with the cold metal barrel of his gun, one of the men motioned for her to move toward the back of the store.

"Let's go," he said with a scowl. His English was clear but with an accent she could do no better than to place as Middle Eastern.

There was no escape here. They either believed she was who she claimed to be and let her do her work or they didn't believe her and killed her where she stood.

As she made her way over scattered books and splinters from wooden shelves, she glanced at the group of hostages seated on the floor to her left. In the quick look she stole, she saw Sean sitting among them, alive and apparently uninjured. Determined not to make eye contact with her husband lest it betray a connection, she stared at the floor with each step. Somehow, she felt his gaze boring into her.

Later, Sean. When this is over, you can lecture me on not getting involved. You can tell me how I had no business making myself a willing hostage even if you could possibly be injured and dying.

In the bookstore managerial office, one Egyptian sat at a desk in front of a laptop, another stood beside him, and a third stood in the corner holding an AK-47.

"You are the doctor?" the standing man asked. He had dark flawless skin and long, shimmering black hair pulled back in a low ponytail. He had broad shoulders and an athletic physique. His wide smile was full of white teeth—a little sinister, not unlike a crocodile's.

"I am the doctor," she replied, which conjured bizarre images of the TV show Doctor Who in which the main character was always introducing himself as "the Doctor."

She eyed the many guns around her with more than a little discomfort.

The long-haired man nodded to the medic bag held by one of the men. Apparently, that communicated to the gunman to search the bag. He set it down and began an inspection of each compartment.

"I am Khait Sadat," the man said, as casually as if he were introducing himself at a cocktail party.

He waited quietly until Lillian realized that he was awaiting her introduction.

"Dr. Lillian Whyte," she replied.

Upon completing her introduction, the man at the computer began typing furiously. Khait glanced down at the screen every few seconds.

"Why do you visit Montreal?"

"I'm on vacation. Here to sightsee," she offered, keeping her answers short.

"And what have you seen so far?" he asked pleasantly as though he were a hotel concierge and not a hostage taker. His demeanor oozed an unexpected serenity.

She mustered a subtle shrug. "Nothing. I flew in last night. I've been waiting all morning on my delayed luggage. Then I was highjacked to come here."

He stared down at the screen for a moment. "You should not put on your Facebook page when you are on vacation. Someone could break into your home while you are away."

Lillian gaped at him for a moment. He seemed to be offering genuine advice. The CIA must have posted something about her trip on her behalf ... after they created an entirely fictitious account in her name.

"You're right," she said warily.

"And your husband?" he asked.

She suppressed the urge to look over her shoulder but tugged at the ring on her finger instead, careful not to twist it. "I am sure he is both furious and worried right now."

"So the authorities came for you, to put you in harm's way, and you agreed?"

"They didn't really give me a choice," she replied, the weight of the truth in her voice.

"You have the option to save your husband or not" was not really a choice.

He looked back at the computer screen and scratched at his jaw. "You work in an emergency room in Atlanta."

She nodded confirmation. She began to think that the background check was taking place at the expense of someone injured and in need of medical attention. Fortunately, that someone was not Sean. He had been sitting among the group, and someone else had been lying on the floor bleeding.

The gunman finished searching the medic bag and nodded an approval to the handsome leader.

In a few long strides, Khait came out from behind the desk and stood so close she wondered if he were trying to smell her fear. He was only an inch taller and perhaps the same age, but he was sinewy and moved like a predator.

"They sent in an American woman?" he asked, evidently still in disbelief of her credentials as a civilian.

Standing tall, she tried to calm her racing heart, lest the lion pounce the gazelle. "They sent an American physician," she clarified. "Something about wanting an American physician to treat an ambassador to the US if he were injured."

He nodded slowly, with pursed lips. Perhaps he was becoming more convinced.

Then he breathed deeply through his nose, leaning closer to the nape of her neck.

"Eucalyptus?"

"Massage oil," she mumbled. She blew air out of her cheeks. "I was getting a massage when they called."

He arched an eyebrow as he looked up and down the length of her body.

"Why do you suppose they picked you?" His eyes came back to hers.

He stepped even closer, reading her eyes for a response. She smelled his cologne, Lacoste Blue. It had an odd calming effect as though reminding her that he was human and not an animal, despite the situation.

"I worked as a physician in a US military camp in Africa treating locals some years ago. My name has been on file ever since," she explained.

Reigning in her fear, she boldly stepped so close to him they were nearly nose to nose. She tried to appear undaunted but thought she only succeeded in seeming seductive. Perhaps, if she were wearing her ER scrubs instead of a fitted dress, she would have achieved her goal of authority.

"I think they keep tabs on me now," she added, then leaned back on her heels.

"Unlucky for you," he commented, his voice more husky. His eyes roamed her face then down to her lips.

Lillian smirked. "No good deed goes unpunished."

Khait barked out a laugh, startling her.

When he recovered, he took a step back and eyed her pristine white dress and asked, "You can treat gunshot wounds?"

She nodded again. "With what I have, I can patch someone up. If there is any metal lodged in any body parts or any organs damaged, I can't do surgery. I can stabilize the patient until he or she can get to a surgeon. I don't have any blood products to transfuse if someone is in shock." She wanted to make sure the expectations were clear.

"Ha," he said with another startling outburst. "Come then, *Tabib*, and stabilize."

Touching her lightly on the elbow, he led her out of the office and over to the sitting hostages.

Details, Dr. Whyte.

She remembered Austin commanding her to absorb her surroundings and assess the situation.

Four guards, four AK-47s, one leader, seven hostages, and a partridge in a pear tree.

She looked from face to frightened face and then, lastly, to Sean's face. As expected, he was less frightened and more furious. He sat rigid with hands and jaw clenched. His hazel eyes blazed as his body seemed poised to spring at a moment's notice. She diverted her eyes to the man lying on the floor. As anticipated, he was the gunshot victim.

Khait motioned to him. "Him first. Then the broken arm over there."

Lillian looked at a man on the other side of the group holding his arm across his chest with care.

The lead Crocodile left and walked back to the office. The nearest guard was posted just outside the office door, glaring at her from a distance with piercingly narrow eyes set in a lion's mane of black hair.

CHAPTER 6

Sean felt a rush of a hundred emotions when he saw Lillian walk into the bookstore, medic bag in tow. The top three emotions had been rage, fear, and disbelief. His intestines had twisted into a ball of painful knots.

She wasn't supposed to be here. If he had a prime objective since his pseudoretirement, it was to keep Lillian safe. Then here she was, in the thick of danger ... all over again. She had come with a medic bag. She had come as a physician.

Khait must have requested medical services—odd considering he was the one who shot Labaris. Austin would have scrambled to provide someone under his influence—someone the CIA trusted and who would be cool under pressure.

Sean's blood boiled.

Austin would have offered Lillian the job, having no other CIA- affiliated physicians readily at his disposal. But why would she willingly walk into danger?

What she had been through in Kenya had taken months to

recover. She'd battled through restless nights of nightmares, and he could do little more than hold her and promise she was safe.

The dreams had fizzled, and by now, they were almost forgotten. Normalcy had come slowly, warmly, like the rising sun. In five more years, Kenya would become a more pleasant memory—their romantic meeting and an experience that made them stronger. Ten years after that, it would take on a dreamlike quality. Did that really happen to us?

Now there would be the Montreal incident—the time she walked into a building full of terrorists. Why?

Damnation.

He knew why. Because when the dust had settled, no one outside of these walls knew who was injured when Khait requested medical support. Fearful Sean was the injured person, Lillian had accepted Austin's proposal. Austin knew she would take the bait.

Manipulative bastard.

That explained the flash of relief in Lillian's eyes when she first saw Sean and he was not the patient. She had come for him.

To save me.

Except that he didn't need saving, and now she was in the devil's grasp.

Taking a long, slow, deep breath, he closed his eyes and saw a vision of her the first time they met. She emerged from the terminal after a long series of flights looking unexpectedly bright-eyed and ready for adventure. He had never been romantically inclined, but he was positively enamored after only knowing her for a few days. Her approach to healing was passionate, and her contempt of authority was amusingly palpable. She pulsed with a radiating energy and captivating snarky attitude. He had wanted to wrap his arms around her and never let go. And then, one night, he had wrapped his arms around her under the stars, and he knew from that moment forward he wanted her in his arms every night.

Then all hell broke loose.

It was as though he'd embraced a dream briefly before it disintegrated in his hold. She had been stolen from him—kidnapped. In the days it took to find her, he already schemed how he could rearrange his career to be with her forever. He was finished with undercover work. Just like that. Chapter's done. Turn the page.

By the time he found her, he had planned how he could live and work in Atlanta where she lived and worked. And if she had reservations because of who he was or things he had done, then he would court her as long as it took.

Luckily for him, Cupid's arrow seemed to have pierced her heart with the same concentrated dose of intoxicating serum. She didn't hesitate in receiving him, all of him.

Certainly, nothing he had done in his wretched past made him worthy of such a woman. Did he still have a penance to pay for their amazing life together because of the evil he had done? He swallowed a bitter lump in his throat that reminded him of a rancid tequila worm. Not today. Not at the hands of these animals. She would not pay the price for his dark deeds.

His eyes fell menacingly on Labaris. He had created this situation, which was rapidly spiraling out of control. He wanted to punch the biochemist in the chest, preferably directly on his bullet hole.

Instead, he had sat quietly, his face a mask of calm, as he waited for his wife to exit the managerial office. If anything happened to her, he would tear this place to shreds. Well, more so than it already was.

SEEING SO many weapons at the bookstore, Lillian thought about the many times Sean had taken her to the gun range. In the unlikely event she found herself in a situation of violence again, he wanted her to be prepared.

Aside from a crash course on weapons in Kenya, she had known more about gun injuries than how to operate one. She had removed a few superficial bullets over the years. Usually, in the ER, she treated soft-tissue injuries from low-velocity bullets, as well as buckshot and bird shot scatter.

The first time he had taken her to a gun range had been north of Atlanta, off I-85, on a warm spring day. Her nightmares from her Kenya experience had finally abated, and she and Sean had been newlyweds.

"This is a Glock 19, a nine millimeter semiautomatic. Semiautomatic means you can pull the trigger in succession, and each time a bullet is released, there is no hammer to pull back," Sean explained.

He was wearing faded blue jeans, a navy T-shirt, and worn cowboy boots. He had been working nonstop on his first book for several days, so he was ruggedly unshaven. She tried to focus on the guns and not her lusciously attractive instructor.

The Glock was small and black. She felt the weight of the gun and then set it back down in the row of four different weapons.

He pointed to a silver gun. "This is a Beretta 8000 or Cougar. This particular one is a nine millimeter also. It's a nice small size for concealment. If you were ever to agree to carry a weapon, this is what I would get for you."

She frowned. She had no desire to carry a concealed weapon. Although she'd had several brief but intense violent encounters, she felt those were extenuating circumstances. She knew from her work experience that guns were twice more likely to be used in a fatal accidental shooting than a justifiable self-defense homicide. Not to mention there were almost a quarter of a million guns stolen each year. What if hers were stolen and used to murder someone else? She didn't want that on her conscience.

"Even if I did decide to carry a gun," she retorted, "it would not be something called a *Cougar*."

Sean smirked.

"Next, a Sig Sauer P226. German made. Also nine millimeter," he continued.

She picked up the big black handgun. The metal felt cool despite the pleasantly warm day. It was too big and too heavy for her to imagine lugging it around, much less shooting it at someone. She set it back down with a thud.

He pointed next to a revolver. "I want you to shoot a revolver too. Not only because you'll be holding a Smith and Wesson—a piece of American history—but because you need to be aware of the kick. Remember, only six bullets."

Lillian nodded as she picked up the hefty, American-made weapon. She took aim at the paper target in front of her. "'Do you feel lucky, punk?'" she said to the target, squinting her eyes and drawing her lips into a thin line.

"Easy there, Eastwood." He put a hand on top of the gun and eased it back onto the table.

"He used a Model 29. This is a Model 10. But I am impressed you knew Dirty Hairy used a Smith and Wesson. It's kind of hot."

She smiled and winked at him.

He had her go through each weapon putting the safety off and on, loading the gun, and firing. The target, a bald black-and-white silhouette, stood just twenty feet away from them.

"Is that standard distance for handgun accuracy, or did you choose that because you didn't want to make shooting difficult and discouraging for me?"

"Bit of both," he replied.

She shot more accurately with the lighter nine millimeters, though she did manage to blow an imaginary paper arm off with the revolver.

Punk.

At the time she had wondered if being the wife of a CIA agent would incur any unplanned encounters. Sean had assured her it was unlikely but not impossible. Since most of his work had been in Africa, he explained that Africa would be the one continent they would avoid in their travels so as not to unearth any ghosts from his past. She didn't protest since she had her own ghosts she wanted to remain undisturbed in Africa.

She had agreed to gun training in the event that his past rivalries came after them, but she had not imagined walking herself willingly into a hostage situation with a room full of terrorists.

Lillian knelt beside a plump Egyptian who lay on the floor looking pale and distressed. Sean appeared, pressing a hand to the man's balled-up coat against his bleeding chest.

"Can I give you a hand, doctor?" Sean asked Lillian loud enough for most of the room to hear.

She nodded, pulling on a pair of gloves.

Then he lowered his voice, still not disguising the displeasure in his eyes at seeing her here. He whispered introductions. "Labaris, Lillian. Lillian, Labaris."

The rotund man nodded.

Lillian only mustered a skeptical glance before evaluating his wound. She detected a familiarity within the introduction, which led her to believe Labaris and Sean were working together.

"I'm Dr. Whyte," she declared. "I'm going to see if I can patch you up."

Amidst the smell of wooden shelves, dusty books, and burnt brake pads, the copper scent of blood diffused the air. With Sean's help, they took off the injured man's shirt. She listened to his breathing with a stethoscope.

After examining the area, she said, "Looks like the bullet went through and through. The back is clotted off."

She doused the areas with topical lidocaine.

Labaris gave a little moan.

"Well, at least it didn't puncture any major blood vessels," she observed.

"How can you tell?" Labaris asked, breathless.

"You're still alive."

She worked efficiently, pulling supplies from the medical bag. "But it did puncture your lung, and air is building up inside your chest."

"A pneumothorax," he gasped.

"Yes," she concurred. The accumulation of air inside the chest could lead to compression of his major blood vessels and lung collapse, followed by death.

"I will die without medical care. I need a hospital."

Is that just now occurring to him?

He could at least act somewhat reassured that a doctor, risking her life to be here, was actively administering care.

"You need a chest tube." Then she spoke in her best infomercial voice as she cleaned the entrance wound with an iodine swab. "Fortunately for you, the military recognizes that chest tubes render a person nearly immobile, which is not what they want their soldiers to be, so they carry the Asherman chest seal."

He gaped at her, which told her she had at least provided temporary distraction from the pain.

After mopping up more oozing blood, she placed the chest seal over the sucking wound. It was a round clear plastic device with a protruding valve. The adhesive side stuck readily to his skin.

"How does it work?" Sean asked.

"This is a one way valve, so when he exhales, air escapes through the valve, but when he inhales, air does not get sucked back in and become trapped."

Labaris looked at her with concern. "I do not feel better yet. It is not working."

"It takes time," she assured him with some measure of irritability at his ungrateful attitude. "Air leaks out with each breath. Eventually, you will breathe most of the trapped air out."

"Most?"

"Look, Labaris. This is a temporary fix. You still need a hospital and a chest tube."

With Sean's help, they applied a bulky dressing to his back. Between the man's hair and profuse sweating, the tape had difficulty sticking.

She asked Sean, "Are you going to tell me the real story or feed me some 'political hostage gone awry crap' like Austin?"

She finally had to apply tape halfway round Labaris's chest to get the seal to stick. It would be a bear to pull off later.

"Political hostage?"

Taking her gloves off, she motioned for Labaris to put on his shirt. As an emergency room physician forced to prioritize emergencies and rapidly triage and treat patients, her bedside manner was generally not as pleasant as it could be. However, being dragged from vacation into harm's way eliminated any empathy she may have been able to muster. It was also apparent that Sean knew this man, which made her think that Labaris was somehow involved in this hostage mess.

She turned to Sean and narrowed her eyes. "I find it hard to believe that the place where you're doing a *book signing* just happens to be where Omar Jabal's kidnappers crashed while avoiding the police."

"Omar Jabal. That's who he is. I knew I recognized him." He looked over at Omar who sat still, nursing what was presumably a broken arm.

"You're right. Labaris was bringing me a package to take back to the US. A good-faith delivery for his defection," Sean explained. "Khait must have known about the meeting and designed this charade to sneak it out."

"Package?" she asked, skeptically.

Sean looked at Labaris and nodded for him to tell Lillian.

Breathing easier, he was now able to speak in complete sentences.

"I took Creutzfeldt-Jakob disease, encased it in a viral shell for delivery, and created an ingestible form that takes effect faster than the sporadic variant."

"You bottled *bovine spongiform encephalopathy?*"

Labaris nodded.

"You weaponized a *prion* disease?" She tried to keep her voice down through clenched teeth. She felt a sickening wave of anger and disbelief roll over her.

He nodded again, but less enthusiastically.

"There's no cure for *prion* diseases," she snarled.

He frowned.

Lillian turned to Sean. "Why did I save his life?"

Sean pursed his lips. "He's going to help us get it back," he explained.

"Get it back?" Her pitch rose. "The terrorists have it?" she asked in a sharp whisper.

Labaris nodded solemnly.

Lillian rubbed at her throbbing temples. She visualized the tiny strands of protein replicating over and over until the brain was nothing but a soggy sponge, incapable of firing a single neuron. It seemed a devastating way to slowly die.

Had Austin wittingly sent her into a biohazard zone, or did the CIA not know he had an actual sample of the disease?

With one last glare at Labaris, she said, "I'm going to go take care of the *innocent* patient."

CHAPTER 7

Austin crossed his arms as he stared at the monitors. The ambulance sat idling outside the bookstore, and he waited with bated breath to see Dr. Whyte emerge. Only fifteen or twenty minutes had passed since he watched her walk into the bookstore carrying the medic bag, white lace dress flowing around her.

He looked at the camera views down the street and up the alleys. The only activity was the Canadian police outside the front entrance. He knew, though, that unseen rooftop officers monitored all exits.

"Friendlies, update," he commanded.

"Twenty SPVM out front, three on the roof. Two choppers are in the air," Mike on coms replied.

The Service de police de la Ville de Montreal—SPVM—had the block surrounded. Austin had a small team at his disposal, but interfering with another country's police and incident response team was not an option. Discretely surveilling such teams, however, was within his purview.

"No change on the terrorist count?"

"No, sir. Still assumed to be five."

Austin nodded at Mike. The SPVM was operating under the assumption that the collision was inadvertent. Austin was not. As Dr. Whyte had rightly and annoyingly speculated, this was not likely a coincidence. As such, there was a chance that the terrorists already had people inside the bookstore at the time of the crash. Since they couldn't see into the bookstore, they couldn't get a more accurate count.

There was no reason to alert Canadian authorities to a covert information transfer conducted by the CIA. Austin could let the SPVM focus on diffusing the hostage crisis while he focused on ensuring Sean, and the information he was hopefully in possession of by now, were safely retrieved.

"Sir," Mike piped in again. "CAAM chatter."

Not surprisingly, the Comité aviseur antiterrorisme de Montréal, or CAAM, would be joining the action.

Mike continued speaking and listening at once. "They're bringing in the bees."

Bomb threat?

That was going to make things dicey.

Shit.

Agent Jennings was already going to have Austin's head for conscripting his wife to enter a hostage crisis. If there were bombs involved ...

He swallowed. He didn't want to contemplate the fallout.

He didn't normally construct a command center in proximity to an information transfer; however, this was particularly sensitive information, and he felt the need to take extra precaution. Austin had had an instinct—a feeling like a lump of undigested food sitting as a stone in his belly—that he needed to be in Montreal. He needed a team in Montreal and an experienced operative in the field. It had not occurred to him that his planning would coalesce into a hostage crisis on foreign soil where he could do nothing more than eavesdrop on Canadian government activity.

Please, let there be no bombs.

Even as he prayed, he knew that the Crocodile Pharaohs had used bombs in the past and they likely would again.

———————

LILLIAN STOOD and hefted the medical bag up to her shoulder. Walking several steps to the man holding his injured arm, she knelt down and introduced herself.

He smiled weakly and said in return, "I am Omar Salim Jabal." His English was crisp, and the last syllable of each word seemed rushed.

She helped him out of his sports jacket.

"I have never met an American woman physician. Nor a redhead," he commented.

She had never considered herself a rare creature to behold. Somehow his expression of intrigue did not convey a compliment.

"And I have never met an Egyptian ambassador," she said.

He raised his eyebrows at her. "You know who I am?"

She nodded, rolling up his shirtsleeve. His bruised forearm did not appear deformed. He winced at her touch.

"They didn't tell me much when they snatched me out of my hotel, but they did mention you'd been taken hostage," she said.

"They who?" he asked, watching her inspect his arm.

She looked at him, considering his question.

He smiled at her with a full, bared-teeth, "Can I have your vote?" politician's smile.

She found the smile unnerving, though she suspected his intention was to convey trust. She shrugged, then dug into the bag. "Government agency, official looking."

Then she asked, "Did these guys rough you up, or is this from the car wreck?"

"Wreck," he said bitterly.

She cycled through some other questions to make sure he wasn't hurting anywhere else she may need to examine. He explained he was fine except for his arm.

The ambassador's face sank into a frown. "You don't seem scared with everything around you."

Pulling out a short splint, she looked directly at him. "I'm terrified," she replied, "but you work long enough in the trenches of gang wars crossing through your emergency department, and you learn not to let little things like armed gunmen and riots in the street distract you from your job."

Omar puffed out his cheeks as though trying to decide if she were telling the truth.

Wrapping his arm snugly, she added, "Don't act like a victim, and you won't be treated like one."

He nodded but seemed surprised that she would have such insight.

"Speaking of victims," she said, "why did they take you?"

He frowned again. "They are terrorists," he replied as though the logic were obvious.

"Yes," she agreed slowly, "but terrorists usually have an agenda other than just, well, terrorizing."

He scowled at her, obviously displeased with her line of questioning, which only piqued her interest more.

"You talk a great deal. Have you been told that?"

That was apparently her cue he wasn't going to answer her question. "I can multitask," she responded sweetly, flipping a strand of red hair out of her face.

She decided to keep talking because he seemed bothered by it. Until she understood why he was so ruffled by her questions, she might as well keep pushing his buttons. "I've been known to suture lacerations while having debates on the wins and losses of the Atlanta Falcons. Once, I put a dislocated shoulder back in place on an eighty- year-old woman while we discussed her home-made apple pie recipe."

Omar gaped at her.

She chuckled lightly then tested the fingers hanging out of the bandage and over the splint. They all moved and had good circulation. She hadn't bandaged it too tight.

Admittedly, her mouth and her redheaded temper had landed her in hot water with her hospital administrator with enough frequency that they were on a first-name basis. She hadn't become an emergency room physician to have her workplace misused by drug seekers and common cold snifflers. She could be compassionate, but many people just needed a reality check. She didn't refrain from telling them their lifestyle choices were killing them.

After multiple complaints about her abruptness over the years, she was immune to the criticism. Quite some time ago, she had been banned forever from the pediatric ER, having gotten into more than one shouting match with parents who had been neglectful about child safety. It was better for her health and her blood pressure if she didn't take care of sick and injured children, so she didn't fight the dismissal.

She would never be dismissed from the adult ER though. For every complaint about her being rude or unprofessional—code for not keeping one's mouth shut—there was an accolade for saving someone's life. She could recognize illnesses and injuries early, and her treatments were timely.

So even if the administration had to sigh and take another nerve pill when she was working, she was the one they wanted in the ER the day they were in a car wreck or had a heart attack. She had mellowed a little over the years. Perhaps, in part, because most of her abruptness didn't really coerce change in people, and perhaps because she had learned in Kenya that life was too uncertain to spend a significant amount of it bitter and angry. Over time, her criticisms had become more witty, more subtle, and more Southern.

"The way your arm has been swelling for the last few minutes, it's probably a nondisplaced radial fracture. You're going to need an x-ray and a real cast. The good news is, I don't suspect any permanent damage."

Omar nodded. "Thank you, Dr. Whyte."

She was impressed by how well he handled the stress of being taken hostage followed by a "vehicle versus bookstore" head-on collision and the pain of a probable fracture. How was he able to remember her name after just one introduction? Then again, she reasoned, he was a politician, and name recollection was part of the job description.

As she stood and turned to pick up the medic bag, two of the villains moved quickly around her and snatched up the Egyptian ambassador. She remained motionless except for a dry swallow as they dragged him into the manager's office, back to Khait—back to the lion's den.

Lillian turned slowly to the nearest gunman. "Can I go back over there and check on his bandages?" she asked, pointing toward Labaris and Sean.

He nodded gruffly.

She dragged her bag back over to Labaris and began to examine his wound with a fresh pair of gloves. She listened with the stethoscope.

"Lung's back up."

"Am I dying?" he asked meekly.

Lillian rolled her eyes. "Most people that are dying don't get the chance to ask if they are dying. You just need a hospital. Besides," she added in a harsh whisper, "where you're going after this life, you don't want to die yet."

"What does that mean?" He looked at Sean.

Sean shook his head but couldn't conceal an amused curling of the corner of his mouth.

Lillian explained, "I'd like to think there's a hell for those who are intentionally evil and then a separate special one for those that do really, really stupid things that hurt a lot of people—like weaponizing a prion disease."

She pulled out a preloaded syringe of morphine, wiped an area of skin on his bicep with an alcohol swab, and injected the pain medication.

"Ow," he pouted.

"Morphine," she explained. "Or maybe just an excuse to poke you with something sharp." She had given him a small dose, and it would only last an hour, but if they needed to make a sudden escape, the morphine would take the edge off the pain enough that, hopefully, he wouldn't slow them down too much.

Labaris started to protest and then shut his mouth.

She took off her gloves and stuffed them into the bag.

"So what's the play?" Lillian asked Sean, hoping that was the right terminology.

Sean's smirk faded, and his CIA face rematerialized. "The agency?"

Lillian shook her head. "They want to continue to appear uninvolved."

She started taking Labaris's blood pressure, not because she cared what it was but because it would help her linger by the two men longer.

For a brief second, Sean's face darkened, and Lillian knew he was considering how Austin had involved her in this situation. The CIA was hardly uninvolved. Then he nodded as though he expected they were not to be relied upon for resolution of this situation.

This was one of many reasons Lillian knew she would not have made a good spy. She would have been furious if she had given the

US government twenty years of loyal service only to not be rescued from armed gunmen.

"Sorry, agent, no can do on the rescue mission, but we'll make sure that pension of yours gets to your next of kin."

Sean, evidently having anticipated that answer, was unfazed and had already worked out a plan. "You need to get your patients out of here. Request they leave for medical attention. Leave me here to figure out how to get the vial back."

Lillian looked at her husband skeptically as she stuffed the sphygmomanometer back into the medic bag. "I can try that," she replied slowly.

She thought it unlikely they would release their kidnapped ambassador since they had only just acquired him. She also didn't relish the idea of leaving Sean behind but couldn't make a reasonable argument for him to be released without betraying a preexisting relationship. If she left with Omar and Labaris, that left Sean, four innocent bystanders, and too many men with automatic weapons.

She drew up two syringes full of the tranquilizer and laid them on the floor. She left the needle on but capped them.

"Tranquilizers," she told Sean.

She sighed and stood but not before giving Sean one more sour look to make sure he knew she was not pleased with the plan whereby she leaves him with armed gunmen. He matched her gaze, which reminded her he was still displeased she came into the bookstore in the first place.

She surrendered and broke eye contact first as she walked away from him.

"May I speak with Khait?" she asked the nearest guardsman.

He squinted at her warily behind robust facial hair.

"This man could die if he is not transported to a hospital," she explained, which was the truth. Even though she had stabilized him for now, Labaris could still die of infection or the chest seal could dislodge and the lung could collapse again. Therefore, death was a possibility, though perhaps not as imminent as her tone suggested.

With his unarmed hand, he waved for her to come with him. She followed him back into Khait's office.

As she entered, Khait was speaking with the ambassador, who was seated in a chair across from Khait's desk. They were presumably conversing in Arabic, as it was the principal language in Egypt, but Lillian understood not a word of it.

The ambassador's tone suggested he was giving Khait a tonguelashing, a gutsy move considering he was the unarmed victim. Perhaps he was taking her advice a little too far.

Khait looked at her with annoyance.

"That man out there has a pneumothorax, which is a collapsed lung. I've done everything I can for him, but he needs a hospital and a surgeon. The ambassador has a fractured arm, which needs to be stabilized if he is going to maintain function of his hand."

Her last statement stretched the truth like a toddler stretching silly putty. Perhaps with reinjury to the arm through her soft splint, loss of function was something she could foresee as a possibility. Yes, without certainty. But she was able to make this claim while maintaining unwavering eye contact with Khait, something Sean had always emphasized to her when trying to convey truth.

Sean had explained to her that, although she was married to a semiretired agent, he still had enemies. With that, he made an effort to train her for verbal interrogation, disguise, and even weapon use in the unlikely event she would need any of it. Right now, she wished he had taught her Arabic.

She glanced at Omar to her right who was looking from her to his arm in disbelief. As he started to open his mouth, she turned to him and gave him a direct stare. Perhaps her current claim of permanent limb injury was in contradiction to the reassurance she had given him only moments ago, but she hoped he was intelligent enough to see her ploy to get him to safety.

Omar closed his mouth and then turned to Khait. He spoke heatedly to him, raising his injured arm as though putting it on display.

Please be making a case for our release.

CHAPTER 8

Sean's eyes followed Lillian as she left. She carried the medic bag as Omar helped Labaris hobble out of the shattered entrance. Her white dress was now stained with dirt around the hem and blood higher up on her hip, but the fit exquisitely showed off her figure. Although he was not sorry he had purchased it for her, he was sorry he couldn't savor her in it under different circumstances.

Relief struck him, knowing she would be in the ambulance driving away and out of danger.

He looked down at the syringes she had left. It was both endearingly sweet and woefully naive of her to think the situation called for tranquilizers. Bullets worked faster, and he had every intention of getting his hands on a gun very soon.

What Lillian hadn't noticed, as she focused on sucking chest wounds and hairline fractures, was Khait's men placing small explosive devices around the store. Fortunately, the terrorists' focus on their work enabled him to speak with Lillian unencumbered. Unfortunately, they would all be reduced to a pile of dust when Khait decided to detonate them.

Four bombs. All near the store entrance.

A rear escape then.

Seemed foolish either way since the Canadian police would likely be watching all exits.

As Sean thought through his own exit strategy, he noticed the bees.

Clever.

He wondered if they were from the Canadian government or his own. There were no more than half a dozen bees spread out inconspicuously in the store. Yet before long, their pattern emerged as they migrated toward the different C-4 explosives.

Trained hymenopterans.

They were honeybees conditioned to detect the odor of explosives—TNT, C-4, gunpowder, and propellants. They flocked to the C-4 as they had been trained to do to await a sugar reward. A computer technician outside the store would be tracking their movement in real time and noting their pattern of assembly. Clusters of motionlessness would indicate they found the smell of explosives.

The authorities would soon deduce the building was wired to explode. They would likely withdraw a safe distance from the area, leaving the exits unattended. Even if the agency or the police noted the bees were congregated at the front of the store, they would probably assume the bees parked their proboscis at the nearest explosive and would not make a risky gamble that there were no rear bombs.

A lack of police presence might work to his advantage, Sean realized. He could follow the gunmen along their rear escape route. Unhindered by police or other agents, he could target Khait and retrieve the vial.

He was still left with the pesky business of how to free the remaining hostages.

As Khait's men were assembling, Sean motioned for the four other people seated on the floor to huddle closer. He opened one of his books and scribbled a quick square map of the bookstore where, normally, he would have been signing his pen name. At the front of the store map, he wrote bombs, and at the back, he wrote EXIT. The bearded bookseller gasped, and the young woman next to him nudged him silent.

"We have to follow quietly behind them as they leave," Sean explained. "Whichever way they go down the back alley, everyone needs to go the opposite direction. Got it?"

There were nods and muffled murmurs, mostly in French.

Commotion became more frenzied as Khait exited the manager's office and began barking orders. Sean, having trained extensively in the Middle East during his more active agency days, knew Arabic, Swahili, and French. While his accent could betray that he was not a native to these countries despite a good physical disguise, he could clearly understand everything Khait was saying.

"Khms daqiqa," he barked. "Everybody out. Ammon, you stay and kill the hostages, then follow us."

A stocky man nodded and adjusted the gun strap on his shoulder.

Five minutes, Sean understood. The lack of reaction from the rest of the hostages indicated he was the only one who had understood they were to be gunned down.

Khait and three of his gunmen dashed down the back hall and out of sight when Ammon raised his gun and shouted in English, "Everyone against the wall!"

The hostages, whimpering in fear, started to stand.

Sean used the opportunity to leap at his attacker. As he knocked him back with the weight of his body through his right shoulder, the automatic weapon erupted. Sean had already maneuvered his left hand on the barrel, angling it up and away from the hostages, some of whom let out screams of terror.

The two men tumbled to the floor, Ammon on his back with Sean on top of him. In close combat, the burly man had no way to reposition the muzzle of his weapon and aim it at Sean. That didn't stop him from trying. Sean punched the assailant in the jaw. His head slammed back onto the wood floor of the bookstore with a thud. The man was resilient—stunned but not unconscious.

Four minutes until detonation.

Sean rolled to one side as the man produced a six-inch knife from his boot with his left hand. Sean simultaneously dodged to the gunman's right, snatched the AK-47 from the man's grip, and yanked the strap off his arm. The man swept his knife at Sean's neck but, with the tumble, caught only his right arm superficially.

With one fluid motion, Sean came up from his roll, anchored the automatic in the crux of his shoulder, and fired a burst of bullets into Ammon's chest. The Egyptian fell back, lifeless.

He turned to the hostages as he stood with the gun securely in his hands. Although he had clearly written bomb on a piece of paper for all of them to see, the hostages had been gaping at him while he was fighting instead of fleeing for their lives.

"Out the back," he commanded. Finally, Sean's verbal command startled them out of their stupor and into action.

He took the lead, in case any gunmen were lingering. The hall was empty.

Three minutes.

They raced down the hall in the dim light of a single bulb, past an employee restroom and several closed doors leading to storage rooms. The back door wobbled, already opened, and sunlight streamed past. Sean poked his head out for a quick look. The gunmen had taken the alley to the right, and he glimpsed them turning down another alley to the left.

He motioned for the people at his back to take off to the left.

One by one, he heard their footsteps clamor onto the cobblestone and down the alley. He raised his weapon to provide cover should any of the fleeing terrorists turn around and open fire.

They did not, which was reasonable since they were running to the sound of their own footsteps and trying to flee from the C-4 that would detonate imminently. Sean would have liked to open fire on them, but if he did, they were certain to turn and see the hostages fleeing. As the last gunman turned the far corner, Sean thought perhaps he had glanced back and seen Sean.

Two minutes.

He stole a peek back over his shoulder. The bystanders were free and running for their lives. With concern for their safety abated, Sean sprinted down the alley toward the gunmen.

Stopping short of the second alley, he leaned with his back against the wall. Then he took a fleeting look to ensure that no one was waiting for him.

Clear.

With gun raised, he advanced cautiously down the alley, the backs of sturdy brick buildings, hundreds of years old, on either side, rising up around him.

One minute.

Sean crept down the alley until a sudden flash of movement caught his eye. He flattened himself in the recess of a back door as one of the terrorists opened fire from far down the alley. Shards of brick, stone, and concrete zipped around him, but he was out of the line of fire from any direct bullets, though ricochets were still possible.

He knew a standard AK-47 would have thirty rounds and, at ten rounds fired per second, the gunfire would be over in a few short seconds.

When the weapon clicked empty, Sean spun and fired. At five hundred meters away with the mediocre accuracy of the weapon, his best hope would be to wound the assailant.

The man let out an enraged growl as a bullet erupted through his kneecap. He fell to the ground, a fresh magazine in hand.

"*Abaq hadiaan*," Sean commanded the man to stay down on the ground.

Then the world turned upside down as gravity seemed momentarily suspended. The deafening roar of the explosion from the C-4 in the bookstore filled his ears followed by hot, suffocating air filling his lungs.

Sean dove against the building for cover and was simultaneously carried by the blast roughly into the exterior wall. The ground and walls all around him shook and shimmied violently, causing loose brick to tumble from the sky. Metal debris from doors and shattered glass from windows swept down the alley.

When the rumbling subsided, he opened his eyes to the dust and debris strewn around him. His ears were ringing painfully. The man he had shot was crushed under a pile of stone rubble.

A quiet stillness settled into the rest of the deserted alley.

The others had escaped.

Dammit.

The vial was gone.

Dammit.

Sean rubbed his head in irritation. Looking at the crumbling buildings around him, he hoped Lillian had been far away in the ambulance by the time the bomb detonated. Based on the time elapsed, she should have been a safe distance away from the exploding building. He clung to that logic, keeping the nagging worry in his mind at bay.

He sighed. He needed to get back and regroup with Austin to see if they had any intelligence on the terrorists and who the potential targets were. He wiped his prints from the gun and laid it down. Time could not be wasted explaining to the Canadian police who he was and why he was holding a gun immediately following a terrorist attack. He would be locked up, or worse, until his innocence could be proven.

Hopping over the rubble, he made his way out of the smaller alley and behind the bookstore to the main street. The air smelled of burnt paper, charred drywall, and the tarry, vinyl smell of C-4.

Taking stock of the damage, he shuddered. The bookstore and the apartment home above it were obliterated. The surrounding buildings were intact but missing pieces of wall like bulky chunks of gray, moldy swiss cheese. Remains of blackened books littered the street like a scene from Fahrenheit 451. Some of those books had been his.

He frowned. How was he going to recoup the loss? He had actually been hoping to sell a few copies of his book today before the information trade turned hostage crisis turned bombing.

Since his confiscated mobile phone now likely lay shattered beneath a few tons of stones and debris, he needed to get to a phone and call Austin.

DEPUTY DIRECTOR AUSTIN lowered himself into a nearby chair, weak and stricken. He felt a twinge of pain in his chest. He rubbed at the ribs over his heart. His physician had warned him he had signs of coronary artery disease. Per his doctor's orders, he consumed daily cholesterol-lowering medication and was given instructions to keep his blood pressure under control.

Hah! What a joke.

Blood pressure control in his line of work was like telling a firefighter not to inhale smoke. He knew it was spiking this moment as he watched the dust settle from the demolished bookstore. He massaged his throbbing temple, but it did little to ease the pressure.

The entire warehouse had fallen silent. Hands rested, unmoving, on keyboards. All eyes locked on the screen where the explosion had just occurred.

The cameras showed an entire block of building damage. Fortunately, all emergency response vehicles pulled back when the bomb bees detected explosive devices. Adjacent buildings had already been evacuated almost immediately after terrorists had rammed their vehicle into the bookstore.

Dr. Whyte had left in the ambulance, so Austin knew she was safe. The sickening feeling that flooded him when he had learned there was a bomb in the building oozed out of him as he watched her climb into the emergency vehicle. Relief swept over him when the ambulance drove her away from danger.

That leaves Sean and the hostages and the terrorists. Alive or dead?

The last images he had seen of them were from an alley camera set up to watch the rear exit. The terrorists fled and headed north, followed by hostages exiting south, and Sean, gun in hand, followed the terrorists. The rest of the alley could not be seen. As the camera was destroyed with the bomb, there was no way to reposition it and ascertain if any of them were within its blast radius.

"Sir," Mike on coms spoke. "SPVM reporting four hostages alive."

Austin sat up straight. Could it be possible no civilian lives were lost in this disaster?

Austin scanned the room. Pale faces stared back at him. Worry. They still didn't know about Sean. Had they lost one of their own? Not only did an agent loss remind them of their own mortality, it would especially heighten angst if they lost Sean. Most of them revered the seasoned agent whom Austin found more annoying than endearing.

Mike said eagerly, "Sir, incoming call from Agent Jennings."

Thank God.

"Open com," Austin said, irritated by how much relief flooded his voice.

"Agent," Austin said.

"Sir, any casualties?" Sean asked.

"No. The hostages are safe. Labaris, Omar, and the physician are on their way to the hospital."

"Yes, sir."

"Jennings."

"Sir?"

Austin noted some strain in his voice. While Sean was no doubt relieved to hear his wife was well, he would be boiling with rage at Austin having roped her into helping.

"We need you back here."

"Yes, sir."

The phone disconnected.

The phone in Austin's pocket rang. The deputy director of the CIA was calling. This one he would not put on speakerphone.

Up goes the blood pressure.

He answered the phone with an immediate statement, "No civilian or agent casualties, sir."

Maybe, just maybe, he would be able to keep his job when all this was over.

CHAPTER 9

Lillian had been sitting in the back of the moving ambulance beside Omar, while the Canadian paramedic tended to Labaris, when the ground shook.

"Oh god," she said, barely above a whisper.

"*Merde!*" the driver in the front snapped as the rumbling shook the ambulance.

As quickly as it had begun, it was over. Lillian surmised there could only be one explanation—a bomb. Sean must have known, which explained why he wanted her far away and fast.

Omar let out a little oomph, as though the jolt had jarred his tender arm.

Labaris's eyes widened, bulging with fear, the white sclera encircling his narcotic-dilated black pupils. He looked like an untamed filly corralled for the first time.

Lillian's fear flared to anger, and she flushed with the sudden urge to shake Labaris and demand to know who took the vial and why. All the danger to her and Sean was his fault. But Omar knew nothing of the biohazard, and she couldn't let her temper result in the leak of sensitive information. So she sat, rubbing the hem of her dress and wishing she had her damn phone.

"You are not so chatty now, Dr. Whyte," Omar noticed. "Rejoice. We are alive."

Lillian frowned. "But we don't know about the other hostages."

A few minutes later, which seemed like hours to Lillian, they pulled into the ambulance bay. Police and government vehicles parked behind and beside the ambulance. She assumed they had escorted the ambulance here as a protection detail for Omar Jabal.

Once the patients were taken into the emergency room, Lillian left Labaris and Omar to find a phone. Neither of them needed her services any longer. Omar would get an X-ray and a cast to replace his splint, and Labaris would be inaccessible for the interrogation she wanted to give him owing to the minor detail of needing a chest tube and perhaps open thoracotomy.

She found a wall of phones and called Sean's phone first. After several rings, it went to voicemail. She hung up and then stared at the black plastic phone on the wall having no idea what number to call to reach the CIA.

Hello, operator, please connect me to the Central Intelligence Agency of the United States. Well, I don't know the number. No, this is not a crank call ...

That probably wasn't something she could successfully do through an operator.

Lillian found herself thinking about Sean as though he were already gone. How could he have survived? He would have had to best four armed men within fifteen minutes from the time she left the building to the time she felt the blast.

She suspected he had killed a man pursuing them at the airport in a bathroom brawl six years ago when they were fleeing from oil thieves. Subsequently, he had shot a man in the hospital where her brother had been staying when the assailants had come to get their revenge on her.

His violent past dated back to his Navy SEAL days, and he, no doubt, had a long list of kills. But she had never witnessed him in any acts of violence. Talking about his violent past was something he seldom did. Though she had not actually ever seen him fight, she was sure defeating a barrage of armed gunmen was beyond the capabilities of any operative, even Sean.

She wanted—needed—more of him. He couldn't be gone now. Not after the love and trust they had built over the last five years. During their first six months together, he supported her through nightmares from Kenya and she gave him time to learn how to let his guard down. They learned to trust and confide in each other.

They enjoyed a small wedding at Callaway Gardens in Georgia, with a few close friends and her brother in attendance. Initially, she had tried to change her name from Dr. Whyte to Dr. Jennings, but her profession was so entrenched in her identity that she never finished the transition paperwork.

She had lost her mother long ago to leukemia and her father, years later, to a cattle stampede. Sean had lost his parents and former fiancé in the September 11 tragedy in New York City. Having each other made them whole again.

Five years is not enough time.

She remembered the first time he had broached the subject of a long-term relationship. Still recovering from the shock of the violence in Kenya, she was just enjoying their time together. She hadn't yet considered what would happen when they both went back to work. She had known she wanted him, preferably all of him, though there was a chance that, with his work, she would only get a few months out of the year. Such an existence would be hard, painful even, but she had her career to occupy her. Snippets of time with someone she loved was more than she'd had before Kenya.

"You have turned my world upside down, Lillian," Sean had said, stroking a finger along her collarbone.

Her body tingled in response to his touch.

"Thank you. That was pretty amazing." She smiled.

"Yes, but I'm referring to more than the last thirty minutes." He licked his lips. He was propped up with a pillow under his elbow as he looked at her intently.

Was that a nervous twitch of his lashes?

He continued, "I'm referring to what we have together. I want to extend this relationship ... into a lifetime."

The healing gunshot graze on her hip had started to ache, but she didn't dare move before he finished his thought.

"I've been working on my PhD. I'd like to finish it and then to write and teach. I want to come home every night to you, or ... well ... I guess, technically, you'd be coming home every night to me.

"I have a lot of demons, Lillian. I have a dark past that I'd bury forever if I could. I can't honestly say I'd do any of it differently because a lot of good came of it, and the unexpected result is that I'm here, ensnared by a phenomenal woman who, somehow, is blind to my many faults."

He gave a weak grin. "If a future with me is something you can even vaguely envision, then I'll make the transition at whatever pace suits you."

She felt a smile spread across her face as she stared into his apprehensive copper eyes. Couldn't be often such a formidable man battled butterflies.

She shifted her weight and ran a hand through his hair.

"Do I have to pace myself, or can we just start this lifetime together now?"

His eyes widened. He cleared his throat. "Just to clarify ... are you saying that if I asked you to be mine forever, you would accept it now?"

"Are you asking me to be with you forever?"

"Yes." His voice dropped to a husky rumble. "Be mine forever?"

"Well, you already have my heart, and clearly, my body

responds to you in uncontrollable ways. So coming home to you every night sounds like a pretty amazing next step."

He leaned forward and kissed her with spine-tingling tenderness.

They had capitalized on their time together. They made up for the deprived lives they had led prior to meeting one another—she as an overworked, burned-out emergency room physician and he as an undercover operative, dehumanized and demoralized. She was saving lives, he was taking them, but neither were living their own lives.

In their time as a couple, they either took trips together or planned the next getaway. They toured great cities and visited exotic destinations. Antigua was her favorite. They had flown out of Atlanta, through Miami, and on to the Caribbean paradise. The island was surprisingly arid owing to its lack of tall mountains and scarce rainfall. Despite the lack of moisture in the air, there was plenty to be had in the ocean, with around three hundred beaches there.

Lillian and Sean made an adventure out of kayaking to as many beaches as they could. The ocean water was a stunning emerald, and they could see the sand, fish, and reefs below. After loading up on food, water, and snorkeling supplies, they would kayak to a remote area, then stop to snorkel or eat or make love in deserted beaches. Mostly, they made love.

It was blissful delight to be in the arms of someone who knew every inch of her body and her most tantalizing spots. And she knew his. Her fingers and her lips knew every inch of his tan skin, lean muscle, smooth stomach, and combat scars. Antigua was the only vacation she had ever taken where she had no tan lines at the end of the trip.

.   .   .

STANDING in front of the phone on the wall, she pulled her emotions back within her, bundling them tightly, refusing to experience the stages of grief before knowing for certain if he was dead or alive.

She ran shaky hands through her red hair, her nails digging into her scalp. She curled her hands into fists full of hair and forced a deep breath. Then she dropped her hands to her side. Looking down, she caught a glimpse of the tainted, white summer dress Sean had picked out for her. She felt a sudden lump of coal her in stomach because she had given him a hard time about his selection. It was beautiful—or it had been before the blood and soot and sweat.

Austin hadn't let her change clothes.

Austin. He has my phone!

She dialed the number to her smartphone.

A man's voice, mechanical and rehearsed, answered the phone, "You have reached the answering service of Dr. Lillian Whyte. How may I direct your call?"

Well, that's new.

"I *am* Dr. Whyte," she said. "Please connect me to Director William Austin."

"One moment," he replied.

"Dr. Whyte," Austin's voice resounded.

Lillian gripped the phone with white knuckles. "Please tell me that wasn't a bomb."

"It was a bomb," he said, but hurriedly added, "but Sean is okay. He was out before the blast hit. We're picking him up now."

She felt like a corset loosened from around her chest. Sucking in a deep breath, she felt the blood rush all the way to her toes.

"Can I get a ride?"

"Car's out front."

Lillian hung up the phone and headed to the front entrance of the hospital to look for a black SUV.

Austin sniffed and wrinkled his nose at the smell of the abandoned warehouse. The scent of rust and dust and mothballs filled the air. They had erected an impressive base in a short amount of time, but the location left something to be desired. He stood behind computer stations with large screens and half a dozen intelligence agents who were monitoring cell phones, street cameras, and Internet traffic. Despite all their technical equipment and expertise, Khait and his men had vanished.

He heard one of the agency's cars park and the door slam. Knowing it was Sean without turning to look, he sighed.

Time to face the music.

He and Sean had been colleagues for almost twenty years now. Though they never talked about their personal lives nor were they seen having beers outside of work together, they had mutual respect and trust. In their line of work, they valued those commodities more than small talk and intimacy.

There was a time when Austin truly disliked Sean because his fieldwork bordered on being a little too instinctual, too messy, and too beyond what he was instructed to do. Austin hadn't trusted Sean's cowboy methodology until he finally had to admit he produced results.

Austin had been disappointed in the Kenya massacre though. For quite some time, he felt Sean should have done more intelligence gathering and less time courting a certain American physician at the camp. Perhaps if he had been more focused, an entire military camp would not have been killed by the oil thief Sean was supposed to be hunting.

Later Austin admitted to himself that none of their intelligence could have predicted such an atrocity. Therefore, the fact that Sean's love interest was captured and led him to the villain's base was a better outcome than they could have hoped.

Damn messy and damn successful. That was Sean.

As the semiretired operative strode toward him, eyes ablaze with rage, Austin knew him well enough to know what was coming. His sport coat was in shreds with dried blood on one arm. If it was Sean's blood, his injury wasn't slowing him down.

Austin could have surrounded himself with guards. He could have ordered his men to restrain Sean, but he was going to need Sean to get past his frustration with his supervisor if he was to be useful with the work ahead of them. Sean needed his moment of retribution in order to focus on finding the terrorists. Austin only hoped his retribution would not result in a broken jaw.

"She's alive and uninjured," Austin reminded him hurriedly, knowing it would not alter Sean's course but hoping it would curtail how much power he would put into his punch.

"You *ass*," Sean snarled.

Then he swung.

Austin felt his jaw explode with pain, and stars swam before his eyes. He staggered back but remained standing, glad to keep at least some of his dignity in front of the team. He rubbed at his jaw and tested its function. Not broken. Fortunately, Sean had kept his impact at half his capable force.

"You'll be written up for that," Austin said without malice. While he accepted he would have to absorb Sean's anger in the form of violence, he also needed to let onlooking agents know assault would have consequence. He was not a punching bag.

Sean kept his fist balled but didn't strike again. "You brought my wife into this!" he shouted.

"And she saved the day," Austin replied flatly, adding, "again." Something deep inside his gut shriveled at having to admit her contribution.

Sean shook his head incredulously. "She could have been killed any number of ways. There were terrorists, AK-47s, and C-4 bombs."

"If I could have seen another way, if I had any other choice, I would not have used her," he explained. He hadn't wanted her for this task for many reasons. In addition to being an untrained civilian, she had a brute for a husband. Oh, and then there was having to deal with her sarcastic and impertinent mouth.

"She's not a choice," Sean growled. "Lillian is never an option. The CIA doesn't get to use her. You don't get to use her."

Sean poked a finger into his chest, which Austin found damn annoying. He took his punch, but he was not going to apologize for his action nor falsely promise he wouldn't do it all over again if it meant improving the outcome.

Sean lowered his finger and looked around at the warehouse, asking, "Who are the terrorists?"

"Al Tamsah Alfaraeina," Austin replied, content to see Sean's anger assuaging and rationality taking hold. He rotated his throbbing jaw slowly. He wanted to put ice on it but knew that would betray weakness before his team.

Sean narrowed his gaze. "The Crocodile Pharaohs? Kidnapping is new for them."

Austin nodded, not surprised that Sean was still keeping up with current events in the espionage world.

"Did they get Labaris's information?" Austin inquired. His mouth grew dry. He really didn't want to hear that his operation resulted in the confiscation of a recipe for a new type of biomedical warfare.

Instead of answering him, Sean glanced around at the busy operations in the center of the warehouse. He tilted his head slightly toward an office in the far corner. Austin followed his cue, and they walked over and entered the worn office, standing behind frosted windows. Sean closed the door.

In a low but enraged voice, he demanded, "Look me in the eye, and tell me you didn't know Labaris was bringing the actual biomedical weapon."

CHAPTER 10

Austin took a few long seconds to digest Sean's words calmly spoken with their icy bite. He felt the blood drain from his face.

"He brought the biohazard?" he asked in a whisper. "And the fact that you didn't just hand it to me means they have it."

Austin felt weak and suddenly old, too old for this kind of stress. He reached into his sport coat pocket, withdrew his pack of antacids, and dropped two into his mouth. He put the pack back in his pocket.

Sean's shoulders sagged slightly as though simultaneously believing Austin's ignorance and reliving the gravity of the situation.

"Sir"—a voice came from outside the office—"Dr. Whyte has arrived."

Although his conversation with Austin was not concluded, Sean's head jerked up, and he took two long strides to the door. He snatched it open.

Austin watched as the beautiful woman threw herself into

Sean's arms, golden-red hair the color of sunset spilling around them. He pursed his lips in a mixture of jealousy and annoyance. Certainly, he had never had such a beautiful and accomplished woman throw herself at him, and their personal display of affection was wasting valuable time.

If there was a biohazard loose in Montreal, he needed to let Canadian Intelligence and CAAM know. He bit his tongue. He needed to give the couple their moment if he was going to get their cooperation.

At last, she pulled away, then took hold of Sean's coat collar and shook it.

"You should've told me there was a bomb," she demanded, but her voice betrayed more relief than anger.

More than one, Austin thought. He kept silent. Of course, Sean wouldn't have told her. She had already been under enough duress with armed gunmen. If Sean told her there were bombs, she might have cracked under the pressure.

Her eyes roamed over Sean, seeming to inspect him for any injuries.

"Then you wouldn't have left me," Sean replied.

She took hold of his chin to turn his face and inspected an abrasion on his forehead.

She huffed, then said, "Damn right I wouldn't have."

"How did you get out?" Noticing blood on his coat, she started to inspect his arm. "Did you get *it* back?"

Sean shook his head.

"You're cut," she said with alarm.

"Not bad."

She shot him a sharp look of reprimand as she roughly helped him out of his coat.

Austin enjoyed their banter for a moment. It was nice to see someone who didn't tolerate any crap from Sean.

He walked over to the agent outside the door, took the medic bag from him, and closed the three of them in the office.

Sean stood shirtless as Lillian cleaned a three-inch laceration on the back of his arm.

"Are you tracking Khait Sadat now?" Sean asked him.

Austin scowled. "He escaped."

"Do you know what he has?" The physician's eyes darted to him as she interrupted. Before Austin could reply, she leaned over to Sean, asking, "Does Bill know what he has?" She cleansed the wound and then began injecting lidocaine under the skin surface.

Austin shot her an irritated glance before speaking. "I knew that he was supposed to be couriering information about a disease that could be turned into a biological weapon." He held up his hand before she started flapping that uncontrollable mouth of hers again. "And yes, I am now aware that Labaris brought the actual disease with him."

"Why is an Egyptian biomedical engineer in Canada giving away his country's secrets?" She laid out suturing supplies and then donned a set of sterile gloves.

Austin pinched the bridge of his nose, trying to alleviate the pressure of a headache that was forming. He wasn't supposed to have to explain anything to a civilian, but since she had just saved the Egyptian ambassador, he felt obliged to share some information with her.

"The International Biomedical Conference is currently being held at the Palais des congrès de Montréal. Labaris is a presenter at the conference. It was our opportunity to get the information while he was under less watchful eyes and then help him defect."

Then he added, "He created the disease under duress."

"*Modified* the disease," Lillian corrected him bitterly. She began to suture Sean's wound. "Modified a prion disease. A disease for which there is no cure."

"He does not want to see it used on anyone," Austin said.

She pursed her lips. "And our government wouldn't possibly do that."

Austin bared his teeth at her, failing to mask his annoyance. "We reviewed what details he gave us early on and decided the disease would be too unpredictable. What if it aerosolized? Could it be transmitted across thousands of miles with symptoms so latent we'd never know until we were all infected? We had no intention of using it."

She tilted her head. "Biological warfare that's not quite tailor-made to the government's liking. Pity."

Her tone of mock sympathy grated on his nerves. He looked to Sean for some measure of support or perhaps to rein in her mouth. But he saw in Sean's expression amusement around the wrinkles at the edges of his eyes as he watched his wife.

She tied the sutures and clipped the extra strings. Then she taped a bandage over the wound.

Austin tried to look unimpressed, but she had just thrown in six stitches in under three minutes. He shook off the amazement and glared at Sean expectantly until he made eye contact and understood.

Sean cleared his throat as he slipped his shirt back over his shoulders. "Regardless of previous plans or intentions, we need to focus on getting that vial back."

Austin scratched irritably at his elbow. "We are working on it," he said.

Hadn't this muscle-laden bronze brute noticed the quarter-million dollars' worth of hardware in the warehouse or the half dozen agents working frantically at the computers?

Austin added, "I need the two of you debriefed and then parked in front of a computer screen identifying Khait's colleagues."

———————————

SENATOR COLE LAWSON plopped into his office chair, staring at the news on the television. His mouth felt parched even as he sipped his tea. The Nigerian black tea was bold and still warm on his lips. Although he was born and raised in the US, he liked to drink the tea and think of his African ancestry. He still had relatives in Nigeria.

"So far," the reporter on television was saying against a backdrop of debris and damaged buildings, "we don't know the cause of the explosion at the bookstore in Old Montreal. A van crashed into the bookstore a short time before the explosion and may have burst a gas line. There is some speculation that the explosion could have been a terrorist bombing. No organizations have yet claimed responsibility ..."

He sighed and muted the television. He liked Montreal, liked visiting this time of year and working away from his usual office. His wife and kids enjoyed the trip as well. There were plenty of sites to see and amusement parks to fill the weeks' activities. His family had been at La Ronde across the river riding roller coasters when the explosion occurred. They had been *safely* across the river. The first thing he had done was call and check on them.

A knock resounded at the door.

"Come in," Cole said.

He swiveled in his desk chair to see his assistant enter the room.

"Parker." He greeted the thin man.

"Senator."

Parker hesitated. "Sir?"

"Yes?"

"Is it a bomb?" he asked nervously.

Cole pursed his lips and nodded. The State Department had

already informed him it was indeed a bomb even if news reporters hadn't been made aware of the facts yet.

Parker looked stricken. His loyal assistant worked like a fiend and didn't mind traveling with Cole, but he had zero experience with real threats.

"Senator, what do you want to do about the dinner party?"

Cole stared past Parker, unfocused eyes on the partially open office door behind him.

"The UN meeting this weekend is still on?"

"Yes, sir."

"Then so are we," he concluded.

Parker started to back out of the door. "I'll let the guests know."

"Thank you, Parker."

Cole turned his attention back to his tea.

The UN subcommittee meeting was paramount in the peace-keeping efforts. Discussions about boosting economies in Africa and reducing political strife were needed to address the rampant terrorist factions, especially in Northern Africa. These leaders needed to have this meeting, but the stakes were high with terrorists here in Montreal.

The meeting was in just a few days, so it was reasonable to assume it could be another target. Why they would detonate a bomb only days before and raise the existing level of security was a mystery. At least, now authorities knew there was a threat present.

For something as important as the UN meeting, perhaps the assumption should be that a threat always existed.

***

LILLIAN PACED THE WAREHOUSE, sipping a double espresso thick with cream. She drank the warm refreshment and felt the delectable liquid warm her chest.

Thank the stars someone made a coffee run.

After two hours, she had finally finished staring at images of Middle Eastern men on a computer screen. She had identified all the gunmen—or thought she had. It was all starting to blur. She wiped at her watering eyes. They had one thing in common—too much facial hair. Except for the leader.

She had reclaimed her phone earlier and had been given a log printout of phone conversations. Her personal operator had spoken with incoming callers and taken messages. Three calls from Kelly and one from her brother. Kelly left a message asking if she had looked at the cakes, and Jonathan's response had been to ask when in the hell had she gotten an answering service. She stared down at her phone on the table beside the laptop, not ready to return any calls.

The agent who had been with her taking notes packed up his laptop and left.

The warehouse hummed with computers and buzzed with activity. Between the faint wafting of diesel fumes from a generator and the incessant clicking of fingers on keyboards, she began to feel light-headed.

She pushed aside fresh memories of nearly losing her husband.

"Dr. Whyte," Austin began, approaching her from his command center with Sean in tow, "there is a vehicle out front when you're ready to leave."

Lillian raised an eyebrow. This was apparently Austin's way of saying "get lost."

Sean must have read her expression because he puffed his chest out defensively. "You brought her into this. You can't just dismiss her like that."

"I can, and I will," Austin replied.

Sean took a step forward.

Lillian stepped between them, coffee in hand. Earlier, she had noticed the red swelling of Austin's jaw and could only assume it had been Sean's handiwork. Austin didn't go into combat, so the only explanation was Sean's outrage at Austin sending her into a hostage crisis and a building full of explosives. Any more violence between them was just unnecessary.

"I'm really wiped." She blinked at Austin.

She swiveled toward Sean. "I've done this rodeo before. I've chased the bad guys. I've been part of the team. I am perfectly content to leave this room of highly qualified experts, seated over there"— wanting to ensure that Austin didn't assume she was referring to him before continuing—"to do their job."

Sean's tension eased visibly as his shoulders relaxed.

"I'm going to go over to that table, eat my turkey swiss on rye, and then go back to my hotel room and take a hot bath." She left them and sat down to eat a late-afternoon sandwich.

As she ate, the sandwich seemed the most heavenly thing she'd had in a week. Her metabolism had burned through the half bagel for breakfast probably just in the time it took for her to ride to the warehouse and learn of the danger to Sean.

She idly skimmed through a stack of papers on Omar Jabal as she ate. Presumably, they had been printed in duplicate when he was kidnapped to see if the kidnappers' identities could be gleaned from his file. Now that the ambassador was safe and the Crocodile Pharaohs fingered as the culprits, the stack of papers sat waiting to be shredded.

Pity engulfed her as she read about Omar's impoverished childhood and struggle to educate himself in a time of upheaval. He had married, but his first wife died of malaria. During his second marriage, he had a son, but he was visiting friends in Port Said on the Egyptian coast when he was killed by bomb shrapnel at the young age of nineteen. Shortly after this tragedy, his second wife committed suicide. Despite these unthinkable hardships, he had earned his way to ambassador. The man had risen from poverty and hardship to travel the world. Perhaps she had been a bit harsh toward him at the bookstore.

She thought of her own hardships—losing her mother to cancer and her father, many years later, in a cattle stampede. She was surprised to have learned cows killed more people annually than sharks. She discovered this fact after his death. Subsequently, it was a conversation she'd had many times with people over the years when they learned of how he died and she saw their incredulous expression.

Despite the misfortune, she had become a physician and her brother a marine. The truth of life was that everyone was fighting his or her own battle every day against previous misery, adversity, and grief in an effort to make life better than it had been.

When she finished her sandwich and light reading, a wave of utter exhaustion hit her. Just then, strong, warm hands sunk into her shoulders. She moaned and closed her eyes as Sean started massaging the tense muscles in her neck. She melted under his touch even amidst the bustling warehouse.

"It's officially released to the press as a bomb now."

"That didn't take long," Lillian commented.

"Better if the Canadian authorities come forth with the truth so they're not criticized later for withholding information from the public or trying to cover anything up."

She nodded. "Are we staying in Montreal until this is finished?"

Sean seemed to flinch slightly before answering. "I need to see this through, Lily."

"Damn right you do." She looked up at him.

He smirked, seemingly reassured she wasn't upset.

She didn't like the thought of him in danger. She liked even less the thought of this disaster being managed by someone less competent. Not to name names, but Assistant Deputy Director Austin was mediocre at best. In all fairness, she had limited interaction with him, so her impression was based on the post-Kenya debriefing and fallout. Since then, Sean seemed to think he had improved. Nevertheless, she would feel better knowing Sean was involved.

He leaned nearer, whispering in her ear, "Go back to the room and get some rest. I'll join you shortly."

Nodding, she patted his hand and then pushed herself up from the chair.

She tidied the pile of papers she had rifled through, then turned and hugged her husband goodbye.

"Love you. Be safe," she whispered.

"Love you," he replied with a kiss on her cheek.

She wanted to hold him longer, hug him harder, but he had work to do and a reputation to maintain.

CHAPTER 11

The driver of a black sedan, an impassive agent with whom Lillian was too drained to make small talk, drove her back to her hotel. She drummed her fingers on her purse. He parked the car and opened the door for her.

She eyed him as she got out of the car. "You didn't drop me off," she observed, "which means that you're staying with me."

"Director's orders," he confirmed.

"Okay, Agent ...?"

"Applegate," he answered.

"Okay, Agent Applegate." She knew better than to argue with him about his orders, though if she were to be targeted by terrorists for her involvement earlier, she wondered what one armed man would accomplish. She hadn't thought to worry about her own safety, but now his presence raised her awareness.

She kept a few paces behind Agent Applegate and his black luggage bag as they entered the hotel. He checked into his room, which somehow managed to be directly across the hall from hers.

When they arrived at her hotel room door, she withdrew her key card from her purse. Agent Applegate fluidly clipped the key from her hand and put his large body between her and her hotel room door. She stood frozen, waiting. The mechanical lock slid open, and he opened the door. Stepping inside, he surveyed her room.

She walked tentatively in behind him and sat down on a chaise lounge as he inspected the bedroom, bathroom, and windows. Her luggage had arrived; she noticed the familiar red suitcase standing at the foot of the bed.

"All clear, ma'am," he concluded.

She nodded in appreciation.

From a pocket of his luggage, he withdrew a small rounded black object. He stood on his toes at the door's entrance and secured the object on the outside doorframe.

She looked at him quizzically.

"This camera will project to a laptop in my room," he explained. "I'll be able to see everyone coming and going. If it's anyone other than Agent Jennings, expect I will come over and introduce myself."

Looking at his boyish face and spiked blond hair, she tried to imagine him "introducing" himself and his Browning HP-35 pistol to any visitors she may have.

When Agent Applegate finished his security detail and withdrew to his room, Lillian felt the weight of silence around her.

Creutzfeldt-Jakob disease.

She shuddered and wrapped her arms around her torso. Instead of the relaxing bath she had planned, she scrubbed herself clean in the shower. Then she dressed in her cotton pajamas and sat in bed with her tablet.

As a distraction, she looked up her Facebook profile created by Austin's team. It was superficial but contained all the key elements

— she worked in an Atlanta emergency room; she liked horseback riding and running. There was a selfie of her and her husband, an attractive tan man with light-brown hair that was not Sean. She knew that photo though. It had been from their trip to Italy. Somehow, they had confiscated the photo from her cloud and superimposed a stranger's face in place of Sean.

There was a picture of her in running shorts after the Georgia's Tri-Cities 10K run. Sean had taken the profile shot and told her it was one of his favorites.

Apparently, she liked to post about health and safety issues. There was a post on child-seat safety, trampoline injuries, and the dangers of all-terrain vehicles. It was almost as though they knew some of her prior patients.

They had also thrown in a shared article about emergency room physician burnout, which seemed especially intuitive as burnout was the reason she had gone to Kenya six years ago. A smattering of posts about recipes she liked were sporadically peppered between the more serious medical posts. How did they know she liked chicken curry? Lastly, there was a post with the Canadian flag and her declaration about how excited she was to be leaving for Montreal.

Frighteningly, Big Brother had created a Facebook account that actually looked quite representative of her. She was going to need to remind Austin to have it deleted.

Her phone buzzed. Jonathan. She had forgotten to call him back. It was out of character for him to call twice in one day.

"Hi," she said.

"What's going on?" he demanded.

Lillian was startled. "What do you mean?"

He couldn't know what she had been through, so she tried to fathom if there was something she had done or not done with regards to her brother.

"A bomb went off in Montreal, Lily. You are *in* Montreal."

Lillian frowned into the phone. "Why would you assume that had anything to do with me?"

"I didn't," he spat, "until I called to make sure you were okay, and I get an answerin' service. You don't have an answerin' service, Lily." His tone rose in an alarmed crescendo, and his Arkansas accent became more pronounced.

She considered briefly inventing a story about hiring a service while on vacation, but she didn't care to lie, especially not to her brother.

"I'm fine," she said, offering no further explanation.

He was silent for a moment, as though deciding whether to pursue her clipped response.

"And Sean?"

Is this an angle of probing or genuine concern for my husband?

"Sean is well. I'm sorry you were frightened. We are both fine. We're still here on vacation."

Sort of.

"Enjoying your vacation?"

"Less so with the threat alert at red," she admitted though it was for many more reasons than just a colored-coded threat scheme. "However," she added, "I am sufficiently distracted from work."

Their last conversation had been about some of her difficulties at work, which he assured her would improve with time and space and relaxation.

"Did you decide to do the leadership training?"

She was relieved he had taken his cue to ask no further questions about the bombing. Six years ago when she had destroyed the oil thieves' compound, they had come all the way to Arkansas to kill her brother. Luckily, they had underestimated the former marine, yet he had still been shot. After that, she owed him the truth that Sean was CIA and she'd had several near-death experiences.

In the months to follow, he had opened up about his own frightening encounters as a marine to help her through her post-Kenya nightmares.

Today, however, she could divulge no secrets and would be forced to dance carefully around any direct answers. Discussing work was a welcomed alternative, even if it was the dreaded leadership training topic.

"I don't know," she said with resignation. "It's a lot of understanding personalities and emotions."

"And that's a bad thing?"

"It's absurdly complicated. If people just do their job, then there needn't be whole bookshelves on leadership. When I'm running a trauma code, I give directions and they follow. In fact, everyone knows their job well enough that they often don't need a lot of direction or hand-holding."

He snorted. "*People* are absurdly complicated, Lily." She heard what sounded like him popping open the top of a beer bottle and taking a swig. "Besides, what works in a trauma code might not work in other daily operations—"

"Give orders, follow orders," she interjected, knowing she was oversimplifying. "Isn't that how you marines operate?"

"In some situations," he said slowly.

She sighed. "When my superiors talk to me about leadership training and hand me books to read, I feel like they are trying to change my personality. Round peg, meet square hole."

She recalled having said as much to Sean in a similar conversation. Since he played so many roles as a spy, he could easily change his demeanor for a given situation. A hat for every occasion. It also meant he couldn't grasp her struggle to change.

"I was thinking square peg," Jonathan teased.

She scoffed.

"Look," he said, his tone growing more serious, "I think you're looking at it backward. They don't want to turn you into a leader."

"They don't?" she asked skeptically.

"No. They already recognize that you are a leader. They simply want you to become a more *effective* leader."

That gave her pause. He must be on his third beer because he actually gave sage advice around that marker. By the fifth beer, though, he made no sense at all.

Effective leader.

Sean had said something along those lines also. "An effective leader recognizes her leadership style and plays to her strengths. She analyzes the different group dynamics and is able to steer them toward creativity and productivity."

"Sounds manipulative," she had commented.

"Not manipulative," Sean had corrected. "It's understanding human nature."

She definitely did not understand human nature. What drove people to do the things they did? Maybe that was why she couldn't comprehend Khait's intentions. He wasn't a bone fracture, a stroke, a heart attack, or a sucking chest wound. She understood those. For complex human motivators, personality characteristics, inner psyche, and nature versus nurture—she was at a loss.

"Perhaps you're right," she conceded to her brother.

"I'm sorry?" he asked, speaking loudly, his voice dripping with irony. "Must be a bad connection. I didn't quite catch that. What did you say?"

She laughed. "You're right."

"If you could just repeat that one more time, I need to get that recorded." He made noises like he was fumbling with something. "Oh, wait, never mind. As your husband is CIA, it is likely this conversation is already being recorded."

She rolled her eyes, though he wasn't wrong.

Then he added dismissively, "I can subpoena the records later."

"Goodbye, Jonathan," she singsonged. "Call you when I get back home."

"Stay safe," he said in a more serious tone before she hung up the phone.

She felt suddenly exhausted, and her eyelids grew heavy.

Cake. Forgot to look at the cakes. Some maid of honor I turned out to be.

She closed her eyes just to rest them for a moment.

SEVERAL HOURS after his phone call with his sister, Jonathan paced the floor in his ranch house. He absentmindedly stuck a hand in his boxer shorts. For the first time in years, he thought about the night he was attacked in his own home.

Automatic weapon fire.

Glass raining down upon him.

An acquaintance dead on his kitchen floor.

He'd been forced to shoot to kill. He took a gulp of his beer. That night he realized how much danger his sister had faced in Kenya against men under orders to kill. Hired humans with no conscience. He didn't even know she was in danger until it was almost concluded.

The news footage of Montreal continued to cycle on the television in his living room. The bomb could be seen exploding at various angles. Entire buildings were brought to ruin.

He found out many months after her return from Africa that she had fallen in love with the CIA agent who helped save her. Well, that was her version of the story. He suspected the CIA agent probably put her in danger to begin with, and Lily just didn't realize it. Then she married the oaf. Supposedly, he was retired.

Writing books, my ass.

He must have dragged her to Montreal on a mission, and now she was in the same city as a group of terrorists who were bombing buildings.

Careless, reckless, son-of-a—

He caught a glimpse of the television and froze. There was a brief clip of the bookstore before the bomb went off when an ambulance was parked outside the building.

A redhead in a white dress walked toward the ambulance.

The image cut back away to the bomb.

Jonathan's heart pounded in his ears.

No way.

He slid into his desk chair and frantically opened his computer. An Internet search on the Montreal bombing led to several videos about the event. Most were of the bomb itself or the aftermath, but he found one where the camera crew captured prebombing footage.

He couldn't see the woman's face from the distance nor the man she was assisting into the ambulance, but he knew that hair, knew that walk.

Lily had lied to him.

He sat back in his chair dumbfounded. His sister had been at the bookstore, just minutes before the explosion. She was doctoring. Was she working for the CIA? Had she been for all these years?

My sister, an operative?

He swallowed hard, unable to assuage the stab of betrayal in his chest. She was evasive sometimes, but he had really believed she was just an emergency room physician all this time.

The biggest mystery of all—why was Lily wearing a dress and sandals?

Lillian watched herself suture a cordis in place in the neck of a patient. Judging by the patient's low blood pressure, she surmised she was placing the large intravenous line because of some form of shock. The patient lay fairly motionless with bloodied clothes around him.

Blood loss.

Hemorrhagic shock then.

She observed from a slightly hovering position as the redheaded physician took off her sterile gown and was back in her black scrubs. Her nametag dangled from one pocket: *Lillian Whyte, MD*, with *Emergency Medicine typed beneath it.*

Below that, in bold, black letters with a yellow neon background, was the word *doctor*. Patients came into the ER in all levels of distress (and intoxication), and most of the ER physicians didn't wear white coats. They were nothing but an extra layer to take off during an emergency and an extra layer to wash. Physicians attached these visible tags to their name badges because patients often got confused about who was who in a sea of scrubs. At best, patients didn't really care, and at worst, they claimed they were never seen by a physician, even though doctors always introduced themselves as such.

The normal bustling of the emergency room swirled around her. Lillian watched herself walk away from the patient and toward the nearest computer.

Everything in the emergency room flickered as though she had poor reception of her own omniscient view.

Great. Satellite interference in my dream.

Dark figures burst into the emergency room. Screams reverberated off the walls as people dashed for cover. Three assailants dressed in crimson outfits with black hoods obscuring their faces fanned out in an attack formation.

Lillian watched as her dream figure took a protective stance in front of her patient. Her black scrubs transformed into a tight-fitting burglar outfit.

Well, that leaves nothing to the imagination.

With amazing speed, she sprinted toward one of the attackers. He took aim to shoot her, but she dropped to her knees. Her momentum carried her forward, sliding across the smooth, laminated floor. She spun around, lashing out a leg and knocking the man flat on his back. She launched a smooth right hook across his jaw.

Whoa. I need to cut back on the superhero movies.

She felt the sudden urge to sit on a sofa with a bag of popcorn and watch herself be a badass.

Her superhero alter ego leaped into the air and brought an elbow down on the shoulder of another man as he was drawing his gun. He let out a grunt and hunched down from the force of the impact. She spiked a knee up into his face. His head jerked, and his spine arched backward as he fell to the floor.

Who needs leadership skills when you've got those moves?

She flicked a strawberry strand of hair out of her eyes as she turned to face the last attacker. By this time, he had his gun drawn and aimed.

No problem.

This was her superhero dream. Naturally, she could dodge bullets, right?

She felt her phantom self pulled into her body. Then she was standing there, dressed in black, facing the bullet that had been fired. She watched it sail with incredible slow speed, inching through the air and sending rippling waves around it.

But she couldn't move. She could not dodge the bullet. It was blazing a course directly toward her chest. At best, it would collapse her lung like Labaris's, but it was far more likely to hit a major blood vessel, if not her heart. Suddenly, it didn't matter that she had known this was a dream. She was terrified of being shot—again. And for what? A patient she didn't know?

She turned her head to look over her shoulder, and her pulse quickened. Sean. They were his bloodied clothes.

No!

Her heart leaped into her throat as an icy shockwave of fear coursed through her, followed immediately by fiery anger.

She turned back to face the bullet as it struck her.

CHAPTER 12

Lillian woke to the sound of Sean entering the hotel room. It was dark, and the bedside clock indicated it was ten o'clock. She sat up and rubbed her eyes with a yawn.

"How did it go?" she asked sleepily.

"They think they've found an Al Tamsah Alfaraeina safe house. There will be a raid in a few hours." He stripped down to his boxers.

"I'm sorry," he added. "I hadn't intended to stay gone so long."

Any apology expressed while she got to see him half-naked was going to be well received. She smiled. "As you can see, I was up the whole time, worried sick."

He paused to look at her sitting up in a bed of ruffled covers. She winked at him. He walked over to a group of plastic clothing bags he had set on the floor as he entered the room. He tossed the contents of one of them to her. It landed on the bed with a thud.

"I'm going to take a shower. Can you get changed, and we'll go out for a walk?"

She peered into the bag—black pants, black shirt, and long black boots.

Just a walk, huh?

"You dressing me again?"

"It's not a *dress*," he replied cheerfully as he shut the bathroom door.

Lillian donned the suspiciously covert-looking outfit for a midnight stroll. At least it wasn't the tight-fitting superhero outfit from her dream.

She rummaged through the other bags of items he had bought — water, flashlights, black gloves, batteries, rope, and a compactly folded backpack. Well, this was vastly different from how she had envisioned spending her vacation.

Not dull though.

Life with Sean was never dull.

She fixed herself a cup of caffeinated tea while she waited. Sipping the tea, she sat in the lounge chair, visited Kelly's website, and scrolled through a dozen cakes. They were large, elaborate, and expensive looking. They were all covered in fondant. She was sure the stuff was just Play-Doh with sugar instead of flour.

Ick.

Sean emerged from the bathroom, clean and dressed in all black. His T-shirt fit snugly against his biceps. He slipped on black boots and adjusted his black jean legs over them.

"Why do I get the feeling this is not a moonlit stroll?" she asked wryly.

He walked toward her, grabbed her at the waist, and pulled her to him gruffly. She smelled the scent of spice with a touch of mint aftershave. She stroked a hand on his smooth jaw.

"Because it is not a moonlit stroll."

He kissed her roughly, sending a wave of excitement from her lips to her toes.

"I want to go back to the bookstore and figure out how they got away. I can't do that from inside a warehouse think tank."

She tapped a finger against his lips. "And you're bringing me for my valuable insight or because walking with your wife makes you look less like a burglar?"

She ran her hands down his shoulders and chest.

He smiled at her. "Bit of both," he conceded.

He handed her a flashlight. She slipped her identification and key card in her back pocket. He put on a blue sports coat and had her wear a pink blazer. She put the flashlight in her blazer pocket, mimicking what Sean did with his. He had wrapped the rope around his torso under his shirt and tucked the collapsible backpack and gloves in his back pocket. He carried the water bottle.

They left their hotel room, and Sean knocked on Agent Applegate's door. It opened promptly as though he were already at the door.

"Alex," Sean began, "we're going to grab a light snack. Can I bring you something back?"

The agent looked back and forth at Lillian and Sean. "No, sir," he said hesitantly. "Thank you, sir."

Lillian and Sean left and took the elevators down to the lobby. They took a cab to the Rue Sainte Antoine just a few blocks from the bookstore. While in the cab, Sean unfolded the backpack and had her roll her pink blazer and his blue sport coat into a ball and stuff them inside the pack. He tucked the water bottle and rope inside and kept the flashlights available.

After they exited the cab, she followed Sean through various side streets and alleys. When they reached the alley behind the bookstore, they had to duck under police tape to get closer. The alley was dark with not even a window light on to provide illumination. Either the explosion had taken out the power supply or the area was abandoned after the terrorist attack or both.

Lillian shined her flashlight around the scene. There was

rubble everywhere—concrete and stone blocks displaced and shattered glass.

"You survived this?" she asked, dumfounded.

"I was here," he began. Then he projected his light down an alleyway. "They ran in that direction. I couldn't pursue because they had left a shooter behind." He shined his light on a block of rubble. "I took him out there and then the bomb detonated."

A chill went down her spine as she remembered the ambulance shuddering from the blast.

Lillian followed Sean to the end of the alley but didn't see an escape route.

"Now what?" she asked.

He held up one finger and silenced her. They stood in the dark alley listening. Street traffic rumbled and beeped several blocks away. Music played into the street from a bar somewhere on a parallel road. Then she heard it. Water. Trickling water.

She followed Sean down a few short steps to a narrow entry into the sewer.

That explains the boots.

She sighed as they crawled through the hole and into a large sewer tunnel. It was eight feet high with gray concrete walls discolored to yellow, green, and brown in areas. Fortunately, the dark liquid at their feet was only a few inches deep. The air had a musty, moldy smell to it.

Well, she could cross off sewer exploration from her bucket list. Oh, wait. That was not on her bucket list. It must be on her other list—the "places she would never consider going" list.

They followed the tunnel north, and it seemed to be diving further underground. The water deepened, forcing them to explore an offshoot to the west. This segment appeared older, with brown stone brick halfway up the sides that connected with the concrete arch of the tunnel.

"So what do you know about the Crocodile Pharaohs?" It

seemed like appropriate small talk while they crept through a tunnel in a foreign country in the middle of the night.

"Al Tamsah Alfaraeina is a small terrorist group with some known bombings and shootings. They don't have the infrastructure to be too much of a threat. Or rather, they weren't much of a threat until today," he corrected himself.

"What's their target?"

She could barely make out the sight of him shaking his head in the dark.

"The CIA has theories, but they don't know for sure."

"They think kidnapping Omar was all just a ruse?"

"Seems that way," he replied, though his tone suggested he didn't think it was that simple. "There is an extra layer of security on him just in case."

She frowned. "Then what's troubling you?"

"Too many pieces that don't fit."

"Like what?"

She knew the pieces of the puzzle didn't fit by her calculation. It didn't surprise her because she had such limited knowledge about terrorists. Because he knew a great deal more than her about the situation, his missing pieces had more significance.

"For starters, the CIA's pegged Khait as the leader, but I can't fit him as a die-hard fanatic. He's a playboy who wants the acclaim of notoriety. I think he's just a puppet."

"And the puppet master?"

He shrugged, and she heard the faint tick of him clucking his tongue in thought. His flashlight swung from side to side, casting long shadows through the tunnel.

"I've been out of the game too long to make an educated guess. I don't know all the players and stakeholders anymore."

"But you don't think Pretty Boy is the king rat," she said, thinking of his crocodile smile.

He looked at her and blinked. "Definitely not."

After another left then right, they came to a large junction and a larger concrete tunnel. Here, narrow walkways lined either side, so thankfully, they didn't have to trudge through the muck of indiscernible depth in this segment of the tunnel. They walked and walked, and Lillian tried to avoid touching any walls or pipes with their grimy layers of deposits. What could Sean be looking for? It would be impossible to decipher which way the Crocodiles had gone in the maze of tunnels.

At a rusted door, Sean came to a halt. A dank metal handle protruded. He put his head near the door and listened.

"The metro," he said at last. "We must be at the northernmost station—Berri-UQAM. This tunnel must run under Rue Sainte Catherine."

How could he have possibly kept his sense of direction in this maze? They could have been back in the United States for all she could tell.

Sean started to turn the circular handle, which emitted a loud screech of grating metal in protest. He stopped.

"Well, I *can* open it, but since I'm not sure if there are security cameras on the other side, I don't want to risk opening it."

"Okay," she replied, concealing her disappointment. She had been looking forward to escaping this cement tomb.

"The UQAM is also part of Underground Montreal. It's a network of city segments with shopping, hotels, pedestrian walkways, and metro connections."

"Oh, shopping and sightseeing—that might be too much like a *normal* vacation."

"C'mon, sweetheart, you like being part of my adventures."

"Only the ones that don't involve sewage," she retorted. But he was right, she knew. She would take a memory-making hike through muck with Sean over a museum tour alone. That didn't mean she couldn't harass him about his choice of nonromantic getaways.

They traced their steps back and then zigzagged a few more times before emerging out to a side street on the Rue La Fontaine, not far from the Parc La Fontaine.

They put their flashlights away and jackets back on before walking down the road to find a taxi.

———

WHEN THEY WERE BACK inside the hotel room and Lillian was rinsing the stench off her boots, she said, "So you know how they got away but not where they went."

He nodded, taking off his shirt.

"Any more exciting sewer adventures at our next vacation spot?" she teased as she washed her hands clean.

She turned to him and noticed the worry lines along his face. It was eating him up that he hadn't stopped the Crocodiles yet. She touched a hand to his bare chest.

"Can I do anything? Do you need to go back to the warehouse?" she asked softly.

It was two o'clock in the morning, but he didn't look like sleep was on his mind. She had known him long enough to know that, right now, he was berating himself. He was trying to fathom how he could have done things differently to keep the vial or repossess it at the bookstore. And he would be calculating how to retrieve it.

She placed a gentle hand along his face and turned his distant gaze to her. His brown eyes focused on her as he smiled.

She smiled in return.

"I'm not really a key contributing agent. It's up to surveillance teams now—Internet traffic, airport and train station security and video, cell phone chatter, and satellite images."

"So not much you can do?"

He shook his head.

"So you need a distraction?"

She ran her hands down to his waist and drew her fingernails across his skin. His eyes turned smoky as he released a low, sensual growl. He wrapped his hands around her and pulled her to him.

———

LILLIAN WOKE a little before nine o'clock in the morning. Sean was already dressed in navy slacks and his sports coat. He was slipping on his shoes.

"Sorry, I was trying not to wake you," he said.

He sat down on the bed next to her and stroked her hair.

"Warehouse?" she asked.

She already knew the answer and expected he would want to go back and see where things stood. If anything, she was surprised he waited so late to leave. She would interpret that to mean she had provided an adequate and exhausting distraction last night.

Sean nodded. "I'll just be gone a few hours to check in and see if I can contribute anything to the search. I'll take you to lunch when I get back."

She watched him go. A little flutter of worry danced along her stomach, but she knew it was ludicrous. The warehouse was probably the safest place he could be right now. She also knew Austin wouldn't send him on any harried missions. Sean had fulfilled his commitment to his country.

He's part-time. Just information transfers. Unless he thinks he can do the job better.

He didn't like incompetence and seemed to think he was more competent than most. Certainly, his experience and track record validated his belief. She believed it too. Would that fact make him embrace something dangerous—an action that would put him in the line of fire?

The room fell silent with his absence.

She reached for her phone, pulled the charging cord off, and called Kelly.

"Hey, Lily!"

"I'm sorry I didn't call you back yesterday, but I have looked at the cakes."

"It's okay. I know I'm bothering you on vacation. Sorry for all the calls yesterday. When did you get an answering service? You need to tell me who you use because he was exceptionally professional and has a really hot voice. So what cakes did you like?"

They talked cake for a few minutes, and Lillian was blissfully delighted to have a friend who wasn't asking about bombs and reading deeper meaning into her missed calls. Kelly was so distracted by her wedding plans that she didn't think to ask Lillian about sightseeing in Montreal.

This worked well for Lillian who would have only been able to describe the burst guts of an old bookstore and the hollowed-out interior of an abandoned warehouse. Oh, and sewer tunnels.

Except ... she couldn't share any of that information with her friend. Kelly knew Lillian had been in trouble in Kenya and the CIA was involved, but that was the extent of it. As far as she knew, everything was done and resolved. As far as she knew, Sean was strictly former CIA and currently professor of history and writer, nothing more.

At last, they agreed on a style of cake that involved ribbons and teal-colored pearls. No doubt Kelly would change her mind several more times before actually settling on what she would buy for the wedding.

They said their goodbyes and disconnected.

Lillian wriggled out of bed and paced in the room for several moments. She tried to watch television, but it didn't hold her interest. At last, she decided she needed fresh air. She had travelled from a wrecked bookstore to a poorly ventilated warehouse to sewer tunnels.

Definitely need fresh air and exercise.

After four days of twelve-hour shifts followed by travel and then stress, her body was practically screaming to get moving. The tunnel had involved walking but not a real cardiovascular challenge. Her muscles felt pent-up, almost as though all the adrenaline from the day before had seeped into them and needed to be released—to be run out of her system.

After slipping into exercise clothes, she pulled her thick red hair into a ponytail. She slipped on her running shoes and stepped out of the hotel room.

She would have to let her surveillance agent know. Before she could knock, Agent Applegate opened his door. He wore the same flat expression on his young face and the same suit on his bulky body as the day prior.

"Morning, ma'am," he said, polite but devoid of cheer.

"Good morning, Agent Applegate," she countered with excess cheerfulness.

She put her earbuds in and connected them to her phone.

He frowned. "That's not a good idea," he replied, having assessed her attire and surmised her intent.

She smiled. "I'm not under house arrest," she assured him in a nonconfrontational tone. "I'm just going for a run. You may join me if you like."

"One moment, ma'am."

He closed the door.

Is he seriously going to run with me?

She waited a brief sixty seconds before he opened the door again, still dressed in his suit. In his hand was a small black band that looked like a fitness wristband.

Lillian looked at it skeptically and kept the same expression when she raised her head to look at Agent Applegate.

"Wrist tracker, ma'am," he explained. "It will allow me to know your location. If you give me your route, then I can make sure you do not deviate against your will or at a speed that would suggest you were no longer traveling on foot."

"Aren't you already doing that with my phone?" she asked wryly.

He didn't deny it but instead replied, "An abductor would likely destroy your phone but might overlook an exercise band, ma'am."

Lillian extended her wrist and let him fasten the band. She bit her tongue to keep any snide comments to herself about feeling like a dog on a leash.

She understood he was doing his job. She should not make it harder for him. Austin was the one with whom she was truly annoyed. Besides, she couldn't really be mean to Agent Applegate's baby face and no–nonsense, endearing *"ma'am."*

"I'm going to Mount Royal," she said.

CHAPTER 13

As soon as Lillian was down the elevator and out the door, she turned on her music and bolted toward Mount Royal—Montreal's peak overlooking the city.

Placing one foot in front of the other, she let the beat carry her forward on the concrete sidewalk. A light mist in the air brushed against the bare skin on her face, arms, and legs. Overcast clouds appeared to be on the verge of parting.

In two miles, her feet carried her off the city concrete and up the trail on the side of Mount Royal. The northern red oak lit up the mountainside like wildfire, while spruce provided a lush green backdrop.

Next, she conquered the stairs. Pushing forward, she felt her thighs burn as she ran up the steps. She passed other sightseers and joggers traversing up and down the wooden stairs. Reaching the top, she panted while peering over the lookout. She checked her phone—2.5 miles, which meant the run would make a nice five-mile round-trip. But first, she needed to catch her breath.

She stopped the music and took out her earbuds to hear the

rustling of leaves. From the overlook, she took in the city of Montreal.

Four million people down there, she marveled.

She couldn't appreciate the more historic buildings through all the more modern ones, but the skyline was breathtaking, with a silver sliver of the Saint Lawrence River behind an expanse of the city. The tallest skyscraper—1000 de la Gauchetiere, with its triangular peak—was nicely accented by other tall modern buildings. None though, by law, could be higher than Mount Royal.

"Dr. Whyte," a silky male voice spoke beside her.

Lillian turned, expecting to see one of Austin's agents. The smile that had started to form at the edges of her mouth dropped when she saw Khait standing next to her.

She fought the urge to scream. Her eyes darted for any signs of a gun and any possible escape route. He was blocking her only means of escape.

Instead of the black tactical outfit of yesterday, he wore a sweat suit with the Canadian flag on the front. His hair was still pulled in a ponytail, but he wore a navy knit hat. He blended in with the other walkers and runners.

The baggy shirt obscured the presence or absence of a weapon. His hands were tucked into his pockets. Probably safe to assume the fanatical terrorist was armed.

Not that he is the sort of man who needs a weapon to kill me.

"Please do not scream or fight. There are many people who could be injured." His soft tone held a gentle plea.

She believed him fully capable of opening fire on the passer-bys. After all, just yesterday he had shot someone at point-blank range in the chest shortly before detonating a bomb that leveled an entire building.

She stared at his flushed face. He was not panting at the top as much as she had been, though surely he had made the same run in keeping up with her.

Lillian felt a rising panic as her heart accelerated. Terrible flashbacks of Kenya raced through her mind—the carnage, the kidnapping, the armed men. Her head pounded as the trees around her began to spin.

I'm having a panic attack.

One of her hands shot out to steady herself against the railing.

She felt Khait bracing her. His muscular body was behind her with one leg and one hip keeping her on her feet. He was positioned to ease her down gently should she faint.

"Are you well?" he asked. Strangely, there seemed to be genuine concern in his voice.

Taking slow, deep breaths, she tried to calm herself.

Don't be a victim.

"I was," she said in a low, raspy voice, "until you ambushed me." Lillian closed her eyes, trying to force the spinning to stop.

Seemingly assured she wasn't about to faint, he took a step to her side.

He stared at her. "You are not an agent." Confusion filled his voice and his expression.

Opening her eyes, she glared sideways at him. Apparently, her panic attack would not be typical behavior for someone who lives, eats, and breathes violence. Did that make him more or less likely to shoot her?

"I thought we already established that," she said.

He flashed a white smile, seemingly relieved that she had reinstated her brassy tone. Her anxiety was under control.

As her calm composure resurfaced, she began to gain the use of her rational brain. When she could prepare for a dangerous or fearful situation, she could be calm and composed, or at least mask her fear with sarcasm. She had escaped her prison in Africa (albeit a mansion, it was still a prison) with tactical calmness because she had days to prepare. Before she had entered the bookstore with armed gunmen, she had time to tap into her inner serenity. This encounter had been so unexpected it was all the more terrifying.

Khait obviously hadn't jogged all the way to her just to put a bullet in her. He was also alive, which meant he had survived Austin's raid. But he wasn't wearing the look of a man whose coworkers (coterrorists?) had just been killed or apprehended.

Does he know?

If he had planned a conversation with her, he must have been waiting outside the hotel all morning. Had stalking her saved his life?

She sighed, more from sudden emotional exhaustion than irritation. "What do you want?"

He placed his hands on the rail, which she found somewhat reassuring. They weren't hiding with a finger on a trigger or on a kill switch.

"Now or esoterically speaking?"

She tilted her head.

Now, right now, with me! she wanted to scream.

But then she was a little curious about both.

"There is something you wish to discuss with me?" she clarified.

"I wish many things, Tabib," he said, gazing at the skyline.

Lillian waited. She decided to allow the armed fanatic to set the pace of the conversation.

He extended a hand. Lillian frowned. Then, reluctantly, she put her phone in his palm. He tucked it into his shirt pocket.

"Tabib?" she asked.

"It is *doctor* in Arabic," he explained patiently.

He added, "You are not an agent, but you are more than you pretend to be."

Since it wasn't a question, she felt no obligation to provide an explanation.

Instead, she remarked, "As are you, I think. What terrorist risks everything for a personal meeting with someone so wholly disconnected from his realm?"

He arched an eyebrow with his half smile, which in a different setting might have been called seductive.

"You entered *my* realm, Dr. Whyte. I am simply trying to understand why."

Somehow, she thought "I already told you" wasn't going to suffice. Since the rigorous truth was not an option, she would have to continue the game of dodgeball.

"I am trying to exit your realm. I left the bookstore. I left the injured at the hospital. I was back in my room then out for a jog. If I were an agent or otherwise involved, would I have gone for a run in the middle of a terrorist hunt? Unarmed?"

Shit.

She just told him she was unarmed. Then again, her spandex provided no place to conceal a weapon; therefore, he had probably already surmised the obvious lack of a gun.

He seemed to think about her words, trying to find something incongruent. His English was so impeccable there could be nothing lost in translation.

"You do not want to be involved in this, or you do?" he asked.

She admitted in a low voice, "If I thought I could stop people from dying, then I suppose, yes. Honestly, I'm not even sure what *this* is."

He nodded with a pensive scowl. "What do you know?"

She had trouble reconciling this conflicted man before her with the fanatical villain he was supposed to be. What was his game?

Sean had been skeptical about Khait being the leader of the Al Tamsah Alfaraeina, but she also thought it unlikely that someone gave him orders to have a conversation with her. Was he leading or breaking rules?

"I was told that the Crocodile Pharaohs—I'm sorry, I cannot

pronounce the appropriate Arabic name—are the terrorists involved."

"Al Tamsah Alfaraeina," he interjected politely. Somehow it flowed gracefully, like satin, from his lips, not the harsh, bitter pronunciation she had heard in the warehouse.

"You are suspected of being the leader of Al Tam-sah Al-far-ae-ina." She tried diligently to pronounce it the way he had. "You kidnapped Omar Jabal only to inexplicably release him. You are in possession of a biological weapon, but your target is unknown."

He listened to her carefully, betraying nothing, until her last sentence when he jerked his head toward her.

"The target is unknown?" he asked with narrowed eyes.

"Yes," she confirmed slowly, worried that she had said too much but oddly wanting to talk to and trust this stranger.

He moved suddenly, but not violently, taking her hand in his. With his other hand, he gently grasped behind her neck and held her head steady as he looked into her eyes.

She froze, spine stiff and barely breathing.

"The target is unknown?" he asked again.

Lillian could feel his breath on her lips as he gazed into her eyes, searching.

She swallowed. "Yes," she said dryly, realizing that he was feeling her pulse and watching for pupil dilation.

"Who do you work for?" he asked slowly.

"I work in an emergency room in Atlanta as a physician." Her voice was gently pleading.

She tried not to tense any further in his grip. While his proximity to her allowed him to analyze her and the positioning of his hands might appear affectionate to bystanders, it would be easy for him to toss her over the ledge should he choose to do so.

Marie Beaulieu walked into Montreal General Hospital and found Room 322. She flashed her badge to the police guarding the room and was allowed to enter.

She sniffed, disliking the distinctive smell of bodily fluids and hospital antiseptic. She preferred the pristine scent of a sterile lab. A revulsion for human scents and the images of patients suffering from all manner of debilitating, decaying diseases was one of many reasons she had chosen to use her medical degree in a research capacity only. She had tacked on a postdoctorate study in biomedical warfare. She could work in a lab or an office and avoid the messier aspect that occurred when disease met with flesh.

"Bonjour, Monsieur Hamdan." She introduced herself to the balding man with his rotund belly beneath his hospital gown.

Intravenous fluids dripped into his veins, and various wires were strung around the bed and connected to a monitor in the room. She watched his heart rate elevate as she introduced herself. She knew from his file that she was just a few years younger than him, but his aged, sagging eyes made him appear ten years her senior. Perhaps the type of duress he had been under had taken its toll. Perhaps he needed a job like hers—working to protect people from biohazards rather than creating them.

"Bonjour, madame," Labaris answered with a nervous swallow.

"Je m'appelle Marie Beaulieu," she began. She went on to explain she was a biochemist with Canadian Intelligence. Sitting down in the chair beside his hospital bed, she adjusted her navy-blue skirt and suit jacket.

"Mon Anglais est meilleur que mon Français," he said.

"English, then." She spoke slowly, her voice thick with her French Canadian. "I need to ask you some questions about your concoction."

Labaris shifted uneasily, which seemed to cause him some degree of pain. He had been in surgery until late yesterday evening and was only recently conscious enough for her to visit him. She had been instructed to ascertain any information she could about his modifications to Creutzfeldt-Jakob disease. Canadian Intelligence needed to plan a containment contingency should the biological weapon threaten Montreal—well, become more of a threat.

"You're Canadian," he commented on the obvious. "I thought I would be in American protection."

She pursed her lips. "You brought an *arme biologique* into this country, Monsieur Hamdan. The CIA cannot protect you from your own actions in a country that is not their own. It would be in your best interest to cooperate with my government whilst you are on our soil."

She omitted that her government and the CIA were fully cooperating in this international incident, and she would, in fact, be directly reporting to her boss as well as the assistant deputy director of the CIA. That information was not relevant to this conversation, as far as Labaris was concerned.

"Did you know that Canadians are pioneers in the field of medicine?" She didn't wait for him to answer. "Sir William Osler, the father of modern medicine, was a Canadian. He trained at Toronto School of Medicine. He was one of the greatest teachers of medicine and the author of many famous medical textbooks.

"And did you know that my country is no novice to epidemics?" She idly inspected the red polish on her fingernails. "In 1535, smallpox ravaged the Iroquoians near Quebec. Seventy years later, Stadacona was a ghost town—*ville fantôme*. Did you know smallpox has a single, linear, double-stranded genome? It starts in the respiratory tract and migrates and multiplies in lymph nodes, moving from cell to cell until it is rampant in the bloodstream. Then the rash manifests. In the malignant form, people die from high fever and sepsis. In the hemorrhagic form, death comes through bleeding under the skin, in the spleen, and in the liver—disseminated intravascular coagulation. They are both terrible ways to die. Are you vaccinated against smallpox, Monsieur Hamdan?"

She let her words linger for a moment, the insinuation of a threat causing the plump man to swallow once. She smiled.

"Madame—"

"Typhus was equally as devastating for us though," she interjected. "In 1746, an outbreak claimed fourteen hundred French sailors at Bedford Basin. That was nothing compared to when over twenty thousand died one hundred years later. Typhus, as you know, is a bacterium rather than a virus, but death is not swift or forgiving. Meningitis and encephalitis are debilitating. The brain —such an *organe délicat*—destroyed by the parasitic bacteria with excruciating pain. I'm told that its victims beg for death in the end."

Labaris sat motionless.

"I will not stand for the threat of another epidemic in my country, *monsieur*, when such a thing may be thwarted."

Several long moments passed before he nodded solemnly. She felt certain he was grasping the magnitude of his situation.

"The CJD is still a prion and will act as such. The viral coating enables more rapid passage through the blood-brain barrier," he offered in nervous speech.

"What is the anticipated time to symptom development?" she asked carefully.

"A few weeks."

Marie shot him a sharp look. That was a far cry from the six- to eight-year incubation period from eating infected meat.

"And what of the *génétique* susceptibility to prions?"

He frowned. "I did not create anything that can bypass the natural selection of the disease. Those who are susceptible will succumb, and those who are not, will not."

Marie felt this was of some reassurance. At least the anticipated death rate was not 100 percent. Genomic studies had found that susceptible individuals were methionine homozygotes at codon 129 in the *PRNP* gene, though there were other susceptible mutations as well. One-quarter to one-third of the population was thought to have this genetic susceptibility. That still posed quite a large death toll should this mutated form be unleashed on the population en masse.

There was no way to test for the presence of CJD short of a brain biopsy or autopsy. However, genetic profiling in exposed individuals could determine if they were susceptible to the prion disease. Unfortunately, testing for genetic susceptibility did not mean they could stop the prion from brain damage and death once someone was infected, especially with such a relatively rapid onset.

"The delivery method is ingestion?"

Labaris nodded, grimacing in pain again.

"Could it be used to contaminate a water supply?"

He licked his lips and nodded again. "It may require a larger sample than what was confiscated, but it is possible."

"Is it capable of becoming airborne?"

He considered her question. "Again, it is unlikely, but the viral casing may make atmospheric survival possible."

She sucked in an irritated breath. She found his scientific irresponsibility most disturbing. Why would he create such a monstrosity and then transport it carelessly around without understanding its propensity for destruction?

"I understand you were commissioned to create this—*arme biologique*—biological weapon?"

Eagerly, he answered, "Yes, yes. I was studying the disease in my lab to see if there were different mutational susceptibilities in Africans compared to Europeans when I was forced to develop it into a weapon."

"Forced?" she asked in a deliberately skeptical voice.

"They threatened to hurt me and my family." Labaris pleaded

for her understanding.

"They?" Her voice was still even and cool.

His shoulders sagged. "I don't know who they were. Egyptian. Muslim. Radicals, I think."

"*Nomes*?" she asked, feeling like she had to make excessive effort to drag the information out of him.

"Only Fazil. That is the only name of one of the young ones I met. I know no surnames."

She nodded. She leaned back in her chair trying to think of other questions, though largely he seemed unhelpful.

Biological warfare was not a new concept. Anthrax and *Burkholderia* were used against animals in World War I—destroy the food supply in order to destroy the enemy. During World War II, tularemia and brucellosis were added to the anthrax arsenal, though most were still in development before the war ended. The Japanese had plans to spread the plague to the Pacific coast. They surrendered before it came to fruition.

The Cold War continued efforts to efficiently weaponize the plague, brucellosis, equine encephalomyelitis, yellow fever, and anthrax. Countries shifted from insect vectors—fleas and mosquitoes—to aerosolized bomblets. Smallpox was added to the mix, and during a testing accident in 1971, a Soviet release of aerosolized pathogen over the Aral Sea resulted in a smallpox epidemic on a small island there. That wasn't their only debacle. They accidentally released anthrax in 1979 outside a biochemical warfare facility, which killed sixty-eight people.

During the Gulf War, UN inspectors found nineteen thousand liters of botulinum toxin in Iraq, enough to kill the entire world population ... a couple of times.

Following the attacks on September 11, 2001, anthrax was used to poison Congress and media outlets. Twenty-two people were ill with weeks of fever, chest pain, and shortness of breath. Five died.

Now over 165 countries had joined the Biological Weapons

Convention to ban this type of warfare. Of course, here was another biological weapon threat with entirely new implications.

Marie blinked a few times and then stared at the unimposing man with his sunken eyes and bandaged chest. He had created a form of a deadly prion that could replicate and cause encephalopathy exponentially faster than the version created by nature. There was no real certainty as to the weapon's capability to become airborne or to infect a large population through mass contamination. Only after he had created this abomination did he think to ask an intelligence agency for help. Then his show of good faith was to actually transport the disease across thousands of miles with untold risk to millions of people's lives.

Ça me prend la tête!

CHAPTER 14

As Khait's facial expression relaxed back into his playboy smugness, Lillian guessed she had passed the human polygraph test. He let go of her neck, though the slight pressure he had applied left behind a tingling sensation. His hand trailed down her back and rested on her hip. He continued to look at her intently, not moving from her personal space. Then he leaned in closer, and she felt the steady strum of his pulse quicken where their hands entwined.

She stood still, spine stiff, feeling like the gazelle in the lion's embrace.

With a dry throat, she croaked, "I am also happily married."

His mouth broke into that wide crocodile smile again as he leaned back from her.

"Of course, Tabib." He bowed his head apologetically and released her. "I made the incorrect deduction that a married woman would not be let out to run the streets the day after she had been added to a terrorist organization's radar."

"Um, first, that was not my intention. I was there to treat

injuries and not make myself a target. Second, I let myself out. No one controls me." Even as she said the words, she thought Sean would not have left her side if he'd known she was going to leave the hotel room.

He would be furious to learn she had an encounter of the terrorist kind. Admittedly, running alone at a time like this was not one of her more intelligent moves. Hell hath no fury like an agent whose loved one breaks tactical protocol. Her days of tagging along to his "book signings" were done.

Khait spoke, interrupting her thoughts. "You are thinking of him now."

Her eyes focused back on his face. She pursed her lips.

"You have been married for how long?" he asked.

"Five years," she answered without hesitation.

Lillian turned her gaze to the horizon. "He is my strength. When I come home after treating abuse victims, drug addicts, and unspeakable traumas, he reminds me of all the good people I have helped, all the lives I have saved." She didn't know why she was confiding in a terrorist, but that didn't stop her. "Then he whisks me away on vacation and reenergizes me."

Khait nodded, listening intently.

She finished speaking and thought briefly about the bombing and how Khait had nearly made her a widow. Before she could suppress it, she felt a flash of anger cross her eyes.

He noticed, but his subsequent expression was more of curiosity than offense.

"And what is it you do for him? No, let me guess," he added quickly. "I think there exists in you a feistiness he must enjoy. You bring him humor and levity and beauty, of course. All these things center him."

She straightened again.

His eyes brightened as he smiled. "A compliment, Tabib. Not a pickup line.

"Someday I should like to have my own pretty creature who speaks her mind and will not be contained." He stared beyond her. "Perhaps when my work is done," he added.

Lillian sucked in a breath. "Why can't your work be done now?" she dared to ask.

His jaw clenched, reminding her that he was a dangerous man and she was treading dangerous waters.

"I have come too far to quit. I must finish."

A heavy silence settled between them.

Softly and inexplicably, she said, "I think you will do the right thing in the end."

He smiled weakly, unperturbed. "Let us hope so, or it is all for naught."

After another silent minute that seemed to stretch into eternity, he spoke. He instructed her to stay on the lookout for no less than five minutes, and then she could descend and return to her hotel. He withdrew her phone and handed it back to her.

He straightened and took a deep breath. "I know you think me a monster, Dr. Whyte, capable of unspeakable violence, and perhaps I have had to become that to some extent." His voice grew melancholy. "But please sleep well. I would never harm you, and I will not seek to corner you again, pleasant though it was."

Somehow, she believed him—every word of it. Every intonation of internal strife and conflict. Yet it didn't make him or the experience less terrifying.

After Khait left, she spent seven minutes at the top of the stairs stretching and shaking and trying to regain her strength and composure.

With knees trembling, she made her descent. She gripped the rail to steady herself.

Did she really just have a secluded conversation with a known terrorist? She was now going to be on every international government organization's watch list. Forever.

How was she going to tell Sean?

He was going to go crazy. Bat. Shit. Crazy.

***

AUSTIN HAD FELT his mouth twitch at Sean's sudden appearance at the warehouse. He was wondering how he was going to keep him occupied and out of his way.

He couldn't uninvite him. After all, this had been his drop. The least Sean could do was show up early like everyone else. If he really was the supreme agent everyone held in such high esteem, then he ought to be able to brawl with a bomb on one day and arrive on time to work the next.

Austin sighed and pinched the bridge of his nose. It wasn't so much the arriving late that irked him at this instant. It was the subtle expression of incredulity when Austin had explained they had not captured any Crocodiles during the raid.

"So it was a six-man team?"

"Yes, Sean."

"And of the six heat signatures inside the building, four escaped and two were killed?"

"You're out of line, Sean. I'm running this op." As it wouldn't do any good to raise his voice, he didn't.

Sean smacked his lips. "Who was on the team?"

"*My* team."

"Who was on your team?"

"Qualified agents."

"*Which* qualified agents?"

Austin glowered at him.

"Their combined field experience equals yours, Sean. Is that what you want to hear?"

Judging by the infuriating smirk on his lips, that was what Sean wanted to hear.

"You're not a field agent anymore."

Despite the fact that you were one yesterday.

Sean bared his teeth in a vicious smile from ear to ear. He was no doubt pleased with himself at provoking Austin.

"I have an opinion and expertise. You might have consulted me."

Austin suppressed the urge to roll his eyes lest Sean count that as another childish victory.

"We think there are still about a half-dozen radicals left."

"Including Pretty Boy."

Austin cocked his head.

"Lillian's name for Khait," Sean explained.

"Not very scary."

Sean shrugged. "She does that with anything or anyone she wants to be less intimidated by. Vanier became French Fries. Ivan became Icy Eyes."

Explains why she calls me Bill.

Sean's phone buzzed. He excused himself to take the call and took a few steps back from Austin.

"Hi, Alex."

Austin perceived a long pause.

"What?"

Austin froze at the alarm in Sean's voice.

"I'm taking a car."

"Jennings!" Austin barked a warning.

"I need an open channel!" Sean called over his shoulder as he bolted for the car.

"For what?"

Sean hurried to a company sedan, dropping the keys out of the visor. He started the engine and sped away in the car.

Austin's phone rang. He jerked it out of his pocket, snarling, "If you are flying off on a solo mission, I'm going to—"

"It's Lillian," said Sean.

The panic in his voice instantly muted Austin and capped his anger.

"Mike, open com," Austin snapped.

Sean's voice projected in the warehouse.

"Alex said she went for a run. She's been stationary on Mount Royal for fifteen minutes. She's not answering her phone. She always runs with her phone."

A run? Now?

Austin's initial feeling was that Sean was overreacting. On second thought—damned if the man's instincts weren't usually right. If he was worried, then odds were there was a problem.

"What do you need?"

"A team on standby and call her again through my line. Keep calling her."

Austin perceived Sean's voice growing steadier as he talked. He was worried about his wife, but years in the field taught impeccable self-control. He managed to sound only mildly harried.

Meanwhile, Austin chewed another antacid.

At last, Lillian reached the dirt-and-gravel trail at the base of the stairs. She felt mentally and physically drained and lacked energy or motivation to finish her run. As she made the trek back down Mount Royal, she looked at her phone. She thought about calling Sean but decided to wait. The worst was over now.

She noticed her phone had been put on airplane mode. Had Khait done that?

She changed it back and quickly saw three missed calls from Sean and two from Jonathan. She stopped at the curb on the Avenue des Pins and pressed the Call Back button.

The sudden screech of tires accompanied a black sedan with dark-tinted windows as it came to an abrupt halt at the curb.

Lillian jumped back and inadvertently dropped her phone.

The passenger-side door flung open.

"Get in," Sean barked.

Lillian picked up her phone, turned the call off, climbed into the passenger side, and closed the door. They were alone in the car.

Sean waited, staring forward with a white-knuckled grip on the steering wheel, as she buckled her seatbelt. She sat motionless with her hands and phone in her lap as he pulled away from the curb.

He remained silent as he drove.

She recognized the turns.

Back to the warehouse.

Finally, he spoke in an eerily calm voice. "Imagine my surprise when Agent Applegate informs me that my wife went for a jog during an ongoing terrorist threat."

Lillian chewed her lip. She hated to see that she had worried Sean. Almost equally infuriating was the fact he was right. She carelessly left the safety of her room and was ambushed by a terrorist, although she was still not sure why. If nothing had happened, she could have defiantly accused him of being paranoid and paternalistically overbearing.

"I'm sorry," she said, her voice thick with remorse.

He turned to look at her as his expression changed from anger and frustration to worry and alarm.

"What happened?"

Damn.

Since she had not reacted by accusing him of being paranoid and paternalistically overbearing, he had correctly deduced that something had happened. He knew her too well.

She wished she could explain what had happened, other than a terrifying, bizarre, and strangely seductive encounter with a criminal.

"Khait confronted me on the mountain lookout," she said quietly.

Sean grabbed her hand. "Are you okay? Did he hurt you? Did he threaten you?"

She shook her head. "I'm fine."

Shaken not stirred.

"He was trying to figure out who I work for. He didn't threaten me. It was as though he was trying to decide if I could be useful to him somehow."

As though he wanted my help, she didn't add.

Sean pulled into the warehouse lot and parked the car.

"What did you tell him?" He turned toward her in his seat.

"Nothing about the CIA," she assured him. "I emphasized that I am a doctor. Then I told him I knew he was a terrorist, that he kidnapped and released Omar, and that he was in possession of a biological weapon."

Admittedly, she left out the part about telling her aggressor she was unarmed, revealing that the target was unknown, and nearly fainting instead of employing the array of defensive measures Sean had taught her.

Minor details.

She could see Sean's mind racing, calculating. He was trying to grasp the strange purpose of such a meeting. A fanatic would have either concluded she was of no value and thus eliminated her or she was an unknown liability and thus eliminated her. Although Lillian had already tried and failed to decipher Khait's motives, she waited as Sean deliberated in silence.

Finally, he turned her hand over in his.

"That's the ring that Austin gave you?"

Oh boy.

She nodded.

Sean withdrew his hands and rubbed his temples. He gave a long sigh before saying, "In the unlikely event that you are in the company of a known terrorist again, can you please alert the CIA so that we might be able to take action?"

"I forgot the bat signal," she admitted.

He revealed no hint of amusement.

He got out of the car and walked around to the passenger side. He opened her door and waited.

Lillian exited slowly and stood silently in the gravel parking lot at the warehouse. The clouds had fully receded, and she squinted against the midday sun.

Sean closed her door and then embraced her. The hug was fierce, a testament to the fear he must have felt from the moment he learned she went for a run, to unanswered phone calls, to tracking her location, to finally seeing her alive and safe, only to then learn she had indeed been in the company of danger.

"I'm sorry," she said again.

He didn't reply as he pulled away from her.

He walked her into the warehouse. "Since your involvement seems unavoidable, how about you peruse our files on Khait, think about what you learned about him today, and see how we can put something together to stop the bad guys." He paused and then added pointedly, "Because that is what we do here. We don't offer ourselves up to them, take scenic tours with them, or deliver state secrets to them. We stop them."

Lillian knew by the forced calm in his voice that he was boiling under the surface. She was beginning to think she would have preferred batshit crazy. She would feel less guilty about having caused so much worry if he had just yelled at her. But he wouldn't. He never had in six years.

His anger was something one felt at a visceral level, like the atmospheric pressure change before a storm. It was never heard. There was no thunder. She imagined his rage for his enemies was barely perceptible before the lightning struck. She was only ever the recipient of barometric change, and there was never any violence to follow. Feeling his anger or frustration was always enough to motivate her to course correction, even knowing he would never escalate to violence with her. Because he tolerated quite a bit of her idiosyncrasies, she changed course before she had pushed too far to make him truly, palpably angry. This was not out of fear, but respect.

CHAPTER 15

Lillian waited at a distance as Sean approached Austin. He led him to a spot out of earshot from the other agents. Their conversation appeared heated, and judging by the irritable glares Austin shot at her, Sean was explaining her encounter with Khait. Presumably, they were also discussing the length of her leash. Austin pulled out his mobile phone and made a call to someone. Sean stood and waited patiently without making eye contact with her.

The warehouse was as frenzied as it had been the day prior—the frantic hunt to find a biological weapon and those who would use it. She tugged at her tight-fitting exercise clothes, feeling a little underdressed in a warehouse full of working men and women in slacks.

When they finished their discussion, Sean leaned over a cooler and plucked out a bottle of cold water. He walked over to her and handed her the bottle. Lillian accepted it gratefully and drank with fervor. He handed her a bag of trail mix.

After leading her to an expanded folding table, he set up two laptops. Lillian sat in the nearby chair. After opening both of them, he powered them on.

With a few clicks, he initiated a video chat.

"Lillian, this is Zoey Cain. She's one of the most knowledgeable analysts on Al Tamsah Alfaraeina and is part of our counterterrorism unit. She is going to share with you what we have on Khait Sadat."

Lillian nodded.

Zoey smiled a greeting. She was sitting and looking attentively at Lillian through the computer screen. She pushed her glasses back up on her nose after the gesture. Her red blouse accentuated her long, blonde ponytail. She looked young, perhaps late twenties. Lillian couldn't place the background—a nondescript pastel painting and curtains in one corner. A hotel perhaps?

On the other computer, Sean logged into a CIA secure connection.

Zoey made a few quick keystrokes. "This is everything I have assembled on Khait," she said.

"I'll check on you in a bit," Sean said.

She watched him walk away, the air still thick with the weight of her error. The least she could do to atone for her actions was try to contribute.

Lillian scooted her chair closer and read Zoey's report on the adjacent screen.

Khait was born in Egypt and was two years younger than Lillian. His father was an affluent lawyer. His mother must have supplied his good looks judging by their 1970s wedding photo. Khait was raised in an upper-middle-class household with two other siblings, older sisters. He attended private school with impressive grades. He could have pursued any career of his choosing. He chose to come to the United States and study law at Princeton. Again, he was an outstanding student. Subsequently, he returned to Egypt and fulfilled the mandatory eighteen-month conscripted service in the Egyptian Armed Forces.

Lillian looked to the other computer screen. Zoey was still online, though it looked like she was working on her own computer while she waited for Lillian to finish.

"Military service is mandatory in Egypt?"

Zoey nodded. "It's shorter for the educated—just eighteen months. It can be up to thirty-six months for some. He had his choice of army, navy, air force, or air defense forces. He chose army."

Zoey pursed her lips. "Dr. Whyte, I would just like to add that it is an honor to meet you. Most of us at the agency really admire what you did in Kenya and the events that followed. Well, we admire what we know about the events. Most of it's classified."

Lillian sipped her water. "Thank you," she replied, surprised to hear that her events were a topic of conversation at the CIA and even more so that she would be admired for her part in it. "I'm just relieved to have survived it all."

"We talk about what you accomplished under duress. There are trained agents who might not have had wits enough to achieve what you did."

"Well, I had a lot of preparation time. I spent time alone developing and refining my escape. It was a lot of planning coupled with a lot of luck."

And it didn't hurt that I'm a physician and had sedatives at my disposal.

Zoey fell silent as though thinking about what Lillian had said.

As she ate her trail mix, Lillian wondered if Zoey had a comprehensive file like this on her. If she did, she could have been the one to have concocted her Facebook page.

Lillian focused her attention back on the dossier. She read through Khait's travels and work, which didn't seem particularly taxing. However, during that time, his oldest sister went through a divorce. She had been married to an American civil engineer and was living in New York. After Khait's military service, his radical days began. He joined different fanatical groups, committing acts of violence, until he seemed to settle in with the Crocodile Pharaohs.

"So what set him off? His sister's divorce? Something that happened in the army?"

"It's not entirely clear," Zoey replied. "The divorce may have been a factor. We also believe he met other fanatics in college."

"At Princeton?" She did not conceal the surprise in her voice.

Zoey's face brightened as she leaned toward the computer camera. She seemed to enjoy having someone with whom to share her research. "Contrary to popular belief, Dr. Whyte, terrorists are not poor, deprived, or uneducated. They are intelligent people with strong geopolitical grievances."

Grievances? I have grievances. I don't kill anyone over them.

KHAIT SADAT FELT REFRESHED after a warm shower. He dressed in clean clothes to prepare for the midday salat. A tranquil quiet permeated his hotel room as the afternoon sun filtered in through sheer curtains.

He stared at himself in the mirror as he pulled his long hair back into a smooth ponytail. He didn't see a monster. Had he become one with everything he had to do? Was there a line he had crossed somewhere between man and monster? He replayed in his mind how the physician's gaze shifted as though seeing him as both.

Why did that bother him?

American women were so brainwashed by their media that they feared all Muslims. They scattered like little white plump pigeons, bobbling in frenzied fear as they gulped their frapalicious mochaccinos. So why would she be any different? But she was different. She vacillated between seeing the man he was and the one he had become. There were things he had done to get to the position he was in now—things of which he wasn't proud, but necessary things. Necessary evils for the greater goal.

As he washed his hands, he cleared his mind of distracting thoughts—the war he faced, the threat of danger and discovery, the wrath of God should he fail, and the enticing redhead who was something of an enigma.

He found a square of carpet and faced northeast. He spaced his feet evenly apart and looked down to see the imaginary location on the floor where his head would touch the carpet. After preparing mentally for his prayers, he performed the *takbiratul ihram.*

Raising his hands, palms forward up to the level of his ears, he said calmly, "*Allahu Akbar*—Allah is the greatest."

With his breathing steady, he lowered his hands and folded them right over left. He rested them gently against his abdomen, below his navel. He recited Surah Al-Fatiha and another portion of the Quran.

Unfolding his hands and placing them on his knees, he bowed, with his back parallel to the ground, and praised Allah three times.

He rose up. "Sam'i Allahu leman hamidah." *Allah listens to those who praise him.*

Taking another deep breath, he said, "Our Lord, to you is all praise."

He lowered himself to his knees with the bases of both feet touching the ground. Placing his palms on the floor, he eased hisnforehead onto the carpet. The stiff, faded green carpet of his motel room was not a comfortable surface. However, humility in prayer was not about comfort.

"*Subhan rabbi al Ala*," he said. Then repeated, "Glory be to my Lord, the most high. *Subhan rabbi al Ala.*"

Rising to a seated position, he kept his eyes fixed on his lap.

"Allahu Akbar."

He turned up his heel, bent the toes of his right foot, and repeated the prostration with prayer.

Rising again, he said, "Allah is the greatest."

He remained seated as he performed the *tashahhud* and said the *duroud.*

WHEN KHAIT HAD FINISHED his prayers, he slipped on his shoes. After checking his weapon and ensuring the safety was on, he slipped it into his holster and onto his back waist. He donned his jacket, pocketed his cell phone, and stepped out of his room. He traveled two flights of stairs down to room 306 and knocked.

"Allahu Akbar," he said to the closed door.

"*Nem Fielaan*" came the response.

The door opened, and a young, thin, wide-eyed, and nervous Egyptian greeted him. Fazil was a good kid, obedient. But he was a pawn like the rest of them in this room. Lost kids taking up someone else's cause that they didn't really understand.

"The safe house on Rue Beaubien has been compromised," Fazil said in Arabic. "Halil and Hamid are dead. The others retreated here."

Khait nodded and produced a frown. He patted Fazil on the shoulder as he entered the room. He was bitter to think of any of his God-fearing brethren dying, but they knew the life into which they had enlisted.

May Allah have mercy on their souls.

The motel stunk of stale cigarette smoke. The blaring television accosted his ears. These were some of the reasons Khait kept a room for himself. Five members of Al Tamsah Alfaraeina sat on the queen beds of the small room, watching the television and puffing cigarettes.

"Who is responsible?" Khait asked.

"American," Fazil answered, closing the door. "CIA."

Khait pursed his lips. That had been his suspicion. His intelligence suggested Labaris was making the transfer to a CIA operative, but he couldn't tell who it had been in the bookstore. His or her cover had been too good.

Then the physician had arrived, and she didn't fit into the equation at all. She was no agent, trembling at their encounter—frightened and unarmed. However, his intuition told him she was more than just an American physician on vacation. Her appearance in the bookstore had some measure of design involved. She obviously didn't want to tell him, and—curious though he was—he didn't want to force it out of her. He preferred the fiery blaze in her eyes when she spoke the truth than the withdrawn darkness they became when she told half- truths, hoping he wouldn't probe further.

"*Alqayid* knows?" Khait asked.

Fazil nodded.

Khait sighed. Two dead, the CIA breathing down their necks, and he still didn't know the endgame.

He withdrew his cell phone and called the leader of Al Tamsah

Alfaraeina.

"Marhabaan," he answered.

"*Ahlan*," Khait greeted him in return. "The infidels are upon us," he added. He always felt a little foolish using that term. Anti-Christian Muslims and anti-Muslim Christians used the term to describe one another. In truth, they worshipped the same God with many of the same core beliefs. Khait used the term loosely in conversing with other members of Al Tamsah Alfaraeina to refer to those without faith, as though the beliefs of their organization were superior. It seemed to be a way to reinforce their dedication to the cause.

Since his agenda was not actually in line with the organization in which he was highly ranked, it was important he act in accordance with their methodology. He had worked hard to achieve his status and calling others *infidels* was probably the least offensive thing he had done.

He was an ardent Muslim—that was certain. It was the reason he was doing the things he was doing. It was why he had his own agenda, separate from Al Tamsah Alfaraeina.

The Crocodile Pharaohs.

At least it was a clever name. It was certainly better than Al Qaeda, which was dully and unimaginatively "The Base." It was better than ISIS, an acronym for "Islamic State in Iraq and Syria."

"Indeed" was the reply. "The first task will be completed tonight."

"How can we be of assistance?" Khait asked. What he really wanted to ask him was what, precisely, the "task" was. The leader was obviously planning to use the biological weapon, but on whom?

And how was Khait to confiscate the biohazard in order to implement his own agenda? Yet he could not appear too curious or too inquisitive.

"I will text you a time and location to arrive and await further instructions."

He hung up the phone.

CHAPTER 16

"What are Khait's grievances?" Lillian asked.

Zoey shrugged slightly as she leaned back. "I think it probably originated when he saw the stark contrast between his country and ours. Take such a shocking awakening and follow it with military service and violence and you create an extremist."

Would it have been a stark contrast given his privileged background and private schools in Egypt to see the same in the United States? It seemed like he went from one privileged life to another.

Lillian continued to let her eyes roam over the screen. She saw pictures of a young Khait in college, sitting on a bench in a courtyard and wearing jeans and a Nirvana T-shirt. In another picture, he sported combat pants in the desert and was holding a UMP German submachine gun. His shirtless torso glistened with sweat under a hot sun. In another military photo, he wore camouflage and a beret with his hair cut short. He was an attractive youth and just as vibrantly alive then as now.

Lillian looked at the counterterrorism expert. Zoey had clearly studied Khait intensely and possessed the qualifications to draw accurate conclusions from her knowledge. She must be right. Yet she hadn't met Khait, spoken with him, and looked into his eyes. Perhaps he was capable of immense deception, but she felt there was more to him than *geopolitical grievances*. Something was missing from Zoey's assessment of him, but Lillian didn't know what it was. Without knowing, she didn't know how to help find him.

"What's your overall assessment of him?" Lillian asked.

Zoey seemed eager to answer. "He's highly intelligent, well-funded, and trained to be violent, which is exactly what I put in my report to Langley."

Lillian took a drink of water. She leaned back in the uncomfortable metal folding chair and snacked more on the trail mix.

"Dr. Whyte, this CJD is pretty bad, right?" Her voice was laced with genuine concern.

"Yes, Zoey. It's named after the German scientists who discovered it in the 1920s, but we didn't really understand details about the disease until the 1970s. It causes proteins in the brain to misform and then replicate infinitely. The brain becomes sponge-like and slowly loses function—personality changes and mood swings eventually give way to psychosis and seizures."

"There is no cure?"

"No. It is one hundred percent fatal for the one-fourth or so of the population with the susceptible gene. Well, genes pleural."

Zoey looked stricken.

Oops.

Lillian provided the scientific explanation she would give a colleague or a physician in training, but it appeared the young girl would have benefited from a more compassionate physician-to-patient explanation. She had, once again, failed to employ her bedside manner.

Too late to offer any words of comfort now.

Lillian decided to change the subject back to their assignment.

"Do you think Khait's capable of using biological warfare?" Lillian asked.

Zoey nodded, reinstating her poised demeanor. "He has the means and the motives. Besides, biological warfare is far more sinister and subtle than using bullets or bombs, both of which he has demonstrated ample ability to use. Yes, he is capable."

"How many people has he killed?"

"We don't have any confirmed kills as a terrorist," she explained, "only his military days. But there have been multiple bombs and multiple shootings as part of Al Tamsah Alfaraeina."

She frowned. No confirmed kills? Was that odd? It seemed odd.

Zoey's face darkened abruptly, and her tone sharpened. "Dr. Whyte, I was under the impression I was sharing this information to see if you had something to contribute to it. Instead, you seem to be trying to disagree or invalidate it."

"I'm sorry. That was not my intention. Your work is thorough."

Lillian thought about the times patients had come to her emergency room for her help and advice only to tell her that they trusted an Internet search engine over her medical training and years of experience. Zoey was likely feeling affronted from the same askance.

"It's just that I've met Khait. It was a strange meeting, but not hostile. I have met evil men before, been face-to-face with them, and Khait felt ... different."

Zoey wrinkled her nose at Lillian's use of the word *felt*, as though she could hardly compare her feelings with the known facts about Khait. She raised a skeptical eyebrow, saying, "A highly intelligent fanatic can be charismatic and deceptive with little effort, Dr. Whyte."

"You're right," Lillian acquiesced. "You're right. Now that I have the evidence of his crimes before me, it seems clear I was deceived."

Lillian sighed. "Unfortunately," she added, "he was also clever enough to not give me any clues that might facilitate his capture."

SEAN LEFT Lillian to explore their files on Khait as he sought out Austin to exchange updates. Before he had been alerted to Lillian's run by Agent Applegate, he had been learning about the morning raid. They had indeed discovered the location of a terrorist subcell, but two died and four escaped during attempts to apprehend them.

Austin had sent too big of a team on the attack. It should have been more covert. An experienced four-man team—two for entry and two for covering exits—would have been stealthy and sufficient. A six-man adrenaline-junkie group of eager beavers was a mistake waiting to happen.

Regardless, here they were. No Khait. Two dead Egyptians. No one to interrogate. A still unknown target.

Austin approached him. "Damn mess," he said, not actually taking responsibility for it.

Sean blinked but didn't reply.

"Director Austin," one of the seated agents said, turning to him, "incoming call from Marie Beaulieu."

"On screen," he ordered.

Sean noticed Austin straighten his posture and his tie. Sean suppressed raising his brows to a conspicuous height.

On the large screen ahead appeared an attractive woman, probably Sean's age, midforties, with a short brown bob cut, and smartly dressed in a navy suit. She was seated in an office with a wall of diplomas and accolades behind her. A miniature Canadian flag was askew to the side of the lens view.

"Bonjour, Director," she greeted him.

"Bonjour, Agent Beaulieu. Comment allez-vous?" Austin returned.

Sean had never, before this moment, heard the man attempt French. It was not entirely butchered.

"Bien, merci," Marie replied with a slight bow of her head.

Sean stared at the scene of Austin smiling and standing tall and trying to speak the native language of a beautiful woman.

Huh. He is human after all.

To be sure, Austin would never cheat on his wife, but that didn't mean he couldn't want to portray himself as an attractive coworker. She was probably ten years younger than Austin, but Sean realized his thought was hypocritical given the eight-year age difference between himself and Lillian.

"What have you learned from Professor Hamdan?" he asked.

Her lips puckered as though she had just sucked a lemon. She continued in English with a thick French accent. "He does not know if it has *aérsolisation capabilities. Mais*, he is convinced it will hold to the *génétique* susceptibilities that it originated with from nature."

"Does he know who commissioned him to create it and what their intent is?" Austin asked.

"*Non et non.* He does not think there is enough for a grand-scale water contamination, but I lack confidence in that *minimalisation*. He gave me *seulement un nom*—Fazil."

Austin nodded with a scowl. He was clearly hoping for some reassurances about controlling the calamity of a biohazard and was getting none.

"Merci," he said.

She nodded again.

"My courier picked up your box," he said.

"You need to fill up the vials, label them accurately, put them in the cooler, and activate the dry ice," she instructed.

Then she added, "My *organisation* has many questions for you in return, William." Her tone was mild and nonconfrontational but conveyed the need for immediate action.

Austin nodded. "I'm on my way."

Sean surmised Austin had confidential information to share that even the warehouse couldn't know. A personal visit.

Austin signaled for the agent to end the call, and the screen went back to a satellite image of Montreal. He turned to Sean.

Sean asked, "Vials and dry ice?"

"When the box arrives, everyone needs to supply a blood sample. We're shipping it off to a genetic lab in New York. Everyone's getting tested for susceptibility to CJD so that if there is a mass contamination, we know who can safely handle it," Austin explained.

Sean scratched his chin. It was a well-conceived proactive plan. He didn't know how to express that he was impressed with Austin since such an occasion had never before presented itself.

"I have to smooth things over with CSIS," Austin continued.

Sean frowned. The Canadian Security Intelligence Service was probably more than a little curious and more than a little outraged that the CIA was killing people on their turf. "Smooth things over" was another way of saying he was going to try to prevent the international incident from becoming a *public* international incident.

"Can you oversee things at the warehouse for a few hours?"

Sean blinked again. Then he nodded.

"Good," Austin replied, which was probably as close to a "Thank you" as Sean would ever get from his superior.

Austin pulled his phone out of his pocket and started texting.

"Does everybody here know I'll be in charge?" Sean asked.

Austin pressed his Send button and looked up at Sean. "They do now."

As Austin left the warehouse, multiple agents looked up from their phones and computers and over at Sean. He realized he knew each of these faces and a little something about them.

Agent Applegate was a good sparring partner who could outmuscle but not outmaneuver Sean. He owned a goldendoodle, and Sean had dog-sat for him in the past.

Marty, a.k.a. Hound Dog, was a good tracker—satellites, traffic cameras, and cell phones. Though he appeared nonthreatening with his round head, round glasses, and round belly, his talents reminded Sean that no one really had any privacy anymore—for better or worse. But Marty had also gone through a divorce three years ago and turned to Sean for support. It made sense. Sean was neither his supervisor nor his direct colleague. He could confide in him about his stress and desolation and not worry about it affecting the way he was treated at work.

Sean even knew Zoey well, though she wasn't present. She had been happily married for seven years, and he even attended her wedding. Her biographical profiles were invaluable, and he always preferred her intelligence reports to any of the other agents'.

Tall, lean Mike had done some fieldwork, which made him useful in relating to onsite agents. He usually ran coms. He didn't last in fieldwork after the birth of his son. He had called Sean on more than one occasion in the last five years to check in on his family when Mike was on assignment. Sean had driven to Washington, DC, and willingly provided protection detail for a few days until Mike's job was done or his nerves had eased.

Barbara was Internet ops—no small feat. She could scan a gazillion words a minute. She never missed a deadline, she didn't tolerate being interrupted while talking, and she made a mean ham quiche.

And so it went with the others in the room. He had some small personal and professional connections with each of the agents staring at him. Some were wide-eyed with looks of surprise at his sudden— albeit temporary—promotion. Others opened gaping mouths of delight. Others gave "attaboy" fist pumps.

Sean grinned and suppressed an all-out smile. Finally, he made a rolling gesture with his right hand and said, "All right, all right. As you were."

CHAPTER 17

As the agents resumed their work, Sean looked down at a text message on his phone.

Cole: *Still coming for dinner?*

He mentally chewed on mixed feelings. He wanted to see his friend and introduce Lillian, but he also knew if he went, he would be distracted with thoughts of the ongoing investigation. He would be with Cole wishing he was helping catch the bad guys. However, he also had Lillian to consider. Since bringing her to Montreal, she had been apprehended by Austin, thrown into a hostage crisis, forced to treat the injured, stalked by a terrorist, and placed under house arrest. The least he could do was take her to a nice social event since the rest of her vacation had been ruined.

Yes, he texted back.

As he stood in the warehouse, anticipating seeing his friend again, he recalled one of their rendezvous seven years ago. They had met at Salamander Cafe in Abuja. The two men shook hands while coming together for a brief embrace.

"Sean, great to see you," Cole said, his white smile genuine and dazzling.

"You look different. Dying your hair gray?" Cole teased.

Sean ran a hand through his dark-brown hair. His natural color was sandy brown, no gray. He had dyed his hair dark for his work in Africa.

Rather than reply, he reached out a hand and smacked Cole's abdomen.

"What about you?" Sean asked. "Growing love handles?"

"Hey," Cole began defensively, "you should see the food you get on the campaign trail. I'm lucky this is all I've gained."

They took a seat at the café table. Cole unbuttoned his sports coat as he sat. He produced a handkerchief and wiped the sheen from his forehead. The Nigerian sun was not even in full force yet.

"Congratulations, by the way, Senator Lawson."

Cole's face lit up, pleased. "Thank you." He tucked away the handkerchief in his coat pocket.

"What about you? Still *not* doing covert operations?"

Sean shrugged. "I'd tell you, but then I'd have to kill you." Sean could joke with his friend in such a manner but only this friend. Others would likely take him literally.

Cole leaned back in his seat. "I would expect nothing less ... even though I saved your life."

Sean blinked at him. "You're still using that nearly decade-old line against me?"

The Georgia senator released a brief chuckle.

"How are Rachael and the kids?" Sean asked, absently looking at a menu.

"Good, good. They are visiting my uncle's studio and getting a glimpse of Nollywood."

The Nigerian film industry was booming. It was expected to become the third most-valuable film industry within a few years. Sean knew Cole's uncle was a director and producer.

"What about you? Any meaningful relationships?"

Sean smoothed his starched white shirt. "Field agents have different meaningful relationships than the type to which you refer."

A waitress took their drink orders and left.

Cole rolled his eyes. "Love, Sean. I'm talking about loving a woman."

"That would also imply a woman loving me," Sean said. He drummed his fingers silently on the arm of his chair.

"That so impossible?"

Sean smirked. "With my track record and my career? Yeah, it is."

"You have the right values," Cole countered. "Someone will appreciate that."

The CIA agent shook his head. "You're such a romantic."

Cole snorted. "I'm the romantic? Who told me to stop dragging my feet with Rachael? Who gave me proposal advice? Who brought my mother-in-law to tears with his wedding toast?" He shook his head emphatically and pointed a finger at his friend. "*You're* the romantic."

Sean glowered at him, unable to refute his claims. He resumed drumming his fingers, eyes scanning the perimeter, as always.

Cole leisurely leaned back, not disguising his pleasure in having won a round against Sean.

"But you're not here to talk about women—or lack thereof. You mentioned something about my cousin?" Cole asked.

The waitress returned with two glasses of palm wine.

Sean waited until she left, then asked, "He still works in import-export?"

Cole sipped his drink. "Are you going to drag this conversation out by asking me things you already know?"

Sean's eyes sparkled. "Daudi is exporting textiles from Nigeria to Kenya for a corporation called Tin Enterprises, which I believe is a criminal organization under a larger umbrella corporation that is stealing and selling oil across Africa."

Sean drank his *kallu*, made from the sap of a flower of a palm tree. It was sour and acidic, not his beverage of choice. He drank the popular beverages in the countries in which he visited to better assimilate with the locals.

"You want to talk to my cousin," Cole deduced.

"I want to talk to him," Sean confirmed.

Cole frowned. "And you came to me because you want me to initiate the conversation."

"I want you to initiate the conversation."

"Uh-huh. Why do I have the feeling you already know when and where you want this conversation to take place?" Cole's eyes flickered irritably away from Sean.

Sean turned his wrist up and peered down at his watch. "According to his electronic calendar, he will be in his office between meetings in seventy-five minutes."

Cole snapped his napkin open and placed it in his lap. "How thoughtful of you to have arranged our meeting early enough for you to buy me lunch." He attempted a tone of mild annoyance.

Sean gave him a nod of appreciation and hid his relief that his request was not rejected. As a stranger to Cole's cousin, Sean's unannounced arrival would be treated as a threat. A person in import- export had means of dealing with threats. If Daudi saw his cousin, he would hopefully give Sean five minutes of his time to ask about one of his business partners. He may not be willing to divulge information about a client; however, Nigerians had a strong sense of national pride, especially middle-class business owners. If Sean could explain his hunt for a masochistic parasite thriving off destabilizing African countries, perhaps he could be persuaded to share information.

Unfortunately, the encounter did not go as planned.

Cole Lawson piddled around his apartment in Montreal while his wife picked up and readied the place for company. He received Sean's text and was practically giddy to know he was coming tonight.

"Hey, honey," Cole called excitedly, "Sean and his wife are coming!"

Rachael walked into the room in her jeans and T-shirt, scowling at him.

"One of us is excited," she said blandly, one hand on her hip.

Despite her bristling exterior, he knew she was at least a little curious to meet the wife of his best friend. Her lack of enthusiasm at Sean's company was due to her dislike of the CIA agent. Her aversion stemmed from some of the same reasons Cole liked him —always the promise of adventure, which his wife saw as the threat of danger.

Sean reminded Cole of the adventures they'd once had. He often pondered on what further adventures he would have embarked on if he had not been injured in Port Said. Although his combat days had ended swiftly, he had gained much in their place —Rachael, the kids, his political career. Rachael would never have agreed to marry him if he were gone for months at a time on dangerous missions. His political career would hopefully enable him to save more lives in the long term than he could physically achieve with stealth and ammunition.

Aside from their Navy SEAL days together, Sean had appeared from time to time under the auspices of catching up with an old friend. Inadvertently, their meetings had turned into something a little more violent than what they were intended to be. Cole knew danger seemed to follow his friend and didn't blame him for it, but his wife certainly held him responsible.

Probably the worst operation or the best, depending on if

Mrs. Lawson or Mr. Lawson was asked—was what they now referred to as the Abuja Warehouse Incident.

Cole and Sean had arrived in the commercial district of eastern Abuja at the warehouse of Cole's cousin. It was late morning, so most deliveries were already on their way. Incoming trucks had not yet arrived. Cole suspected Sean had planned it that way.

Although Cole had family in Nigeria, he only visited every few years. He had been to his cousin's warehouse once before, but it wasn't much to behold then—or now.

They had taken Cole's rental car and parked it in the visitor parking lot outside a six-foot razor wire–topped chain-linked fence. The large aluminum gate was open since it was business hours. There was no security at the gate. Had there been previously? Cole could not remember. The security was not robust, meant mostly to deter petty thieves. Such trespassers were unlikely to be skulking around during the day.

They walked past the warehouse toward a trailer on the grounds where his cousin Daudi's office was. As it was the only place on-site with air-conditioning, Daudi would most likely be in there.

The warehouse doors hung open, revealing a large and cluttered space with crates and cardboard boxes. It stretched up two stories, the upper level mostly offices and catwalks.

They had almost reached the trailer when a gunshot rang out from inside the warehouse. Cole hadn't been in combat in ten years, but he knew the sound of gunshot when he heard it. Single-shot, handgun.

He instinctively kneeled. Sean was already in a crouch with his gun drawn. He shuffled to the front of the warehouse behind the aluminum wall. Cole followed him silently, stirring a cloud of dirt in his wake.

Sean peeked his head into the warehouse briefly. "I count three assassins. They have Daudi pinned upstairs."

Cole nodded, scowling.

"You have a gun?" Sean asked.

"The hell, Sean. Of course I don't have a gun," he retorted in a sharp whisper.

Sean grinned at Cole, which only irritated him more. The CIA agent knew he was unarmed. He just wanted to force Cole to admit that, despite being a former SEAL, he found himself unprepared for a violent situation.

"Be right back."

"*What?*"

But Sean was already inside the warehouse, leaving Cole unarmed and exposed. He looked around the flat barren landscape searching for threats, but he saw none.

He heard a few thuds, and in two minutes, Sean crept back out of the warehouse. He brushed a smudge of dust and rust off his white shirt. Then he handed Cole a Glock.

Cole reached out his hand to take the gun by the handle, but Sean didn't release it. Cole blinked at him.

"You gonna use this thing if you have to?" Sean asked.

Cole rolled his eyes. "I want world peace, man. That doesn't mean I won't defend myself or my family."

Sean seemed satisfied with the answer and released the weapon. Cole checked the chamber. It was full.

"You go in first. Stairs are on the left. I'll cover you then come up the stairs on the right."

Cole nodded and huffed a few breaths to calm his nerves.

Sean appraised him skeptically. "You're not going to shoot me on accident, right?"

Cole glared at him and bared his teeth. "If I shoot you, it won't be on accident."

That made his friend smile again. He seemed reassured that if Cole had his wits about him to give back the same gibe he was getting, then he was stable enough to enter a gunfight.

With one last full exhalation, Cole sprinted for the far stairs. He heard one shot come from behind and to his right. True to his word, his friend had covered him, firing somewhere above him.

As his eyes adjusted to the darker interior of the warehouse, he noticed an unconscious Nigerian in blue jeans and a pale-blue T-shirt, presumably the former owner of the gun he was holding. Reaching the stairs, he scurried about midway up them. He crouched and spun to cover for his friend.

As Sean dashed for the opposite stairs, Cole scanned the warehouse with his gun poised to shoot. On the catwalk above them, a figure looked to be taking aim.

Cole fired. He missed but disrupted the man's composure. The gunman turned his aim at Cole instead. Another shot fired, and the assassin on the catwalk fell. Cole looked incredulously at his friend who had managed to fire a deadly shot fifty feet away while running upstairs. He couldn't be sure in the dim light and with the distance between them, but he thought he saw Sean wink.

Cocky, Cole thought. *Some things never change.*

That leaves one, right?

Hopefully, Sean's count was correct. There were plenty of places for an abundance of assailants to hide. Straight ahead of him, about two hundred feet, was a small room with hazy plexiglass windows. He could hear movement inside the office.

Sean was making his way toward Cole, about to cross the catwalk.

Cole flattened himself against the wall and shouted, "Daudi! It's Cole! Sit tight! There are more gunmen out here!"

His cousin did not respond.

Another gunshot sounded. Cole looked toward the sound to see another thug on the far catwalk firing at him. He was a difficult target as he was between support beams.

Cole felt a sharp pain in his side. He looked down at a pool of blood coloring his shirt.

The hell?

Sean fired, hitting the shooter in his shoulder.

Looking around, Cole spotted a dent and chip on the railing.

Ricochet.

He stuffed the gun in the back of his pant waist. As he took off his shirt, his eyes tracked Sean making his way to the injured man, presumably with a laundry list of questions.

Cole used his shirt to wipe the wound, and then he inspected it. Not bad. He would probably need a few stitches, but the bullet had mostly grazed him. He held the shirt against the wound to stop the bleeding.

Sean approached, captive in hand. Judging by the bruising on the Nigerian's face, he had attempted to resist.

Sean looked down at Cole's side. "I leave you alone for one minute..."

"Screw you," Cole snarled.

"You always did look for an excuse to take your shirt off," Sean added.

Cole glared at him.

They crept toward the office where Daudi was hiding.

"Daudi!" Cole called again. "It's okay. We got them. We're coming in."

"Wetin day happen?" Daudi asked in Pidgin English.

"I no saba," Cole replied, though he suspected Sean might have an idea.

They entered the small room, which had a few dusty swivel chairs and a small metal desk. The corner was stacked with spools of wire.

Cole looked at his scrawny cousin cowering in the opposite corner.

"Daudi, Sean. Sean, Daudi." Cole gave abbreviated introductions.

"Make you no vex me!" Daudi said standing straight and

approaching. "You bring that hambakman to me?" he asked Cole as wrinkled his nose at Sean.

Cole could think of worse things to call Sean than annoying.

"That man just saved your life," Cole explained. But just as quickly, Cole turned to Sean and jabbed a bloodied finger at him. "But not mine. Just so we're clear. You dragged me into this gunfight, so it doesn't count."

Sean raised his hands in a gesture of incredulity. "I disabled all three of them. How does that not count?"

"We are *not* even for Port Said," he said pointedly.

Sean smiled and shrugged. He plopped his perpetrator in one of the chairs and started rolling a strand of spooled wire around him.

He didn't have anything to cut the wire with so the poor Nigerian gunman was tethered to a chair, which was now tethered to a fifty-pound spool of wire.

"Stay here. I'm going to sweep the perimeter," Sean said as he walked out of the room.

Standing in his apartment in Montreal, Cole absentmindedly scratched at the scar on his side. To this day, Rachael still held a grudge against Sean for the Abuja Warehouse Incident.

Sean had detained Cole and his cousin for two days after the incident. He questioned his cousin about his business. Out of concern for Cole's political career, Sean had insisted he make sure that Cole was not in any way associated with the event. He didn't want some sort of leak to ruin Cole's political career. "Pacifist Senator Lawson Caught Armed in Warehouse Shootout" would have been unfavorable press. It would not have mattered that he didn't injure anyone. Cole was fairly certain that when Sean filed his report, he left out the part about Cole being at the warehouse. To this day, Sean, Rachael, and Daudi were the only three that knew Cole had been there. His secret lay dormant. That still didn't make them even for Egypt.

CHAPTER 18

Lillian stood and stretched. The uncomfortable metal folding chair had played havoc on her back and hips after sitting in it for two hours.

She had reviewed everything on Khait—twice. Still the best she could come up with were pieces of a puzzle that didn't fit together.

Geopolitical grievances?

She couldn't decipher what his motivation was, only that he thought he was trying to do the right thing—whatever that was.

She didn't keep Zoey on the video link much longer after their first discussion. She was sure the young agent had better things to do than deal with Lillian's ignorance and skepticism.

"Let us hope so, or it is all for naught," Khait had said.

What was he struggling with? Did a man who could bomb a building with the intention of killing those inside have a conscience with which to wrestle?

She pulled off the Band-Aid on her arm where they had drawn blood. She agreed to provide a sample even though she wasn't particularly keen on the CIA having some of her DNA. It was supposedly being shipped to a research lab. Of course, as she was previously involved with the CIA and married to an agent who was clearly working for them full-time at present, they probably already had infinite access to her DNA.

At least, if Khait ever did come back around and had the prion, she would know if she was susceptible.

Her phone buzzed.

Kelly was texting her. *Can U talk?*

Lillian let out a low groan.

She sent back: *Call you in 10 min.*

She walked over to Sean, who was engrossed in conversation with one of the older female agents.

He looked up at her and smiled. It was a relief to see him smile at her so soon after her morning blunder.

"I'm going to head back to the hotel. Grab a shower," she said.

He stepped closer to her and placed gentle hands on her arms and massaged them. Looking intently at her, he asked, "Are you still okay to go to Cole's dinner party?"

She blinked. With all the commotion that had been going on, she had completely forgotten about the dinner event.

"Yes," she replied. "Absolutely. It would be a nice distraction." She mustered a smile.

Is it safe to venture out?

Surely, there was no safer place than beside Sean. Hadn't Khait assured her she wasn't a target? There wasn't a reason for him to lie to her. Was there?

Sean nodded. "Agent Applegate will take you back. I can't leave just yet."

"Sounds good."

She gave Sean a peck on the cheek, not really knowing or caring if it was frowned upon by the CIA.

. . .

Fifteen minutes later, Lillian dragged her tired body through the hotel. Fortunately, Agent Applegate was of a professional caliber, and he had refrained from saying "I told you so" in regards to her run earlier that day. In fact, they did not speak at all on the drive back to the hotel.

Her phone buzzed, and she glanced at the screen. Jonathan. She couldn't summon the energy for another quizzing session, so she sent his call to voicemail.

As she entered her hotel room, she froze. A silver-topped food tray sat on the small round dining table near the window. It hadn't been there when she had left. Her heart quickened.

She turned hesitatingly to the young agent.

"Cobb salad, ma'am," he explained.

He walked past her, lifted the silver top, and confirmed the presence of the salad, a roll, a glass of lemonade, utensils, and nothing more sinister.

"Thank you," she said, feeling foolish.

He replaced the lid. "Following orders, ma'am."

"Sean?"

He nodded. "Anything I can get you, ma'am?"

"No. Thank you very much."

He left, closing the door behind him. The room became a calm silence. The sound of the bustling warehouse still echoed in her ears. Suddenly alone, she shivered and hugged herself.

Her phone buzzed, causing her to jump.

"Hello, Kelly," she answered.

"Oh, Lily, I think I'm getting cold feet. I don't know if I can do this. What if I can't do forever with Devin?"

"Okay. Okay. Slow down. What happened?"

Lillian sank into the chair by her Cobb salad and sipped the lemonade.

Kelly's voice rang frantic. "We were at the department store working on our registry. We got through the china just fine, but then we couldn't agree on the ceramics. I liked the stoneware, and it's durable, but he liked the ironware, none of which is going to match our kitchen. And the colors were so bland." Her pitch rose. "So this is not a good beginning. How can we spend a lifetime together when picking out dishes is impossible?"

"Okay. Take some deep breaths."

Lillian stared at her salad. She was hungry, but munching in her friend's ear was probably not the way to convey her concern over the situation.

"First of all," Lillian continued, "this is not the beginning. You and Devin have had plenty of disagreements along the way, and he still proposed and you still accepted and you still both want to get married."

They had been dating for four years.

She paused, giving Kelly time to agree.

"So you don't agree on dishes. Big deal. It's not a foreshadowing of impending marital doom."

"No?"

"No."

"What do you and Sean fight about?"

Hah! Not being mindful of terrorist stalkers and not remembering to alert the CIA.

"Well, our laundry basket has been in the same spot for five years, and the man cannot seem to find it. His clothes are always strewn about the bedroom."

"Does it drive you crazy?"

"It did. And then I let it go."

"You let it go?" Kelly's words tumbled out slowly.

"There are things I do that annoy him, but he doesn't fuss at me about them."

Sean doesn't fuss about anything.

Lillian continued, "I got a cleaning service and just told them anything not hanging in the closet goes in the laundry bin. So six of seven days, I step around the clothes, and one day a week, there are none."

"Devin never picks up his shoes," Kelly noted soberly. "And they're never up against a wall somewhere. No, they're always in the open, waiting for me to trip over them."

Lillian chuckled. "There will always be little annoyances like that. If you get caught up with them, it will interfere with being able to appreciate the things that really matter."

"Like the way he holds me when he knows something is wrong," Kelly said.

"Like the way he can stare at you like there is no one else in the world and nothing more important than being with you at that moment."

—even in the middle of a terrorist hunt.

"You're right," Kelly conceded.

"You're going to be fine, Kelly."

"Thanks."

Zoey poured over her brief. It was the culmination of countless hours of work over several years. She had assembled many such detailed reports about other terrorists—all of them with similarities such as strong educational backgrounds and military training. All of them were deadly threats to national security.

And enter Dr. Whyte from stage left, searching for information.

She had scoured her brief, frowning. Frowning as though the information was somehow faulty. Frowning in disbelief.

She—with no counterterrorism training whatsoever—doubted my work.

Questioning my conclusions, she thought incredulously.

She had wanted to like Dr. Whyte. She was, after all, the legendary physician who brought down the empire of oil profiteer and warmonger, Dominique Vanier. According to the rumors, Dr. Whyte had not only escaped his fortified compound, she had demolished it. Then when the Frenchman had sought vengeance and came to the States to assassinate her, she had foiled that plan as well. Apparently, she defeated him by stabbing him with a fork and then shocking him with a defibrillator.

That was real character. Real grit.

The icing on the cake was when she outshined a room full of CIA specialists by deducing where Vanier kept his hidden oil stash. Assistant Deputy Director Austin had been dumbfounded that she had proven so useful and resourceful. Though he would never admit to it, she had been a true asset. The experience had changed him, Zoey had observed. He was still a hard-ass, to be sure, but he did better at team management and accepting input from others.

Lastly, the physician had married one of the most respected field agents. Sean Jennings had thirty-two kills and sixteen successful missions—including his future wife's help on the Kenya mission. Dr. Whyte had to have exceptional tenacity to love someone with that level of calculated brutality and that many demons.

But she had *questioned* Zoey's work.

She had pitted her *feelings* against Zoey's hard-earned intelligence gathering.

Just because Khait had no confirmed kills, his allegiance to terrorism was no less likely in the same way that being a devout Muslim did not incriminate him as a terrorist.

But the doctor had felt something was missing. She had subtly suggested he was something more (or less?) than a violent fanatic. If that were the case, he would be less predictable. Would that make him more dangerous or less dangerous? Zoey scowled and then had to push her glasses back up on her nose.

If she thought the physician was wrong and if she was truly

upset with her, why was Zoey reviewing her own work? She couldn't stomach thinking she could be wrong about Khait. Determined to work past her initial affronted feelings, she decided to do another in-depth look at him. There were a few other contacts she thought she could reach out to, but that required permission from Assistant Deputy Director Austin.

She looked down at the signed memo on her screen. In the current crisis, when she had asked his permission to follow through on a few other leads that came to mind after discussing Khait with Dr. Whyte, Austin had agreed without hesitation.

SEAN FELT like his heart went limp and spongy when Lillian left. He had been furious when he found out she had gone for a run. A suffocating wave of fear had struck his lungs. His entire world would have imploded if he hadn't found her unharmed. Despite the tsunami of relief that rushed over him when he saw her on the curb, it took a substantial amount of time for him to recover. The adrenaline and fear morphed quickly into anger, but the anger was slow to dissolve.

He avoided her while she sat working at the warehouse. He didn't want to hear her half-baked comments about him being paranoid or overprotective. His anger was too near the surface to be restrained with that type of careless disregard.

Yet she hadn't said anything to that effect. Her eyes held no defiance. Quite the opposite. Remorseful. Yielding. She had been alone and frightened. Her encounter with Khait taught her more caution than any harsh words he could have delivered.

No sense verbally beating a beaten person.

Instead, he found himself wanting to comfort her, quell the terror, but he had to relinquish his anger before that could happen.

He looked around the warehouse. The team ran smoothly despite Austin's absence. Although Sean hadn't overseen an operation of this magnitude before, he had worked with and relied upon other operatives through the years. He had gained enough leadership sense over time to know people responded best to limited guidance on a platform that encouraged autonomy and creativity. Micromanaging, threats, and coercion were counterproductive.

Marty utilized facial-recognition software at his console. The algorithm analyzed the position, size, and shape of a person's eyes, nose, and cheekbones. It would compile faces from various camera images he was collecting and compare them to the US State Department and FBI databases. The software had limitations; for instance, if people were making different facial expressions or if a profile view was captured instead of a frontal view, the software couldn't make a match. In fact, it had failed to track Lillian when she had traveled out of Africa and to Paris six years ago when they were searching for her.

Nevertheless, it could be helpful and was how they had discovered the first hideout Austin sent the team to raid this morning. Marty was also employing 3D facial recognition, but the database was less robust. In addition, it required several different camera angles to compile a more detailed image.

Barbara walked up to Sean and handed him her tablet.

Sean stared at the map on the screen. Fifty different-colored dots were pinned at different locations.

Barbara explained, "These are all the possible targets over the next ten days. It includes the names and locations of all the UN members in town. The UN meeting itself in three days is the red dot."

Sean nodded as his eyes scanned over the map. "And the tunnels?"

He had instructed her earlier to compose this map as well as a map showing the tunnel system and a third map with just Omar's schedule because it was plausible he could be targeted again. She leaned over and swiped her finger across the screen. The street map became a less prominent gray, and a series of colored lines appeared. The dots, or potential targets, were still visible.

"The orange lines are the sewer tunnels. The purple lines are Underground Montreal," she explained. Then, as if anticipating his next question, she added, "Swipe again, and you'll get the same except with just the ambassador."

Barbara hovered a moment. "Sir?"

"Barb, it's still just Sean." He smiled at her.

"Agent Jennings. What made you think of the sewer tunnels?" Her lips twisted at the last words as though saying *sewer tunnels* invoked the smell of them.

"Just before the bomb, they disappeared at the end of an alley. I went back to the scene that night and found the tunnels. It was the only means of escape down that alleyway. I think it is plausible they will plan further travel through the tunnels."

Sean drew his finger across the screen. He tapped on each of the locations. It seemed the only upcoming meeting Omar planned to attend was the large UN meeting. They would focus their efforts on the UN subcommittee assembly.

Three days.

CHAPTER 19

"Ya hello, '*akhtaa*," Khait greeted his sister on the phone.

"Brother!" she cried.

He smiled into the phone, pacing the small carpeted floor of his motel room. It was good to hear a friendly, familiar voice. His Crocodile Pharaohs—brothers in arms, as it were—possessed obedience; however, they were kids—not friends, not family.

"How are you?" he asked.

"I'm well."

"And the kids?"

"Good. Wonderful. Do you want to talk to Seth?" He heard her, more distant from the receiver, say, "Seth! It's Uncle Khait. Do you want to talk to him?"

"No, no," Khait said quickly. "I can't talk long." He worried the call would be traced. He was a well-known terrorist on the news now, thanks to the bookstore fiasco. Any spy agency worth a piastre would have his sister under surveillance, a fact that made him concerned for her and her family's safety. That fact didn't change the work to be done.

He twirled a Canadian half dollar in his fingers, feeling the precious seconds of the phone conversation tick by.

"Khait," she began in her big-sister, cautionary tone. "You don't sound right. What's going on?"

Perhaps she was not watching the world news. That was good. She would worry less.

"Just my job, *'akhtaa.*"

He heard a sigh. "I know your job, shaqiq." She dropped her voice lower. "I am proud of you, but I want you safe back here, playing with your nephews. They want their uncle back alive."

He didn't reply. It was good to hear the concern in her voice, to know that someone loved him deeply. But he couldn't vouch for his safe return. He couldn't make promises he wasn't sure he could keep. He was already uncertain if he could keep the promise he'd made to himself. In the silence, his heart ached miserably to be near his family.

"When is the job done?" she asked.

He was glad she was remembering to talk vaguely over the phone. No specifics.

"When it is done," he replied. Only then would they talk more. *"Insha Allah,"* he added. *God willing.*

"Fi *Amanillah*," she said, wishing him God's protection.

"Thank you."

He hung up the phone but was still filled with pent-up emotion—anxiety, apprehension. He needed to work through his feelings and clear his mind to be ready for the imminent challenges.

He needed to pray again.

———

LILLIAN HAD SOAKED in a hot bath to relax. Breathing in the scent of vanilla from the bath soap, she closed her eyes against the steam. She willed away flashing images of the bookstore rubble, Labaris bleeding on the floor, men with AK-47s, and Sean with his tattered shirt and bleeding arm. It would all be over soon.

After the bath, she scrolled through her tablet reading about Canadian medical history. It would have to do in lieu of being able to actually tour the city.

She read about two famous researchers from the University of Toronto—Banting and Best—who isolated insulin from the pancreas of dogs. They were able to purify it and successfully test it in diabetics. Banting and Macleod, another researcher who helped in the development of insulin, won the Nobel Peace Prize in 1923 for this monumental medical achievement.

Insulin advanced from being collected in animals to being biologically produced. The human DNA code to make insulin was imbedded in bacteria where it used the human DNA instruction manual to produce insulin—a protein chain. Tweaking the amino acid sequence led to different onsets of insulin: fast-acting, slow-acting, and intermediate.

Today, one in four adults lived with the affliction, meaning they either couldn't produce enough insulin or the insulin they produced couldn't efficiently activate cells to uptake glucose. This left high sugar content in their blood. She tried to imagine what it might feel like to be the scientist whose work saved lives on a daily basis for hundreds (thousands?) of years after his own death.

How many lives had she saved? Maybe a hundred per year.

That would have to suffice. She possessed neither the interest nor passion to be a medical scientist. No major cure discoveries in Dr.Whyte's future. No major disasters either. She wasn't tinkering in a lab somewhere making more virulent strains of swine flu or creating human forms of animal diseases.

Or creating more frightening forms of prion diseases.

She'd had a few different outbreaks they were able to manage through her emergency room. Fortunately, when the Ebola scare was in full force, they were not on the receiving end of any infected patients. The staff training alone cost hundreds of man hours and hundreds of thousands of dollars in supplies—protective equipment, isolation rooms, decontamination rooms, dedicated ventilators, and the like.

They had designated, trained teams that would care for infected patients within select isolation rooms. In reality, a true outbreak on US soil would have quickly outstripped isolation resources. Such a calamity might necessitate that an entire hospital be the sole treatment center for all Ebola cases. Given the financial suicide that would be, no hospital was likely to volunteer for such duty. She had heard of one hospital in England that had dedicated a wing to potential Ebola patients, and it was rumored to have cost almost a half million a year just to keep it ready with trained staff—without any sick patients.

The threat of Ebola wasn't gone, only suppressed. There were other equally frightening diseases lurking, ever on the precipice of an outbreak—anthrax, the plague, and smallpox, to name a few. A mass-scale infection would overwhelm the health-care system. Lillian may know enough to recognize the symptoms and make a rapid diagnosis, but that would only be helpful in the unlikely event that the patient who arrived to her emergency room was the first case—patient zero.

She thought about Labaris's prion disease. Mad cow in a viral shell. Unstoppable. Incurable. Unpredictable. A biological nightmare.

Her phone buzzed.

Be back soon to clean up for dinner, Sean texted.

Okay. Love you, she texted back.

She held her breath.

Love you too.

She hoped that meant he had forgiven her for earlier—what would that be called? It wasn't a fight or an argument. She couldn't even call it a disagreement because she agreed with him that she shouldn't have gone for a run. Poor judgment? Yes. She hoped his text meant he had forgiven her poor judgment.

Lillian heard the key card slide through the hotel room door and the grate of metal as it slowly opened. Without turning to look, she knew it was Sean.

She stayed bundled in her robe, staring out the window. The great maple leaf waved in the distance—*l'Unifolié*, the Canadian flag.

She took a sip of her lemonade. The half-eaten Cobb salad was still on the table.

He came up behind her and kissed her cheek.

"I'll just get cleaned up."

She nodded.

When he was finished showering, he opened the door, releasing steam out of the bathroom. Standing in his boxer briefs, he shaved his stubble. Lillian's eyes roamed over his abdomen and lean, muscular physique.

He always opened the door while he shaved, and they usually used the time for casual conversation.

She really needed some type of normal small talk. She needed to pretend for a little while that they were just a couple on vacation. No terrorist threat. No lingering disappointment with what she should or should not have done earlier that day.

Maybe he would play along.

"Did you know that the first practical electron microscope was invented in Canada?"

He rinsed lather and shavings off his razor.

"I did not," he replied, his voice casual.

"University of Toronto, 1939. And suddenly the mysteries of the cell were unlocked."

"And a whole new side to forensics," he added.

"Oh, right. Like matching fibers at a crime scene or paint flecks."

"And gunshot residue or bullet markings."

Lillian chewed on her lip. Naturally, she would consider the medical applications, and he would consider the criminal ones.

"I was reading that electron microscopy was used in the 1940s to observe the difference in the viral structure of smallpox versus chicken pox. A bunch of others were first seen by EM too. Parvovirus, poliovirus, norovirus, and even the first Ebola virus outbreak in the 1970s."

Lillian fell silent. Her imagination drudged through electron microscope images she had seen in her medical school pathology textbooks of Creutzfeldt-Jakob disease and protein malformation leading to spongiform encephalopathy.

Sean must have sensed the conversation was veering back to the dismal infectious disease. He asked, "How are the wedding plans coming?"

Lillian groaned. "If I were ever to consider a second career, wedding planner would not be one of my choices."

Sean grinned, his smooth jaw glistening with aftershave.

"My own wedding was less stressful," she added.

"That's because you know what you want. Helping other people figure out what they want when you yourself are a fairly decisive person is challenging."

She considered his words, trying to recall the last time she struggled with a decision. She knew she wanted medical school, and choosing the fast-paced shift work of emergency medicine was an easy decision. After that, she wanted to live in a big city and was already familiar with Atlanta. Marrying Sean required no intellectual pondering. The academician in him spurred hours of enriching conversation, the romantic in him made her feel adored, and the fighter in him assuaged her need to feel safe and secure.

It occurred to her, after a lifetime of decisiveness, she was being indecisive about the leadership course. This out-of-character behavior had her out of sorts. Taking the course committed her to nothing. She could choose to use or not use the information she learned from the course.

Leadership training, so be it.

SEAN ENJOYED Lillian's silhouette as she looked out the window of the hotel. One knee was curled up to her chest. He knew a storm was brewing behind those sapphire eyes. Once again, he admired her strength even after all the grim happenings. She had endured a hostage crisis, a medical emergency, a bombing with the fear of losing him, and a confrontation with a known terrorist. After all that, she was in her hotel room trying to replace violent thoughts with medical ones. Some with less fortitude would be curled in the fetal position whimpering until the fear subsided.

Of course, Lillian wouldn't do that—not the woman who kept her wits enough to escape a heavily armed compound in Africa without help from anyone. Surprisingly, she repeatedly amazed him.

In addition, she had amazed her brother, except not in a good way. Jonathan also did not curl up in a fetal position, but he did get belligerent.

Mike had interrupted Sean's work at the warehouse. "Sir, Dr. Whyte's brother has called several times. He is irate, claiming he can't reach his sister and demanding to know where she is."

Sean was still at the warehouse studying the terrorists, trying to track them and predict their next move.

He sighed. Not surprisingly, Lillian probably didn't feel like talking to her brother. He could be abrasive.

Like brother, like sister.

"What's his location?"

"Looks like he's outside of Little Rock, Arkansas."

Good. He's safe at home.

"Put him through." Sean had turned on his headset with a touch of his finger.

"Jonathan, it's Sean."

"Where's Lillian? I want to talk to my sister," he demanded.

Or what? You'll run over us with your hay baler?

"She's resting at our hotel." He kept his voice calm.

"But you're not with her?"

"I'll join her soon."

There were a few heavy breaths on the line, and Sean couldn't tell if Jonathan was trying to calm himself or rile himself.

"Sean," he said through gritted teeth, "I saw her on television. I know that she was in that building minutes before the bomb went off."

Ah. Hence the angst. Good.

Sean preferred the truth.

"Yes, she was."

"What's going on?" Jonathan's voice faltered. "Is she working for the CIA?"

So he is battling fear for his sister and fear of betrayal and a little jealousy toward me. That's a lot of emotion for this man to handle in one day.

"No."

"No, but you have her going into hostage situations?"

Not my choice, but that's not relevant here.

"Jonathan, you know Lillian. You know two important things about her. First, would she ever join and take orders from the Agency?"

Jonathan snorted. "No."

"Second, what's the one reason she would willingly go into a dangerous situation?"

Jonathan hesitated. "If she thought someone needed medical attention."

"Exactly."

There was a noise as though Jonathan were scratching stubble on his face.

"I don't like it."

We have something in common.

"Neither do I."

"You damn well better keep her safe."

"That is my primary objective."

As much as this woman will allow me to keep her safe.

Sean shook off thoughts of the previous phone conversation. He decided to wait to tell Lillian about her protective brother calling.

Lillian turned and gave him a smile that lit up his world.

CHAPTER 20

Lillian wore an emerald-green cocktail dress with matching heels and clutch. She fastened her red hair up with a few loose curls dangling.

"You look beautiful," he said, looking stunning in his tuxedo.

"And I like how you look in a tux," she replied.

"Only for you," he said, winking at her.

"I thought you spies wore tuxedos all the time to infiltrate the rich and famous?"

Sean let out a short, sharp laugh. "Only in the movies. No one has ever accused me of being a gentleman spy."

She ran a hand along his smooth coat. "So you've never introduced yourself as 'Jennings, Sean Jennings'?"

"Uh, no."

He adjusted his sleeve, adding, "Besides, I'm retired."

"Right." She drew out the word, slowly shaking her head. "Hmm.

It's hard to remember, what with you being involved in a

hostage crisis, then a bombing, and now a terrorist hunt. But I can see where you would somehow consider yourself retired. Sure."

He wrapped his hands carefully around her torso. She looked up at him whimsically.

"Tonight, we'll leave all that behind us and enjoy a nice social event."

She could leave anything behind when he looked at her with eyes brimming with a mixture of adoration and desire.

"Agreed," she said.

He kissed her briefly, and they left the hotel together.

They took a taxi to a luxury apartment complex overlooking Parc La Fontaine.

"Okay, I need the cultural handshake primer again," she told Sean.

He nodded. "Middle Eastern, right handshake and only if offered by the man. Russian, expect a kiss on the hand. French and English, light handshake. South Korean, soft grip."

Lillian tried to commit all of it to memory. "Chinese is by age, right? Oldest first and bow?"

"No Chinese here tonight," he replied.

Lillian blinked. "You've memorized the guest list."

Sean shrugged. "I don't attend social events without knowing all the attendants."

"But it's just dinner," she countered.

"Well, it turns out that Omar Jabal is on the guest list."

She thought about him for a moment. The Egyptian ambassador might find it odd that the author from the bookstore was also at a political dinner gathering. He would probably surmise Sean was not present by chance. Then add her by his side, and Omar might be thoroughly confused. Confused or bemused? She had, after all, secured his release from the terrorists. She might have saved his life.

"What does that mean for you?" she asked.

"Nothing." He shrugged. "He is on the list, but his office canceled given what he went through the other day."

"Oh. So your point was if you weren't so thorough and he hadn't canceled, it might have been awkward."

He tapped his fingers silently on his knee. "Yes, perhaps. But once he saw you there, I expect he would just be grateful."

"Not sure he needed an ER doc for his minor injury."

"Well," he said, holding his hands palm up, "you convinced Khait to let all three of you go."

Lillian bit her lip. "I'm still not sure why that worked," she mumbled.

Sean returned to drumming his fingers as he shifted his gaze out the window. He didn't reply, didn't agree or disagree. He offered no theory or explanation. She knew he pondered the same question, and by the slight way his eyes narrowed, something he couldn't quite grasp or comprehend troubled him.

Lillian looked at the ring on her finger as the car pulled to the curb.

"*Shoot,*" she said.

"What's the matter?" Sean asked.

"I forgot to exchange Austin's costume jewelry for my *real* ring."

"That *costume jewelry* costs more than the ring I bought you," he said.

She smiled sheepishly. "Then I will be sure to return it in the same condition in which it was given to me."

***

SENATOR COLE LAWSON inspected the catered table of appetizers and taste-tested the marinara sauce for the penne pasta. Rachael had made the main course, and it pleased the palate as always. Italian cooking was her forte.

Guests trickled into the apartment. The senator positioned himself at the foyer to greet them. He smiled at his wife, Rachael, who looked fabulous in her purple dress. She had worn his favorite. She had also arranged for the kids to stay with her mother at a hotel so that their sleep schedule would not be disrupted by the guests. The politicians may begin mild-mannered, but after a few drinks, there would be passionate and rambunctious political discussions and debate.

No doubt, there would also be conversation about the recent bombing in Old Montreal. The State Department had given him a debriefing on the incident. Omar Jabal—the Omar Jabal—Egyptian ambassador to the US and one of the leading proponents of the upcoming subcommittee peace talks, had been kidnapped.

Kidnapped.

He had known Omar for several years now. He knew the man's passion and unwavering commitment to peace. He knew his determination seemed to stem from losing his son in a bombing some twelve years ago. Cole shuddered and felt a sudden clench in his stomach thinking of how he would lose his mind if anything happened to his children. He shifted his thoughts away from such a dark, unimaginable place.

Then Omar had escaped, and the terrorists had detonated a bomb that miraculously harmed no one, despite causing a half million dollars' worth of damage. It must have been terribly stressful to have a bomb explode where he had just been held hostage.

Cole was surprised when he had received a call from Omar's assistant a short while ago informing him Omar decided to dine with the group. He relayed some party line about not letting the terror of terrorists create pervasive fear and disrupt much-needed peace proceedings.

Much to Cole's relief, Omar Jabal had arranged for additional security to be present before and during the dinner party. The Homeland Security Advisory System was currently at a code red terrorist alert—severe threat.

When Cole had relayed the kidnapping and bombing incident details to Rachael, she had obviously been concerned.

"He has a target painted on his back, and he's going to expose the rest of us to the risk of being collateral damage?"

"As politicians, baby, we're always at risk of being caught in someone else's crosshairs."

"I don't like it," she added.

Cole sighed. "I cannot uninvite the Egyptian ambassador to the United States."

"And Sean's invited tonight?" She arched one eyebrow to a razor-sharp peak. She already knew the answer.

Rachael was an amazing wife and phenomenal mother, but she was not a forgiving woman. She had never forgiven Sean for the Abuja Warehouse Incident—or the other minor incidents.

Cole nodded and placed reassuring hands on her shoulders. "It will be fine."

The eyebrow was unmoved by his claims.

She tilted her head to one side and put a hand on her hip, shrugging off his hands.

She spoke in clipped sentences. "Sean is in Montreal. Terrorists are in Montreal. A bombing happened in Montreal while Sean is in Montreal."

He blinked at her.

"You don't think he's neck-deep in this mess?" she snapped.

Cole chose to ignore the tone in her question insinuating he was dense. He had already considered her conclusion. Sean had told him that he was coming for a book signing, but he also knew he was still CIA. He probably was involved, though how entrenched was questionable. Something this big would require an entire team. Sean was more likely to have a peripheral role. He had over ten years of service, but he was still a field agent. He didn't lead teams and wouldn't be a one-man show for this sort of severe threat to international security.

"He is likely involved," he conceded slowly. "He is likely *helping*," he corrected himself. "But he won't have a pivotal role in something this big. Besides, if he was mission critical, he wouldn't be taking time for a social dinner."

She pursed her lips, and Cole knew he had not assuaged her angst.

He swallowed and thought, for Sean's sake, his friend had better not bring trouble with him.

Lillian and Sean exited the cab and walked to the double doors of the apartment complex. After the entrance and before the elevators, a security detail was checking identity. Lastly, the security team waived metal detectors wands around them before they were allowed to proceed to the elevator. They rode the elevator to the fifth floor, and Lillian commented on the level of security.

"I'm sure it's because of the bombing," Sean explained.

"You knew not to wear a gun?"

He nodded calmly.

"Let me guess. You are your own weapon?" She tried to tease him to lighten the mood. His stiff body did not respond.

He's still in operative mode.

She knew he would be until the crisis abated. He was sweet to keep the dinner reservations on her behalf, knowing that he would struggle through a dull night of socialization when he would rather be part of the active search.

She gently rested a hand on his and whispered, "I love you."

His eyes sparkled as he regarded her for a moment. He seemed to be about to speak, but the doors opened. They exited the elevator only to see two more guards outside of Cole Lawson's apartment. Like the four men downstairs, they wore navy suits, starched white shirts, and communication pieces on one ear and wrist. A bald security guard opened the door for them.

Jazz music played inside as the smell of pasta diffused through the air—basil, thyme, and garlic.

Magical.

Lillian's stomach lurched with anticipation.

A tall, attractive black man and his beautiful bronze wife entered the foyer to greet them.

"Sean Jennings!" Cole exclaimed. The two men in tuxedos shook hands and then hugged briskly.

"Good to see you, Cole. This is my wife, Lillian."

Cole extended a meaty hand to Lillian. "I'm told it's Dr. Whyte," he said.

"Please, Senator Lawson, call me Lillian," she replied, shaking his hand.

"And call me, Cole." He turned to the woman at his side. "This is my wife, Rachael," he said.

Rachael wore a dashing purple velvet dress. The women smiled at each other.

Then Sean shook hands with Rachel. "Good to see you again," he said warmly.

"I'm just glad it's under peaceful circumstances, Sean," she said with a forced smile.

Lillian noted something of disapproval flash in Rachael's eyes. Her words rolled out as more of a threat than a welcome. Lillian would have to unearth that story later.

She set her clutch down on an empty table as Rachael escorted her into a living room where Lillian accepted a glass of wine and a small plate of antipasti appetizer. She took a bite of prosciutto and looked around the expansive apartment. It was elegantly furnished with a leather couch and recliners and an oak coffee table. Vivid contemporary acrylic paintings adorned the wall. Splashes of reds, blues, and greens formed a shapeless image of beauty. It made her think of crushed petals from an array of brightly colored flowers molded together in stunning vibrancy.

While Sean and Cole got reacquainted, Rachael escorted Lillian around for introductions. There were prime ministers and ambassadors all dressed in splendor. They seemed intrigued to have someone from a nonpolitical career join their dinner party. They expressed how refreshing it was to have someone in their midst without an agenda. It occurred to Lillian that, at such a meeting preceding the UN conference, influential discussions and political power plays would take place that would then shape the larger assembly.

"You have known Sean for some years now?" Rachael asked her when they were alone in a corner.

Lillian had finished her antipasto, and her wine glass was half empty. "Yes. Six years now. He has a lot of respect for Cole," she added.

Rachael sipped her red wine, looking over the glass to glimpse the two men still talking. "And Cole tells me he is retired now?"

"Mostly retired," Lillian answered truthfully.

"Mostly," Rachael sneered.

"Sean tells me he owes Cole his life," Lillian said cautiously.

She snorted. "Yes. And apparently his form of repayment is to pop up from time to time and create mayhem in our lives."

It took all of Lillian's restraint to remain silent and wait for Rachael to explain.

"Ask him sometime about our dinner at the Atlanta Seafood Company or the time he *borrowed* Cole for three days in Nigeria." She shook her head bitterly. "It's always a mission with him. He is always trying to save the day. And he doesn't stop to think who he's tangling in the web he spins."

"I will definitely ask him," Lillian agreed with brewing curiosity. "In the meantime, let me free up your husband so Sean isn't occupying all of his attention."

She walked over and stood beside Sean as he laughed and conversed with Cole.

CHAPTER 21

Lillian watched the apartment door open as a new guest arrived. Omar Jabal stepped into the room. He wore a tuxedo with his right arm in a cast. He looked a little nervous as his eyes darted around the room, perhaps still shaken from his kidnapping.

Lillian turned and smiled.

"Ambassador," she greeted him.

He gave her a puzzled glanced before his eyes landed on Sean next to her. Alarm filled Omar's widening eyes.

Lillian frowned as time seemed to slow down, and she considered his reaction. An innocent man would probably see his treating physician and another survivor from the bookstore and feel relieved. An innocent, clever man might wonder about the same two people being at another event and inquire as to who they were, especially since one had been instrumental in saving his life from a bomb. A bomb, she now recalled, that didn't seem to surprise or shake him.

Omar's reaction at seeing her and Sean was more like that of a man who thought he had just been discovered—a man guilty of something. This was a man with his hand in the cookie jar. Images of the background she had read about him flew through her mind. Upper class, educated. Devastation. The loss of his son in Port Said.

Port Said.

The same place Cole had earned his Silver Star and had henceforth pursued a peacekeeping career. Cole's dinner gathering posed an enticing terrorist target with ten national peacekeeping leaders, including one that had perhaps been involved somehow in his son's death.

Sean must have assembled all those facts faster because, with lightning speed, he splashed his remaining wine in the Egyptian's shocked face, spun him around, and pinned him against the wall. He held Omar's left hand twisted behind him.

"What the hell?" Cole gasped.

"Spy!" Omar squealed.

Sean frisked Omar.

Lillian tucked herself close to Sean. "They will attack *you*," she pleaded to her husband in a harsh whisper. Sean was the outsider here. The rest of them were politicians that knew one another. With his free hand, he pushed something cold and metallic into her hand and then pushed her away from him.

"Terrorist!" Omar yelled.

Lillian stumbled back several paces.

The security guards came through the door with a clamor, guns raised. Everyone stared at the spectacle of Sean restraining the ambassador as the guards threatened to shoot Sean. They advanced past her, shouting.

She could stay and watch Sean get taken captive, then Omar would turn the security guards on her, and the vial would probably be taken back by Omar. Alternatively, she could walk away unnoticed at this moment during the commotion, as Sean had clearly intended her to do.

She slipped out the door the guards had left open and quietly walked to the elevators. The doors opened swiftly in response to her pushing the button. Heart pounding, she stepped inside and pressed the button for the lobby.

As the doors closed excruciating slowly, she heard Omar shouting something in Arabic. His voice grew louder as he approached. Through the narrow sliver of the closing door, she could see he was yelling into a cell phone. She only understood one word—*Khait.*

Tentacles of ice snaked through her veins.

Would he be waiting for her?

She looked down at the vial in her shaking hands. It was small and metal and not menacing appearing. It chattered faintly against her wedding ring.

No. Not *her* wedding ring. Austin's ring.

As her cocktail dress had no pockets, she stuffed the vial in the only place she could—her bra. Then she twisted the diamond on her finger.

Time for the cavalry.

There was no noise, no flash of light, no indication she had activated the alarm. But then, she supposed, that was the point. One must be able to activate it without alerting the enemy that it had been activated.

The elevator doors opened.

KHAIT SADAT HAD BEEN MEDITATING OUTSIDE of American Senator Lawson's apartment building when Omar called. He closed his eyes and breathed deeply, smelling the scents of the city through his open car window—fragrant freesia from the park nearby, curry from an Indian restaurant down the road, and diesel fumes from a passing delivery truck.

Omar, leader of the Al Tamsah Alfaraeina, was already inside the building before Khait had arrived. Just twenty minutes ago, he had called Khait to let him know where he was heading and ordered him to be on standby if assistance was needed. Prior to that, he had not known where Omar was staying or what his target would be.

He suspected the UN peacekeepers would be the target but nothing more specific. Still, with that limited knowledge, he had studied the details and locations for all the events ongoing in Montreal before and after the main UN meeting. As such, he knew tonight's event was hosted by Senator Lawson, and there would be about a dozen UN peacekeepers present.

In the time it took the phone to ring once, Khait beseeched Allah for strength and wisdom. He was tired of being someone else's pawn—appeasing the whims of a broken, shattered politician. Omar was a dangerous, unstable man with the funds to achieve his twisted mission. Although Omar's instincts were serving him well to not trust the younger Egyptian, Khait was growing impatient.

He needed to get his hands on that vial.

He answered the phone.

"Khait, the doctor has the weapon, and she is coming down the elevator!" Omar's voice was rushed and panicked before the call was disconnected.

My Tabib?

Though she had convinced him of her unwitting participation in all this, here she was back in the thick of the action.

And with my vial!

His mind raced. She *had* been truthful. He knew it. *Felt it.* She had almost fainted in his arms.

Ya Allah!

But somehow she knew to be here, at this specific place, on the specific night when even he had not known.

Now Omar's identity was no doubt exposed.

Jayid. Good.

Khait wanted no more to do with the unhinged politician.

He needed to find Dr. Whyte and confiscate the vial. This was the opportunity he had been waiting months to accomplish.

He exited his car and walked toward the apartment building. Adjusting his automatic weapon, he readied his mind for the kill.

LILLIAN STRAIGHTENED AND stepped out of the elevator. There were two guards at the entry desk and two more just outside the set of glass doors. They looked up at her as she walked toward them.

No Khait.

"There is some commotion upstairs. I think they need more help." She tried to sound calm but suspected there was still a trace of alarm in her voice.

The two men rose and walked toward her. They drew their weapons, eyes hostile and unfriendly.

She took an uncertain step back from them.

Suddenly, the sound of an automatic weapon erupted, and Lillian saw the two front guards fall. Bullets flew, and glass rained down the front of the building.

Lillian spun and bolted for the back of the building. She found an emergency exit and shoved it open.

The cool night air engulfed her. Street lamps dimly lit the Parc La Fontaine as a few people strolled along the trails beneath the trees and further away at the edge of the lake.

Lillian ran. She didn't know in which direction she was going, and she wasn't able to be stealthy in her heels. Nonetheless, she ran for her life. If she could reach the road, she could flag a cab.

She couldn't pay for one, since she didn't have her clutch. The driver wouldn't know that until she was far away from the park.

In the distance through the foliage, she could see a road.

Taxis.

Adrenaline surged her forward even faster.

"Dr. Whyte," a voice called to her. She recognized that voice and knew it all too well by now.

Her spine stiffened, slowing her to a halt. Khait's voice was within shooting range. Her legs frozen, she stood gasping for breath and trying to slow her racing heart. Reluctantly turning around with open hands raised shoulder high, she faced Khait and waited for him to fire. He no longer had the AK-47 but now held a Glock aimed directly at her chest. He was panting after having chased her through the park, and his dark eyes burned with anger.

"Where is the vial?" he demanded. The soft, nonthreatening voice he had used last time to speak with her on Mount Royal was replaced by volatile hostility.

Lillian allowed herself a long exhale. He hadn't shot her because he needed to see the vial first. He needed to regain possession before he could shoot her. For all he knew, she stashed it somewhere in the park.

Oh, damn. That would have been a good idea, she realized.

If she had deposited it somewhere, then the biological weapon would not fall into the wrong hands again. Better yet, she could have placed the vial and the ring together—maybe under a park bench where the CIA could have retrieved it. Instead, she was stupidly running with it in her lingerie.

"Khait, do you know what's inside that thing?" she asked, panting.

A rational argument with a fanatic was probably foolish, but she needed time for the cavalry to arrive. She had no idea what response time they would have. She thought about the street layouts and the warehouse location. Ten minutes?

Lurking pedestrians had started to peek from around trees, watching the armed gunman. Khait glanced around nervously before walking closer to Lillian. He took her firmly by the upper arm and burrowed the barrel of his pistol into her side.

She felt his hot breath and smelled his cologne again—Lacoste Blue.

"Of course I know what it is," he replied with contempt.

He pushed the gun further into her, motivating her forward. She walked beside him as he led the way by the vicelike grip on her arm.

"I just do not know what *you* are, other than clever enough to fool me into thinking you were a physician."

"I *am* a physician," she replied. "And I know enough about Creutzfeldt-Jakob disease to know it has no business being turned into an uncontrollable weapon."

"On that we agree."

They walked down narrow steps and onto the muddy bottom of a drainage system leading to the sewer.

Shit. Literally and figuratively.

Would the ring beacon work underground? Austin's team might never find her. Sean knew about the tunnels, but he was probably buried beneath three hundred pounds of security guard muscle right now.

Khait sensed her hesitation and nudged her forward. She was going to have a bruise from that gun barrel, but that would be nothing compared to the bullet hole he was going to leave her with once he got what he wanted.

The familiar musty smell engulfed her. She felt as though she was walking into a concrete tomb. This segment of tunnel had gray brick and casted a golden reflection when Khait flicked on his flashlight. Mud, silt, and an inch of putrid water layered the bottom. The top of the tunnel had tiny stalactites, making it look more like a cave than a sewer.

S EAN HAD HEARD the heavy footsteps of the guards outside Cole's apartment storming the room. They had come in quickly, drawing their weapons when they saw Sean's hold on Omar. He knew their location from their heavy steps, and the bald one came in too close. Sean released Omar and spun, capturing the man's gun. He dislocated his shoulder with the force of his body against the guard's arm. Rolling back with his full weight, Sean landed on top of the grunting brute.

The second guard had been trying to maneuver for a clean shot. Sean twisted and kicked out a leg. His knee buckled unnaturally at the force of Sean's foot to it. The man fell to one knee. He tried to readjust his aim through the disabling pain, but was too slow for Sean who was back on his feet. He gave a swift kick to the man's head, knocking him unconscious.

Rachael screamed.

The onlooking politicians stood back aghast.

"Sean, what is going on?" Cole demanded.

Sean hated to see the look of fear and apprehension in his friend's eyes directed toward him. Not surprisingly, Rachael was glaring at him menacingly.

He handed one of the guns to Cole. Judging by the expression on Cole's face, the offering had reestablished trust.

"Omar came to kill you. I can't explain everything right now. Stay here in case he has other men out there."

"What about these guys?" Cole asked of the guards, looking down at the gun he had accepted.

Sean shook his head. "Unless you know them personally, don't trust them. Better yet, just don't trust them."

Sean left, closing the door behind him.

Omar backed frantically away from the elevator as Sean approached.

Qutil, Omar had said on the phone to Khait while Sean was disarming the guards. Omar had given the kill order. Khait was going to kill Lillian, and it was Sean's fault for having given her the vial.

He had wanted to put a bullet in Omar's head. No one would question him after saving the lives of the UN peacekeeping leaders. But the infuriatingly rational part of him knew secrets from Omar could finish the disbanding of Al Tamsah Alfaraeina. In lieu of killing him, he threw the round man against a far wall and watched him crumple into unconsciousness.

Clock's ticking. Got to get to Lillian.

Sean bounded down the stairs, which seemed to take an eternity. Reaching the bottom of the stairs, he emerged with gun raised. The scene was a massacre. All four of the bodyguards he had seen alive less than one hour ago were dead on the floor. Blood and glass were smeared together across the tile. No Lillian.

As he speed-dialed Austin's number, he looked out the front of the apartment. There were no waiting vehicles and no skid marks from urgently departing cars.

"Sean." Austin's voice came quickly.

"Omar targeted Cole Lawson and UN members at a dinner party tonight. Lillian has the vial and escaped. Khait's after her. Can you ping her cell?" Even as Sean asked, he was sure that she left without her clutch, which meant she didn't have her mobile phone.

"I've got one better," Austin said. "She activated the ring. We traced it down Parc La Fontaine, southeast corner. We're already en route."

Good girl, Lily.

Sean spun and ran back into the apartment complex, crunching over broken glass. He grabbed a flashlight off one of the bodies then darted to the back exit. He sprinted on the trail through the park as his eyes adjusted to the dim light. There were people out for an evening stroll, but he didn't see his wife's green dress.

He put the phone back up to his ear. "How close am I?"

Austin replied, "You were heading in the right direction, but her signal fell out. She must have damaged the ring."

Sean stopped, breathing heavy, thinking.

No, she hadn't damaged the ring. She had gone underground. The sewers were how Khait and his men had escaped previously. It was how they would try to escape again. It was not, he was certain, how his wife would choose to escape, which meant she had been apprehended.

Dammit.

"Sewage system," he barked into his phone to let Austin know.

"Sean, one more thing. Zoey dug up more information on Khait. He's Mukhabarat."

Egyptian Intelligence? Because things weren't complicated enough.

"I don't want that vial in their hands any more than Al Tamsah Alfaraeina's hands. I also don't want an international incident either. So try not to kill him."

Sean muted his phone and pocketed it.

Can't promise that.

Mukhabarat or not, the son of a bitch had still cornered his wife yesterday and took her captive today.

It was unlikely that Austin would be able to track his phone underground, but he left it on just in case the signal could make it through the concrete tunnel walls.

When he reached the entrance to the sewer, he saw where Lillian's high-heeled shoes had sunk in the mud with each step. Accompanying her were treads from a man's boots. One pair. Only Khait.

CHAPTER 22

———————————

Zoey reclined in her chair at the hotel room and stared at her computer. After setting her glasses down on the desk, she lifted a glass of Shiraz to her lips and drank slowly. Her hands were still shaking.

She had done fieldwork. Real fieldwork. And her work might make a difference today.

She was in Cairo on a different assignment. She had paused gathering information on a different bad guy—Ivan Kleist, a wanted German gun for hire whose last known whereabouts were in Cairo, in order to pursue a different tangent. As it happened, Khait's sister and her family lived just an hour away from where she was staying. She had decided to make an unannounced visit.

Zoey had smoothed her skirt and pushed her glasses back up on her nose before approaching the woman's townhouse. Swallowing, she rang the doorbell and nervously waited. She had already surveyed the place, inspected satellite images, looked at power usage, and downloaded phone logs. She knew that Addy, Khait's sister, was home while her children were in school.

Addy answered the door, and immediately, her expression flickered to disapproval as she appraised Zoey's appearance.

"I don't talk to American reporters." She bristled. "You all just keep getting rich inventing lies about my brother."

Then she began to close the door.

Zoey felt her heart race. She couldn't let this conversation end before it had even begun. Furthermore, she was on a deadline. It wasn't as though she could just ring her tomorrow, the next day, or the next week.

"Because he's not a terrorist," Zoey stated.

The door stopped one inch from closing.

"I'm not a journalist. I'm an analyst," she added quickly.

And I'm not a field agent, yet here I am in the field.

The door remained still. Not opening but not closing either.

"I did a profile on your brother, and I think maybe he's not a terrorist." Zoey hated to hear the shaking urgency in her voice. Agents weren't supposed to sound desperate. It was unprofessional.

We're supposed to be the epitome of calm—like Agent Sean Jennings.

She added, "But his cover is so good that I can't prove it."

"Why do you think he's not a terrorist?"

Large brown eyes gazed at her from the doorway, which was wider now.

"Despite his involvement in Al Tamsah Alfaraeina, he has avoided actually killing anyone. And he has shown himself nonhostile in situations when most fanatics would have just pulled the trigger." At last she added, "It doesn't *feel* right."

Ugh.

She was using the doctor's words, but she needed an emotional connection here. It would be worth it if it worked.

She added, "His life is in danger, and we don't know which side he's on."

As soon as Zoey said the words, she realized his life was in danger, whether the CIA knew which side he was on or not. Could he be in less danger if he was identified as an ally? That was the assumption she was making, the reason she was here. It might change their strategy if they could establish an inside ally.

The wide-eyed Egyptian woman opened the door all the way. She looked up and down the street and then motioned for Zoey to come inside.

Zoey was relieved but also filled with a sickening feeling Dr.Whyte had been right. Khait was something more than his file indicated. His sister knew it and was protecting him.

Addy boiled Koshary tea, and the two women stood in her kitchen. She steeped the black tea and let it sit for a moment.

"Who do you work for?" Addy asked.

Zoey looked at the single mother in jeans and a tank top. Addy added cane sugar and mint leaves to the tea before handing her a cup. She took a sip and was struck by the strong licorice flavor.

"Probably better that I don't tell you, but a keen woman like yourself can deduce something accurate."

She eyed Zoey warily over her teacup. Then her face became more neutral, and she shrugged a bronze shoulder.

Zoey leaned in over the counter. "Please, Addy, who or what is Khait? Who is he really working for, and what are his real motives?"

***

"Explain yourself."

Lillian flinched at Khait's demanding voice.

They had wound through a dizzying array of tunnels. Blisters were rubbing on her muddy feet. Rather than trying to avoid the soft silt on the sewer floor, she walked on it, trying to sink in her heels to leave a trail. Her parched mouth longed for a drink of water.

She struggled with the meaning of his question. She could only assume he wanted to know why she was still in the middle of this mess. "I went to Cole Lawson's party as a guest. As soon as I saw Omar Jabal, something about his reaction was wrong. The CIA agent with me, my protection, seized the vial. I escaped with it during the fight."

"Omar, that clumsy oaf," he mumbled, but he was more bemused than angry.

They stopped in a larger tunnel, one that Lillian recognized—Berri UQAM.

"So now you have it?" he asked.

Lillian swallowed.

"The disease is deadly. It can never be released," she pleaded, bracing for an angry outburst.

Instead, he scratched his head with the barrel of his gun and paced in a circle. Much of his hair had loosened during his run and was flowing about his head.

"I know that," he replied emphatically.

She decided he had reached the right distance away from her and the right level of distraction. If she lived through this, she wasn't going to have Sean accuse her of being too warm and fuzzy to the enemy again.

She lashed out a foot, striking his gun hand. Unfortunately, it did not jar the gun loose, but it did startle him enough that she was able to move in closer and give a strong upper cut to his abdomen.

He released a grunt of pain and surprise.

One more move, and she would have the advantage. But as she thrust her weight at him to strike him in the jaw with her elbow, he had already recovered and deflected her blow. He used her own momentum to spin her and snag her body and arm in his grip. The cold steel of the gun was against her skin again. This time, it was grinding against her jaw.

"Dr. Whyte, you are trying my patience and making it difficult for me to keep my promise earlier about not hurting you," he said, a little winded.

She swallowed. *Gazelle, meet lion.*

After a moment, he seemed to come to a decision. "I am Mukhabarat, Egyptian Intelligence. I want the vial destroyed as well."

Lillian's mouth fell open. She turned to stare at him as he loosened his grip. That had been his conflict all along? He was an undercover agent within a terrorist organization trying to figure out whom he could trust?

"You shot a man. And then the guards." The words fell out of her mouth.

"Labaris was a bumbling miscreant who made a biological weapon, so I had no misgivings about shooting him." His face soured. "It wasn't fatal. The guards were all working for Omar."

"But," she stammered, "the bomb."

He paced again. "I did not know who Labaris's contact was, another government agency in all likelihood. I needed to prove my loyalty to Omar. So yes, I detonated the bomb. I knew one of those people was an agent, and any agency worth a piastre would have sent an Arabic-speaking spy. So I announced the bomb and the countdown and left the weakest, slowest member behind. Fortunately, it worked. It is less blood on my already-bloodied hands."

"You didn't know if they would escape or not," she said, incredulous.

"Make no mistake that if they had not survived and I was still able to stop Omar, then it would have been five lives to save thousands."

Lillian licked her dry lips and swallowed. Her mind was churning even as he explained things. "You also needed a way to get Omar out with the vial."

Khait pursed his lips and nodded. "Yes. We had planned that

he would *miraculously* escape after we had possession of the vial, but then his arm was broken. He demanded medical care immediately. *Luti*," he spat. Then he added, "Getting him out with someone critically ill was all I could come up with on short notice."

"And I gave you what you needed by demanding they both come with me?"

"Yes," he confirmed.

"Now we have the vial," she said.

He nodded, looking at her keenly.

"Well, the CIA is on its way—" she began.

"I have high respect for you, Dr. Whyte," he interrupted. "Please do not make me think you are a fool that trusts your government's secret agency to do the right thing with that poison."

He had a point. She didn't like the idea of anyone or any government in possession of a potently destructive form of a prion disease.

"What was your plan?"

"Get it. Burn it," he replied simply.

OMAR FELT the room spin around him as he regained consciousness. His arm throbbed worse than it had since the original injury. The break must be damaged further. His back hurt as well. Something was strained or perhaps worse. But he could still stand, still walk.

His brain seemed to be trying to expand within his skull as he tried to grasp the turn of events. The author had been the spy in the bookstore. Khait had failed to kill him. Somehow, he had discovered Omar's identity, his secret, his mission. He had ruined his plans.

Ya dawety! He wanted to scream.

He got on the elevator.

Forcing the fury to abate, he calmed himself enough to think of the safeguards he had put in place because there were always incidentals, always unexpected events, though not quite as radical as this.

Omar knew if he could get the vial back, he could use his resources to escape and plan a new attack. But this one had taken so long, so much planning. He had built an infallible reputation and earned his way to ambassador. He had worked in shadows to conceal his alter ego as the leader of Al Tamsah Alfaraeina.

He could not go back into the room without a gun and with a former Navy SEAL armed and on high alert.

Omar had secured the guards' services for this event. All six of them were in his pocket. The two the spy had disabled were now useless, but four more awaited downstairs. If they were halfway decent at their job, they could detain an unarmed woman and one spy. Or was it two spies? He had done a background check on Dr. Whyte after the bookstore encounter, and she seemed to be whom she had claimed. In light of recent events, she was clearly some-thing more than her file represented.

La yusaddiq! *Inconceivable!*

In addition to the guards, there were the remaining terrorists on standby. He had already alerted Khait who, by now, should also be downstairs with the captured spies.

The elevator brought him to the lobby, and the doors opened. He stepped out to see blood and bodies strewn across a sea of broken glass. Four guards. No spies. No Khait.

He stared at the bodies. The nauseating scent of blood filled the room along with the stench of terminal defecation, which often happened as one died. It made him think of his son, and suddenly, the air was as suffocating as it had been the day he'd lost him. A vice squeezed his chest as he thought of the horrendous, undignified death. A bomb. The life ripped from his son in an instant when he had been a teenager, a lifetime of love and discovery ahead of him.

The United Nations had sanctioned the invasion to "infiltrate an enemy base." What business did they have invading another country—his country—and furthering violence? The bomb would never have detonated had it not been for meddling forces. Old men with their old ideas—idealists trapped in their own simple-minded spheres. They thought only of what was best for them or their country or their children. No one thought of his son, of his loss.

Tonight's plan was going to be retribution for his country and for his son. The small gathering of UN peacekeepers was vulnerable and exposed. The ones affected would have had a slow and terrible death. Senator Cole Lawson, former Navy SEAL and one of the despicable men involved in the invasion of his land and death of his son, was hosting the event. Exceptionally fortuitous.

Now his plans were foiled, and he had to get that vial back.

Sirens in the distance motivated Omar to hasten again. He tugged a flashlight and gun out of the belt of one of the dead guards. He put a sleeve to his mouth and fought back the urge to vomit.

If Khait was able to confiscate the vial, he would use the tunnels—filthy sewer rat. The tunnels had been Khait's idea from the start, and Omar had accepted it as long as it meant he didn't need to go plunging into them. Events unfolding as they were, he was going to need to plunge into them after all. Fortunately, in his meticulous planning, he had memorized the tunnels.

He pulled his phone out of his pocket and texted the group. He instructed them to divide themselves at the three known exit points they had been using for the tunnels. Khait would arrive to find the reinforcements he may need.

Turning, he exited the building into the Parc La Fontaine. The brisk breeze eased the bile back down into his stomach. It was still queasy but manageable for the task at hand.

His back ached even more as he took the few stairs into the dimly lit walkway. There would be no rushing after anyone. There would also not be much shooting on his part since his dominant arm was the broken one.

Every aggravation of the last fifteen minutes seemed to swell his anger to a boiling rage that propelled him forward despite the pain.

CHAPTER 23

Cole scowled at his captives and the gun in his hand. He hadn't held a gun since the Abuja Warehouse Incident. It felt sturdy yet cold and menacing. Holding the gun reminded him of his SEAL days. Although they had been numbered, the violence of them still haunted his dreams. He had held true to his anti-violence campaign, but he would defend himself tonight if needed.

He raked his free hand through his hair and then loosened the tie on his tux. Looking around at his surprised guests, he set his expression in stone. There really was no politically correct action to take in this instance. One of his guests had assaulted the Egyptian politician and brutishly rendered two guards impotent in the span of sixty seconds.

By appearance and action, Sean looked guilty, but Cole knew his friend and his loyalties. He also couldn't exactly burn his friend and out him to the group here by telling them he was CIA.

His eyes fell to his wife beside him. Her face was as purple as her velvet gown, and her eyes flared with anger. Thankfully, that spite was directed at the guards and not at him. She stood in her heels with legs spread shoulder-width apart and a crackling Taser in her hand.

He did not conceal his surprise.

"I actually bought this thinking I might have the opportunity to use it on Sean," she said with genuine disappointment in her voice.

Then she asked, "Didn't Omar hire this security team?"

"Yes," Cole said, the same thoughts racing through his mind.

The men on the floor could not be trusted, and unless Sean managed to kill or disable four of them downstairs, more may be coming up to them.

After everything he and his Navy SEAL buddy had been through, four armed guards didn't really seem like they would pose much of a hurdle to Sean. Then again, the agent's wife was here. Or at least she was, until she fled. Why had she run? Not fear. Cole considered the look on her face as she slipped out the door—determination, resolve. She was involved somehow. Helping?

If her life was in danger, Sean's ability to calmly and effectively neutralize this national threat seemed bleak. Cole ground his teeth, silently acknowledging that he was not in a position to chase after his friend and help. His responsibility was to keep his family and his guests safe.

Cole locked the door.

"Everyone, stay calm," he urged. "I think all this is related to the bookstore bombing and the terrorist group. We'll wait here until authorities arrive."

Was it more or less reassuring to them that he would say this with a gun in his hand?

"I LIKE YOUR PLAN," Lillian admitted.

Khait smirked.

She pulled the vial out of her dress.

Khait stared at the silver tube but didn't take it.

They walked a few steps farther to the hatch that Sean had found two days ago.

"Could we have had this discussion without having come to the sewer? It might have saved me a pair of shoes."

Khait turned the hatch, unfazed by the screeching noise of it, like nails on a chalkboard.

"We could have had this discussion two days ago if you had told me you were in the CIA's pocket when I asked you who you work for, Tabib."

"I'm not in their pocket. I just ... know a guy who is."

"Hmm," he replied, displeased, "I'm beginning to think this connection is the one who is interfering with you and me."

Lillian arched an eyebrow. "There is no you and me," she reminded him politely.

Khait shrugged. "I think there could have been if you didn't *know a guy.*"

Lillian shook her head but couldn't help smiling at his charm and audacity.

He swung open the hatch and motioned for Lillian to enter ahead of him. She climbed up the two steps and pushed herself through the hatch and into a brightly lit, tiled underground walkway. Light reflected off the shiny surface of pale-yellow and eggshell tiles. The room was a stark contrast to the dark, dank muck they left behind. The rumble of the metro sounded nearer.

Lillian froze, petrified. She slowly raised her hands in the air. Four armed gunmen stood with weapons aimed at her. Once again, she found herself face-to-face with a room full of terrorists.

She felt Khait come in behind her. He began barking at the

men in Arabic. Then he forcefully grabbed her by what was left of her updo.

She let out a gasp of surprise as he pulled her by the hair closer to him. "They are true terrorists," he whispered into her ear. "Let me deceive them a little longer, and then we will get you to safety and destroy the disease together."

The men holstered their guns.

Lillian closed her eyes and blinked away tears from the pain of the sudden wrenching on her head. She wanted to believe Khait.

She gripped the vial in her hand tightly.

Oh God, please let him be who he says he is.

Her fate was in his hands.

"Khait Sadat! *Laha hurr!*"

Though the words were Arabic, Lillian knew that voice—Sean. Relief mixed with a whole new round of fear coursed through her.

Khait released his grip on Lillian's hair and spun to raise his gun at the intruder.

Lillian moved quickly, instinctively protective. She put her body between Khait and Sean and firmly but gently grasped Khait's wrist, moving his arm with the gun off aim from Sean. Then she placed her other hand on his chest.

His face furrowed in confusion.

"Khait," she pleaded, "he is my husband."

She saw his eyes transform from narrow slits of anger to wide surprise. He faltered, lowering his weapon as he looked into Lillian's eyes. Then his face softened as though he understood it all now. The undercover agent at the bookstore had been Sean, and Lillian—true to her word, an actual doctor—rode in on a white horse to save him. She had been protecting him all this time.

Lillian kept her body against Khait's and turned to look at Sean. He had shifted his gun from Khait to the terrorists who had not had time to react and redraw their weapons. They seemed to be waiting for orders.

Sean bellowed something in Arabic, presumably some type of command to drop their weapons or put their hands on their heads. They remained motionless, seeming to weigh their odds against a lone attacker.

Then Lillian saw Omar burst through the hatch, and she heard the all-too familiar sound of a gunshot. In that instant, something hard struck her chest with the force of a baseball bat. Searing pain tore through her left shoulder, and the force of impact sent her closer to Khait.

He caught her in his arms even as he fired a shot at Omar. They fell together, striking the tiled floor hard and knocking the breath out of her. Khait tried to brace her fall but, in doing so, struck his head on the floor. His gun clattered on the floor. She felt the rest of his body go lax as his eyes fell shut.

More gunshots.

She heard the shuffling of feet and knew Sean was fighting in hand-to-hand combat. Her eyes shifted to the light on the ceiling above her. She struggled to sit up, but that was impossible through the pain. She couldn't help Khait or Sean. She couldn't help herself.

She rolled onto her left side and felt the blood from her gunshot wound gush down her arm. She didn't need to look at it. She knew where it was based on the pain and knew it was fatal. Beneath the clavicle were major blood vessels—the subclavian artery and vein, to be specific. They were surely wounded, and their contents poured out of her chest with every heartbeat. It took effort just to breathe.

Lillian looked at Sean, trying to focus. He was on his knees before her, overtaken by three men. There was a gun to his head, but his eyes were only filled with anger. He glanced in her direction, eyes a mix of fury and remorse.

He knows I'm dying.

She wondered how much longer he had to live as well, and

tears welled in her eyes. Having imagined so much more life with him, it was hard to believe that this was where they should part.

She heard shouting and realized the men were shouting at her but keeping a hesitant distance. She followed their gaze down to her hands and looked at them. With her left fingers, she had managed to ease Khait's gun closer to her. She felt the warmth of the recently fired weapon.

Good, a Glock and not a revolver.

In her right hand, she held the prion disease. She hadn't realized she had flipped the top and pulled it out of the metal case. Looking closer through her tears, she saw the rubber top was missing.

Omar was yelling at her not to spill it and to hand it to them, but he was afraid to come too close. She saw red on his right arm where blood was saturating his coat. Khait's bullet had hit him but not fatally. Omar's men couldn't shoot her lest she spill it. Based on their rough gestures toward Sean, they were threatening his life. Surrender was death. Resistance was death.

Devil ahead, devil behind ...

What if it aerosolizes? She recalled Austin's words.

She couldn't spill it. No way to burn it. Thinking about its intended victim, she recalled the magazine picture of Cole Lawson with his wife and family. Smiling children.

Forfeit something for the good of another.

Ridiculous that a fortune cookie would have predicted her future.

Why am I hesitating?

She was dying anyway. With that thought, she put the vial to her lips and drank the prion disease. She saw Sean and Omar grow wide-eyed. They screamed for her not to drink it.

A flurry of motion danced before her eyes. Sean had gotten loose in the commotion and was in hand-to-hand combat once again. Omar Jabal was aiming for a clear shot at him. The room seemed to slow as only Omar came in to focus. She saw his round head, not unlike the bald head of the black-and-white target images she had shot in training with Sean. Blinking once, she inhaled deeply, raising the gun. Then, on exhalation, she pulled the trigger.

Bull's-eye, punk.

Omar crumpled to the floor.

She used the last ounce of energy she had. The last ounce of life. She did not even have the strength to open her eyes.

Patient zero. I am the beginning and the end of this genetically engineered nightmare.

She waited in darkness for them to shoot her again.

Moments later, she felt excruciating pain at the site of her gunshot wound. Sean was cradling her, putting pressure on her wound. He pressed his hand down on her clavicle, and she screamed.

He was alive. She felt a morsel of relief, knowing she had provided the distraction he needed to regain control and kill them all. Sadness flooded her mind as she lamented the time she would miss with him. All the future plans they had made were spilling onto the tiled floor.

"I'm scared," she admitted, her eyelids flickering.

He looked down at her solemnly and kissed her lips. His face was twisted in an anguish she had never seen. His hazel eyes were brimming with tears.

"I'm cold," she choked. She was so thirsty. He held her closer, but it only hurt more.

"No, no, no . . ." Sean kept saying, but his voice became distant.

Feeling herself slipping into a deep, dark abyss of cold and pain, she imagined that she was hell bound because, surely, heaven would be bright lights and pain-free. It was probably poor form to kill someone right before one's own death. It left no time for atonement, and she wasn't in a remorseful sort of mood. If drinking a deadly prion wasn't a ticket to heaven, then surely nothing else she had done in her life was worthy either. Perhaps it was natural to question everything in the end.

Then she remembered telling Labaris that people dying didn't have the wherewithal to ask if they were dying, and that made her chuckle.

Ouch.

Guess I was wrong about that one.

She surrendered to the blackness that consumed her.

———

"GOD IN HEAVEN."

Sean didn't take his eyes off Lillian when Austin gasped. He knew the scene of carnage around him was shocking. Khait lay unconscious from his head striking the ceramic tile. A gash somewhere was bleeding profusely the way scalp wounds did. Omar's body was crumpled in a heap with a bullet hole in his head. Lillian's shot had been deadly accurate. There was blood and other particulates splattered on the wall. Despite her pain, her fatigue, and her fear, she had taken the kill shot and saved Sean's life.

Four dead Crocodiles lay on the floor. Sean had shot one when Omar took Lillian with his bullet. The remaining three had subdued Sean briefly until Lillian drank the poison, the *prion*. But her ludicrous distraction had enabled him to get free.

He had spun and kicked one of the men, knocking him back. He pivoted around the man behind him who had been holding him and swept a leg under the man's legs, knocking him to the floor. With a wicked, abrupt twist of his hands, Sean broke the man's neck.

The last man standing was reaching for his gun. Sean leaped at him, grabbed his hand with the gun and wrenched it down then up into his abdomen. He fired the weapon into the terrorist's gut just below his Kevlar vest. The man released his grip, enabling Sean to secure the gun. He spun again and fired a shot into the nape of the neck of the man he had kicked earlier.

So it was not surprising that Austin should be taken aback at the sight of so much death in such a small space and in the span of about sixty seconds.

"Medic team," Austin barked.

Two male agents came forward and started administering first aid to Lillian. Four more agents checked the bodies for signs of life and found none. Sean recognized Agent Applegate among them. His face looked stricken as he glanced at Lillian. The team took up defensive positions around the perimeter.

"Helicopter evac is two minutes away," Austin added.

Blurry eyed, Sean looked up at Austin, puzzled. It seemed too fast for the helicopter to arrive.

"I expected I would be evacuating injured terrorists, not Lillian," Austin said solemnly.

Sean stepped back as the medics inspected the wound. They applied a sponge of hemostatic medication to stop the bleeding and then bandaged her wound with a pressure dressing. One started an intravenous line and administered fluids while the other positioned her to roll onto their aluminum scoop stretcher.

It's my fault.

He had handed her the vial. He had placed a target on her back. Desperate and hurried, he pushed the vial into her hand, knowing she would run.

She did what my body language and my eyes had told her to do.

She ran.

But I was supposed to catch up to her first.

He had been in agent mode. Eliminate the national threat. He had never intended for her to sacrifice herself for her country, for the world. He should have put a bullet in Omar back at the apartment. The weight of guilt crushed every bone in his body.

Lillian lay pale and limp as a dying white lily. He looked down at the blood on his hands and fell to his knees, silently pleading for her to live.

CHAPTER 24

While Lillian was in the operating room, Sean called Cole to make sure he was safe. Cole insisted on details; however, Sean was unwilling to provide them over the phone. After several angry curses at Sean, Cole said he was coming to meet him

"Where are you? I want answers," he demanded. "My family's life was endangered, and you give me some bullshit agency line about restricted information?"

Sean could feel Cole's anger through the phone, but it didn't faze him. It couldn't faze him. He had to contend with larger worries.

"I'm at Saint Mary's," he said solemnly. "Lillian is in surgery. Bullet wound." He swallowed down the lump in his throat at having said it out loud.

"*Christ*, Sean," Cole responded. The anger in his voice instantly deflated. In a low baritone, he said, "I'm on my way."

Sean sat utterly alone in the waiting room. Waiting and waiting.

He remembered the first time he'd met Lillian. When she had first arrived in Kenya, he had needed to go to Nairobi to check on a source and arranged to ride back with her from the airport to the camp. He introduced himself as the camp translator, which was what the military personnel knew him as at that time. He had been instantly enamored by her spunk and how awestruck she was by Africa.

He remembered the first time he knew he wanted to find a permanent way into her life. A pregnant Swahili woman found her way to camp, dehydrated and preeclamptic. Lillian approached the woman's cesarean section with calm focus despite the fact that she'd never previously performed one solo. She explained to him the medical aspects involved. He was sure it had been her way of maintaining composure. Her treatment was methodical, and both mother and infant survived.

Wanting to be alone with her, he had arranged a day off for Lillian, and then drove her to the southern coast of Kenya to a beach getaway. She confided in him about all of her struggles at work—burnout, patient noncompliance, changes to healthcare, and the litigious atmosphere. She stared at the aqua-blue water and struggled to think of how she would be able to return to that toxic environment. He fought the urge to embrace her, to promise to fix everything even if he didn't know how.

He remembered the first time she was in his arms. They were at a Swahili camp, sleeping under the stars. She curled into him, and he smelled her sweet lilac scent. He wanted to open up to her then, but the timing wasn't right.

When all hell broke loose and the camp was slaughtered, she kept her composure. He was forced to reveal his identity under those stressful circumstances. He was certain she would never forgive him. She would never want to be a part of such a violent world, a violent man, a violent liar.

Weeks later, after her escape from the compound in Kenya,

the CIA had tracked her down to a hotel in France. He rushed to her as fast as he could and found himself standing at her door, afraid to knock. He, who had efficiently killed men in armed and unarmed combat, hesitated before knocking. He stood in the dark hallway in the middle of the night, unsure if her reaction would be anger, distrust, animosity, or something better. She could hate him for lying or for not saving her or for finding her now. He had swallowed, heart beating rapidly. Finally, he knocked.

She answered the door in her nightgown, silky strawberry hair cascading down her shoulders. She threw herself into his arms and planted sweet and passionate kisses in place of words. Caution and apprehension went up in flames as they consummated the love that had grown so quietly and secretively during their month together and their weeks apart.

She didn't hesitate when he proposed to her six months later. Their life since they married had been fulfilling work interspersed with blissful romance. The toughest decision they had faced had been where to vacation next.

Not knowing if she would survive this calamity was killing him. He felt like someone was corroding his organs from the inside out—as though he had ingested a slow, poisonous acid.

Ten minutes later, his friend Cole arrived. Sean barely had the strength to stand and shake his hand. Cole's expression was panicked and worried. He was still wearing his evening attire.

Sean had taken off his tux coat and cleaned the sewage silt off his shoes. There was nothing he could do about the blood on his shirt. The staff had assumed it belonged to his wife, and most of it did. Some, though, belonged to the men he had killed in his faulty attempt to save her life.

This late in the evening, the two men were the only ones in the waiting room outside of the operating room. Sean led Cole over to a corner where they sat down.

"I was in town for an information trade that turned violent," Sean began.

"The bookstore bombing," Cole surmised.

Sean nodded. "The information trade was actually a biological weapon transfer, and the terrorist organization that pretended to kidnap Omar Jabal confiscated the weapon. We didn't know their intended target." He leaned forward in his chair and ran his hand wearily through his hair. "Until I saw Omar at your apartment and the panicked look of being discovered that struck his face, I hadn't realized he was part of the terrorists' plot. The CIA didn't know." He added, "Apparently, your party of UN peacekeepers was the target, perhaps the first of many."

Cole leaned back in his chair, eyes glazed with the enormity of what had happened.

"Your wife?" Cole asked, barely above a whisper.

"Wounded. Omar shot her." His mouth suddenly felt parched. He clenched and unclenched his fists repeatedly, feeling like he needed to punch something or someone. Again.

"Sonuvabitch," Cole murmured.

That was an accurate assessment, Sean thought. He fought back tears that threatened to emerge.

"And Omar?"

Sean smirked. "Dead. Lillian's got better aim lying on the floor with a bullet in one shoulder than Omar had standing at close range."

Cole let out a whistle. "You did find your kind of woman after all." He slapped his friend's leg.

"She's going to be upset with herself for a long time for shooting someone—oath and all, being a physician. She's also not going to forget the image of a bullet she unleashed exploding the back of a man's head," he said somberly. His voice cracking, he added, "If she physically survives this, I don't know if she will mentally."

He thought about her six-month-long recovery after Kenya. This trauma might last much, much longer.

"We all eventually get over our PTSD. She's tough as nails, man. She'll be okay."

Sean looked up at Cole through blurred, watery vision. Had his friend had post-traumatic stress disorder after Port Said? He had wondered at one point if that was what had lengthened some of his recovery time from the physical wound.

He decided not to tell his friend about the prion disease—that Lillian might have a deadly protein circulating in her system and replicating. An internal, ticking time bomb.

"I gave up undercover assignments after I met her. Easiest decision I ever made."

Cole nodded.

"I almost thought I lost her one time," Sean continued, staring at the square pattern on the tile floor. "Damn warmonger came to the States to get his revenge on her, and I didn't see it coming. He almost executed her."

He rubbed his fingers over his scraped and bloodied knuckles.

"You saved her?" Cole asked.

Sean snorted. "Hardly. She stabbed the prick with a fork. A fork!" He let out a short laugh. "Then she shocked him with one of those classic defibrillator paddles."

Cole let out a long whistle.

I saved her brother though. Not that he's ever been grateful.

"She tells me I saved her from the dismal, obscure life she was living working too many hours and feeling unappreciated."

"Sounds like you saved each other from the same vacuum," Cole observed.

Sean leaned back and tried to shake off the suffocating dread of losing her that was threatening to destroy him.

"Rachael pissed at me as ever?" Sean asked, needing to change the subject.

Cole nodded. "Maybe this time when she learns you were actually saving our family, she'll be more forgiving." He seemed to reconsider what he had just said and added, "But it's not really in her nature to do so."

Sean chuckled slightly.

"So what's the party line?" Cole asked.

Sean frowned. "What do you mean?"

"Well, I know you're not going to pitch to the public that an Egyptian ambassador and UN peacekeeper turned into a vicious terrorist, true though it may be." He lifted his hands in the air, palms upward. "So what's the party line?"

The politician emerges.

"That's above my pay grade, Senator. You'll have to take that up with the deputy director. Figure out how you two want to spin it."

AUSTIN LOOKED DOWN at Lillian sleeping in the hospital bed. She looked better than she had lying on the floor near the metro, dying, but an element of the undead still lingered in the dark circles around her eyes. Her face looked thin, and she seemed small in the large hospital bed. Even her red hair seemed blanched.

Her arm was in a sling, and she was connected to all sorts of monitors. From what he could tell, she wasn't on any form of life support. She was just sleeping. A pale, redheaded sleeping, wounded warrior.

"She's my knight in goddamn shining armor," he admitted.

He looked over at Sean, who rubbed his hands over his face and then through his hair. Austin had never seen him look so fragile. His hair was disheveled, and his face gaunt. He looked as though a strong gust might blow him into the wind.

Austin had received a report that Lillian had been out of surgery for a few hours. Sean had been by her side since then. The night had come and gone, and morning sunlight streamed in from a narrow window in the corner.

"How is she?" he asked Sean.

"She'll be okay," he said meekly, not taking his eyes off Lillian. "The bullet tore up the shoulder, so she'll have a lot of physical therapy but nothing wholly irreversible. She'll probably suffer chronic pain the rest of her life." His voice cracked at the last sentence.

Austin wondered if she would still be able to practice medicine, but he dared not address that with Sean at a time like this. He chewed his bottom lip for a moment.

With some hesitation, Austin asked, "And Creutzfeldt-Jakob?"

"They are still running DNA tests to see if she is susceptible or not to the prion disease."

Austin nodded with a frown. He seemed to recall Marie—Agent Beaulieu—saying that the testing would take several days. Maybe he could do something to put a rush specifically on her blood sample.

"Status update?" Sean asked, looking from his wife to his superior.

Austin flicked his head toward the exit. "Let me give you an update in private." He knew Sean needed to talk business and get his mind off Lillian lest he implode from the worry, anger, and self-flagellation.

Sean nodded, stood slowly, stiffly, and followed Austin out the door. They walked down the hall and into the stairwell. The heavy door swung shut, and silence engulfed them. The beeping of hospital equipment was still ringing in Austin's ears. How did Lillian work in an environment like that? How did anyone?

When Austin was certain they were alone, he said, "We've quarantined the subway tunnel. Khait's alive, in our custody. I've got seven dead terrorists in three days, and I need the names and locations of every other contact in Al Tamsah Alfaraeina. I have agreed to release Khait back to Mukhabarat if his cooperation leads to the terrorist organization's disembowelment."

He omitted the part where he learned Omar had already contracted to have someone mass produce the prion disease once he tested it on the dinner party. He also omitted that Mukhabarat agents had already raided Labaris's lab and confiscated his recipe. Ideally, they would destroy the recipe and any premade prion concoction; however, he knew the Egyptian government would do the same thing the CIA would do—file the information and the biological weapon away for "safekeeping."

"What about Khait's carelessness?" Sean demanded in a sharp, cold voice. "What about answering for leading my wife into a tunnel full of fanatics?"

Austin suppressed the urge to roll his eyes. Instead, he scratched an irritated elbow.

As though every operation you run goes smoothly without collateral damage, Austin wanted to retort. But he knew Sean was hurting and on the edge of a breakdown. He didn't need to hasten his demise.

Instead of dignifying Sean's bravado with a response, Austin calmly observed, "You haven't slept in two days, Sean."

Sean let out something like a low growl.

"I am ordering you to take the agency car to your hotel and get some rest. Take a tranquilizer if you need to. You're not any good to your wife if she wakes up and you're unconscious from exhaustion." He could tell that Sean was on the verge of disagreeing with him, so he added, "I'll stay with her. I'll call you if her condition changes."

Sean's shoulders slumped.

"Agent Applegate is out front," Austin said.

Sean nodded, a lost and destitute sort of surrendering gesture, which Austin instantly wished he had never seen. As much as he had begrudged the field agent over the years for his smug self-confidence, he much preferred that version to the struggling, half-broken man before him.

Sean patted down his pockets with a long, slow exhalation like the sigh of a diesel engine after a cross-country road trip. Seemingly content that he had his phone, he went down the stairs as Austin reentered the ICU.

CHAPTER 25

Lillian took in the smell of antiseptic, hand sanitizer, urine, and plastic. Lots and lots of plastic—IV bags, catheters, hospital beds. Bustling sounds and mechanical beeping offended her ears.

Definitely not heaven. Could be hell, she surmised.

She opened her eyes slowly. She moved and felt sharp pain course through her body, especially her left shoulder.

Yep. Must be hell.

She looked around, and her eyes fell on the weary, worried love of her life. "You look terrible," she said, knowing she must be the real wreck between the two of them. She could tell her hair was in snarls. She had lost blood, so she was probably ghostly white. Her lips felt cracked, and she hadn't showered in—how many days had it been?

"You look beautiful," he replied, gingerly holding her hand.

She chuckled slightly, but the motion sent spasms of pain into her arm. She winced and drew in a sharp breath.

"You've got a pain pump," he said. "You want me to push it?"

Judging by the alarm on Sean's face, she was going to have to buck up if he was going to fall apart every time she hurt.

Lillian shook her head and adjusted herself in bed, careful not to let her expression reveal how much pain she felt. "I'm already itching like I've got fleas. Besides, I don't need to add narcotic addiction to my list of problems."

He nodded solemnly. It pained her to see him so forlorn.

"I got the bad guy," she said meekly. "I didn't let him get away this time."

That earned a small grin. "You did good, Lillian," he said, kissing around the IV in her right hand.

She inspected the intravenous lines running to her—looked like it was just saline and a bag of antibiotics. No blood products, at least not currently. Nothing to maintain her blood pressure, which meant she was holding her own.

Sean picked up her tablet out of his lap and handed it to her. "I thought you might enjoy this," he said.

Blinking, she focused on the screen. She read the newsclip.

Montreal—Terrorists shot and killed Egyptian ambas-sador Omar Jabal during a botched attempt to assassinate United Nations peacekeepers at Georgia senator Cole Lawson's Canadian condo-minium. An attempt on Omar Jabal's life had been made just two days prior to this latest terrorist attack during a bombing of a bookstore in Old Montreal.

Witnesses to Wednesday night's attack report Omar fled from Senator Lawson's dinner gathering, drawing the attackers away from their other intended victims. No other UN peacekeepers were injured, and UN spokesperson Paige Lamb reports this will only fuel the need for tighter travel restric-

*tions and promoting better economic stability to
thwart dissension. Senator Lawson states he has
been informed by US government officials that all
the terrorists involved in the attack were killed
during attempts to apprehend them. A candlelight
vigil will be held in honor of Omar Jabal's commitment to peace prior to the UN commencement
ceremony.*

Bordering the article were captions and links to other articles: "Talk Show Host Gigi Holmes Criticized for Comment about Politicians Only Having Two Lives," "Egyptian President Lowers Flag to Half-Staff," and "US Escalates Travel Threat Alert to Red."

She shook her head and handed the tablet back to Sean.

"So the Crocs are swept under a rug, and Omar gets to look like some kind of hero?" She was too tired to infuse much anger or feeling into her question.

"That's how we roll," he replied blandly. "I suppose it accelerates the peace movement to make him a martyr rather than confuse everyone with a peacekeeper turned terrorist."

She shrugged and instantly regretted the motion as the pain stabbed in her shoulder.

"Damage report?" she asked, licking her dry lips.

"Physical therapy for the shoulder," he explained. "Turns out you can eat all the mad cow you want. You don't have the susceptible gene."

She sighed. "I'm sorry I scared you."

"Scared the hell out of me," he agreed, squeezing her hand.

"I thought I was dead either way," she explained.

"Well," he huffed, "apparently, Austin knows my propensity for carnage, so he had a medical helicopter on standby."

"Huh. So I saved your life, then you saved mine, then I saved yours, then Austin saved mine. So who owes whom when the dust settles?"

Her head throbbed.

"At the agency, we call that doing our job," he said wryly, the corners of his eyes wrinkling with his small smile.

"Damn. I thought I was somethin' special," she drawled.

He kissed her hand again. "That you are. That is certain, even without the heroics."

AUSTIN WATCHED as Lillian returned to her private hospital room after walking the halls as part of her physical therapy. She was making progress and had moved out of the trauma ICU. Her ponytail sloppily left red strands hanging out about her shoulders. It didn't make her any less attractive. Her skin looked less pale now, less deathly. He had heard she was doing better, making rapid improvement, but the relief that filled him now could only be achieved by seeing her with his own eyes.

The physician eyed him warily as she took a seat on the edge of her bed. She gave a long exhale as she seemed to be struggling with pain.

His jaw tightened as he fought the urge to grimace or offer some form of assistance.

She waited expectantly.

He had tried to imagine what to say to her while he waited in the hospital room chair as she walked the hall doing her early physical therapy. He shifted in his seat.

"On behalf of the country, I want to thank you for what you did."

She arched an eyebrow.

"And I want to thank you—from me."

"Bill, I accept your thanks. But if you keep looking at me like you give a damn, it's going to screw up our antagonistic relationship." She leaned back in bed and closed her eyes. "I really value our antagonistic relationship."

Austin grunted and smirked. That he could easily do. All the time she'd spent in peaceful, drug-induced sleep, he'd spent cleaning up the fallout from dead bodies on Canadian soil as the result of US involvement. What was supposed to be a simple information exchange had mutated into a diplomatic nightmare.

He cleared his throat. "Next time, Dr. Whyte, I would appreciate it if you could create less of an international incident while you're saving the day."

He watched her open her eyes, flashing sparkling blue eyes at him.

"I have dead bodies to contend with, and I have to smooth things over with both the Canadian and Egyptian governments."

She crossed her legs as the corners of her mouth curled upward. Then she leaned her head back again, closing her eyes.

"I believe that's all part of your job description, Bill."

He stood and nodded.

Obstinate woman. God love her.

"Besides," she added, "there won't be a next time."

He scratched his elbow. "That is what I thought six years ago, but it seems that you are destined to simultaneously be a torment to me and a savior to us all."

For once, she didn't disagree with him.

He headed toward the door to leave.

"Thanks for the flowers."

"Those aren't from me," he answered over his shoulder as he left.

. . .

Lillian stared at the lilies decorating the side table. After admiring them for a moment, she leaned over and plucked the note from between the flowers.

She opened it, which was more of an ordeal than it would have been had she had full use of both arms.

> *Tabib,*
> *It is a great honor to have known you and a great relief*
> *to know that you are alive and well. I am returning*
> *home, though I imagine duty will call in short order.*
> *I think our paths will not cross again, and I believe*
> *it will be to your benefit and my detriment.*
> *—KS*

She harrumphed. She thought he might be a charismatic and intriguing acquaintance to know outside of his terrorist role. For her own safety, she had no desire to form a friendship with him. One agent was quite enough in her life.

Before she could ponder that thought further, her phone rang. Private number.

"Hello?"

"Dr. Whyte, this is Jim. I'm your answering service."

"I see."

The CIA is always watching.

"Hi, Jim."

"Your brother is calling."

"Okay, thanks. Please put him through."

She heard a clicking noise.

She put him on speakerphone as that was more comfortable than holding the phone to her ear.

"Hi, Jonathan."

"You have an answerin' service again," he grumbled.

"Nice to talk to you too."

"According to the news, all of this shit has blown over."

"Yep."

"You're not going to tell me to what extent you and Sean were involved, are you?"

"Nope."

"You can at least tell me that ya'll are okay?"

"We are well."

Minus the bullet wound.

Minus shooting a man, which I vaguely remember.

She remembered pointing the gun and remembered the target didn't look like Omar. It didn't look like a person. It looked like a two-dimensional, black-and-white outline. She pulled the trigger, and then the world faded to black. She wasn't sure what it said about her character, but she didn't feel particularly bad about it.

Jonathan remained silent for a long skeptical pause.

Probably, it would be Christmas before she saw him again, which meant she had time to heal and get her arm out of the sling. She didn't enjoy being secretive toward her brother, but there really was nothing he could or would do but worry. Why spill national secrets to accomplish nothing more than worry?

"Okay. Enjoy the rest of your vacation."

"Absolutely." She hung up the phone and closed her eyes, suddenly fatigued and thinking a nap was in order.

A knock resounded on her door.

"Come in."

Agent Applegate entered, his boyish cheeks bulging from a humble, closed-mouth smile. His smile seemed to falter a bit at the sight of her, probably having something to do with her pasty skin and her arm in a sling.

"Dr. Whyte, Agent Jennings told me what happened." He swallowed hesitantly. "You are a real hero. You saved a lot of people the other night."

"It turned out okay," she replied, a little uncomfortable at the praise.

"I know hardened men who might not have made the sacrifice you did."

"Thank you."

He continued, "And it's tough because this is all covert, so you'll never get the recognition you deserve."

Lillian smirked. "Not sure I want to go down in history as the physician that drank mad cow disease."

He snorted. "Yeah. Guess not. Anyway, thank you. And if you ever need anything . . . anything . . ." His voice trailed off as he looked down at the floor.

Her tablet started making a strange beeping noise. She looked down and saw that it was an incoming video chat request. Curious. She had never used that function on this device.

She looked up to see that Agent Applegate had left.

She pressed the Accept button.

ZOEY PEERED at her computer screen at a haggard, gaunter version of the Dr. Whyte she had come to know. She pushed her glasses up on her nose and stifled the urge to gasp or make some other unprofessional noise of surprise. Despite the hell she had been through, her sapphire eyes were still vibrant with life.

"I just wanted to check on you and see you're okay."

"I'm getting there." She shifted her weight in the hospital bed, which looked like it caused some discomfort.

Then she added, "I heard we have you to thank for figuring out Khait was Mukhabarat."

Zoey frowned. "I think we have you to thank. All I did was confirm your suspicions."

"They needed confirmation, Zoey. You're the one who took the initiative to dig further."

Zoey smiled.

"You're still in Egypt?" Dr. Whyte asked.

Zoey nodded. Under no circumstances was she going to divulge her project to Dr. Whyte. The physician had been through enough. Zoey wouldn't tell her that her current intelligence gathering was focused on Ivan Kleist, the German gun for hire. He was one of Dr. Whyte's captors from Kenya. He had been working for Vanier at the time and had been at large since she had destroyed Vanier's enterprise.

"Any chance you know who put together that disturbingly accurate Facebook page about me? I was hoping to have it taken down."

Zoey beamed. "I'll take care of it."

CHAPTER 26

———

Kelly's wedding day arrived in full splendor and with only a touch of pandemonium.

Kelly had chosen a château setting in the luscious green Georgia mountains for an outdoor wedding. White chairs were nestled under decorative white lattice. Bouquets of flowers wrapped in teal foil were scattered among the green foliage of the gardens. There were walking trails meandering through a manicured lawn. The trails wound around a small pond with an elegant fountain, and a quaint stone bridge arched over it.

It was picturesque, or at least, it had been before the rain began to pour.

Lillian stared out the window, frowning. Looking back over her shoulder, she saw her best friend, white dress spilling around her as she slouched in the chair of the dressing room.

"It's an omen," she pouted. Kelly was trying not to cry so she would not ruin her makeup.

Lillian forced a smile. "It's not an omen. The rain will stop and leave a rainbow, and then you'll have good luck the entirety of your marriage."

That was the presumption, right?

Kelly sniffed.

Lillian adjusted the strapless top of her dress, grimacing slightly. The shoulder wound was healed enough that she was out of her sling, but she was still participating in physical therapy. Fortunately, she was able to disguise it with industrial-strength makeup. She walked to the dressing room door and swung it open.

"Where are you going?" Kelly asked.

"To make this wedding happen."

They had been waiting thirty minutes for the rain to abate, and it showed no signs of relenting. There were nearly two hundred people down in the ballroom. Lillian decided they had absolutely nothing better to do than transform this into an indoor wedding.

She only knew a dozen or so of the guests, but that wasn't stopping her. She strode across the ballroom floor, high heels clicking against the polished wood floor. Working her way through the crowd, she caught a glimpse of Sean in conversation with Kelly's father.

Wow, he looked delicious in his suit. He gave her a bemused look as she winked at him.

She reached the disc-jockey station where a goateed man in a sport coat was setting up equipment.

"Can I get the mike?" she asked.

He looked up at her quizzically and then looked around the room, scratching his bearded chin.

"Yeah, okay."

He handed her the cordless microphone and switched it on.

"Ladies and gentlemen," she said calmly, testing the microphone. Her amplified voice carried through the ballroom.

The guests looked at her.

"Good afternoon. I'm Lillian Whyte, the maid of honor. Welcome to Kelly and Devon's wedding. Who is excited to be here?"

There were a few yelps and whistles.

"Who's ready to watch this wedding?"

Murmurs of agreement and a few shouts resounded.

"Who's ready to make this wedding happen?"

The cheers grew a little more lively but weren't quite the fervor she was seeking.

"Who's ready to make this wedding happen so we can get to the open bar?"

Genuine excitement filled the room.

Lillian proceeded to divide the guests into thirds. One-third to bring the dining chairs into the ballroom for audience seating, one-third to bring the dinner table decorations into the ballroom to create the walkway, and one-third to construct the altar where the DJ was presently located. She added that they needed to remember their assignments so that they could perform it in reverse to restore the ballroom dance floor and the dining area after the wedding vows.

"Let's get this couple hitched!" she added playfully.

Thirty minutes later, the new wedding setting was complete.

Take that, leadership training.

She didn't spend time asking each individual his or her goals. There were no drawn-out personality tests. She didn't need to take into account the best way to motivate individuals or psychoanalyze the group.

She had agreed to the leadership training and was one month into lectures and books on effective leadership, emotional intelligence, group dynamics, and more. Somehow knowing her Myers-Briggs personality was supposed to help her realize her strengths and weaknesses as a leader. Apparently she was an ENTJ—extrovert, intuitive, thinking, judging—personality. She already knew she was frank, decisive, and annoyed by illogical policy and inefficient people. She did not need an hour-long personality test full of redundant questions to tell her this. She felt being forceful with her ideas was important in her line of work. Apparently, as a leader, such continued tendency at overbearing behavior would sideline the introverts and alienate the feelers—those empathetic souls attuned to the emotions of themselves and others.

Since much of her empathy seemed to have been whisked via vortex into another dimension sometime during her years of eighty-hour work weeks, she needed to not alienate those with such intangible power if she hoped to restore her own empathy.

Right now, however, she had a wedding to run. Maybe she didn't know shades of teal or what a wedding cake should look like, but she did have the skills to get this thing in gear—rain or shine.

Fifteen minutes later, music was playing, and the wedding party stood at attention at the altar.

The bridesmaids consisted of Lillian and two of Kelly's friends from work. The groomsmen were Devon's college buddies.

Kelly appeared, looking stunning in her wedding dress as it elegantly trailed the floor behind her. Her father escorted her, looking stately in his tuxedo.

Lillian felt a sudden pang of sadness thinking of her own father and how he hadn't been alive to see her get married. Sean's hadn't either. She scanned the audience until she saw him— tailored blue suit, thick brown hair, and tan, clean-shaven face.

He smiled at her and winked. She blinked away a tear and turned back to the bride.

Kelly looked at Lillian, her blue eyes brimming with a mixture of joy and gratitude.

She mouthed a "thank you" through perfectly rouged lips.

Lillian blinked away another round of tears.

Okay, now this is just getting ridiculous.

She took a deep breath and focused on Sean. She thought about the years to come, the adventures yet to be shared, though she was hoping those adventures would be more like Antigua and less like Kenya and Montreal. When she was fully healed, they planned to hike Kilimanjaro and sail to the Galapagos Islands.

By the time the ceremony finished, the rain had subsided. The outside chairs would have still been too wet for the guests, but the walkways were now acceptable for pictures.

Lillian sprang back into action, coordinating the disassembly of the ballroom wedding ceremony and reassembly of the dining hall. Given that the two rooms were adjacent, the chairs didn't have far to travel.

When endeavors were set in motion, she joined the wedding party on the bridge over the pond. Kelly and Devon were taking pictures and looking adorable in each other's embrace.

Lillian looked up at the parting clouds lined in golden sunlight. A rainbow shimmered. Between poses, Lillian caught Kelly's eye and pointed in the direction of the rainbow. The bride gasped in delight and moved the photo session to where the camera could capture the rainbow in the backdrop.

When the couple was done with their photos, the rainbow saw fit to depart with the dispersing clouds. The bridesmaids and groomsmen reconvened at the bridge and dutifully struck various poses.

At last, the photographer declared the shoot complete. Lillian tried to wriggle the muscles in her face free of the tension from so much smiling.

Kelly approached her, blonde hair glistening in the sun.

"Thank you so much, Lily."

"All this time, I tried to figure out why in the world you wanted me for the maid of honor. Now I know."

Kelly smiled. "I knew you'd be the one to come through when I needed your help."

Kelly couldn't accept hugs in her billowy dress, which suited Lillian, who couldn't supply them easily with one injured shoulder. They settled for a brief squeeze of their hands.

AFTER SEVERAL TOASTS of champagne and a three-course meal, the dance floor filled with numerous smiling guests.

At last, Sean had an excuse to have Lillian in his arms all to himself. He led her to the dance floor and gingerly lifted her arms onto his shoulders.

"Thank you."

He knew if she had tried to get her left arm that high using her own muscles, her shoulder would have protested with waves of pain. With his help, she experienced only a little discomfort.

"Is that okay?"

She nodded.

Once her arm was resting around his neck, the uneasy expression in her eyes relaxed.

He said, "You've been so busy, I haven't had the chance to tell you how amazingly beautiful you look."

And she did. The teal dress flattered her waistline, and the diamond jewelry made her sparkle like royalty. She had appeared downright queenly when she strode across the dance floor and took control of the wedding guests. She had put everyone to work just as if she were commanding a trauma code.

The crowd yielded, and not because she had saved untold thousands of people from a horrible death—which they didn't know—nor because the sooner the wedding happened, the sooner the bar opened—which they did know. They obliged because people responded at a visceral level to a true leader. A true leader helped people see the benefit of their work, the impact of it on themselves and others. A true leader helped people feel good about the work they did and made them feel valued. True leaders acted to benefit others, just as Lillian had done, and those actions garnered respect.

Lillian made sarcastic jabs about the leadership training she was doing, but that was because she made sarcastic jabs about everything. Truthfully, he believed she was absorbing the information and would improve because of it.

He curled a strawberry strand of loose hair behind her ear and looked into her blue eyes. There was nothing more beautiful than watching this already-dazzling woman blossom.

As THE SONG ENDED, Lillian thought of a hundred things she wanted to express to Sean. She was grateful for the love and support he had given her. She didn't blame him for anything that happened in Montreal and hoped, with time, he would stop blaming himself. She appreciated him coming to a wedding with nearly two hundred people neither of them knew. She also wanted to tell him she was looking forward to the rest of their lives together.

Lillian didn't get to say any of those things because Jonathan appeared. Her brother looked uncharacteristically composed and clean-shaven in a charcoal suit. He also looked annoyed.

"May I have this dance?" he asked Sean gruffly, confrontationally. His tense shoulders appeared ready for a fight should Sean refuse.

Jonathan was a former marine and a few inches thicker all around than Sean. In every situation Lillian had ever been in with Sean, he was the deadliest man in the room. Such men knew this about themselves and never felt threatened or pressured by ego to prove it.

As such, Sean smiled at Lillian, gave her a reassuring kiss on the cheek, and lowered her arms, sliding his hands gently down the sides of her arms to minimize her pain. He turned to Jonathan and gave a bow and a subtle, condescending smirk.

"Certainly."

Jonathan stood before Lillian as Sean walked away from them. His back was fully to them—again, not in the least threatened by her brother's annoying display of testosterone.

As the music played in the background, Jonathan looked at her with appraising eyes and made no motion to lift her hands in his.

She took his left hand with her right hand, but he then made no countermove to lift her left arm to his shoulder with his right hand.

Sighing, she shot him an annoyed look. Then she gritted her teeth and raised her left arm to his shoulder. The pain cut through her measly doses of ibuprofen and acetaminophen from an hour ago as her shoulder protested the rotation. She swallowed down the pain while maintaining steely eye contact with her brother.

"I knew it," he sneered, grinding his teeth in irritation. "I could tell you were injured from across the room." He squinted in the dim disco light at her left shoulder. "You've got some kind of movie-magic makeup on that thing, but that's a gunshot wound, Lillian."

His face grew redder the more he stared.

"I'm fine, Jonathan."

"You can't raise that arm past twenty degrees without it hurting. You're not fine."

She shook her head. "I'm still in physical therapy. It will continue to improve."

"Can you even work right now?"

"I'm teaching and doing the leadership training course."

"You didn't tell me something happened to you in Montreal."

Sean had told her that Jonathan saw a newsreel of her in the bookstore parking lot and questioned him about the extent of her involvement.

She pursed her lips. "You couldn't have done anything."

"You should've told me."

"Told you what?" She lowered her voice. "Oops, I accidentally got mixed up in a terrorist attack."

He scowled. "This is all Sean's fault."

He looked over at Sean like he wanted to grind him to a pulp.

Go ahead, big guy, keep telling yourself you're even on his level. I watched him kill three armed men. Well, I heard it. I was too busy thinking I was dying to watch it.

"Sean is the reason I'm alive. And the two of us are the reason a good portion of the United Nations and Montreal are still alive."

"No shit?"

"No shit. So pocket your machismo, and treat us with a little courtesy."

Jonathan frowned as he seemed to consider her suggestion. He didn't agree or apologize, but at least his bravado seemed to deflate.

"Thanks for coming to Kelly's wedding," Lillian said.

His mouth quirked as he shrugged. "She's been an important friend to you. We always got along the few times we met."

JONATHAN'S EYES cut away from his sister to glance at Sean who was talking casually with the bride's father. He really was a piece of work. All debonair and casual by appearances while missing nothing in his surroundings.

Jonathan had him easily by twenty pounds, but who was he kidding? His marine days were over a decade behind him. Although he kept in shape working on his farm in Arkansas, fending off snakes from his chickens and opossums from his trash hardly kept his fighting skills at peak level.

Sean had the walk and glinting gaze of a predator with honed skills—except when he looked at Lillian. With her, his eyes were all adoration and admiration. He had noticed the consistent fondness in his eyes on the few holidays they had spent together. It was part of the reason he tolerated Sean.

He looked back at his sister, red squiggles of hair in an updo and shimmering dress cascading around her. She only needed wings to be a fairy. She was positively glowing in a way she never had before Africa, before Sean. Something about their relationship and the life they lived together vanquished years of misery and dissatisfaction. It was as if Sean had somehow pressed the release valve on the pressure cooker of her life.

She's better with him, Jonathan reluctantly admitted to himself.

But life was good and bad, yin and yang.

Balance.

The cost of the enrichment she gained from her life with Sean came at the risk of being sucked into his dangerous work.

He looked again at the faint purplish scar on Lillian's shoulder.

She definitely knew the risk. It seemed she was willing to keep taking it.

Guess I can stop being an overprotective ass.

"You look beautiful, sis."

She smiled.

With a wry smile he said, "So leadership training."

Of course, he could still be an ass about some other things.

Lillian rolled her eyes.

"How's that going for you?"

"Ugh," she groaned followed by a long list of gripes.

L illian threw a left hook and felt the twinge of pain in her shoulder, but she didn't let the discomfort slow her down. Her opponent ducked, which she had anticipated. Since her surgery, it was jarring to strike anything with more than a little force with that arm. Better to use it for distraction than a real punch.

As Lillian's opponent dodged the left hook, she brought her arm back into her body for balance and shot out a sidekick with one long, bare leg. Her opponent blocked the right kick trying to grab her sneaker, but she was too fast.

She spun with the momentum of her kick from the lack of impact and brought her center of gravity low to the ground. Still making a circular motion, she lashed out her left foot, sweeping the tall man's legs out from under him. Her long red ponytail swung out around her.

Sean let out a grunt as he landed on the sparring mat. His head hit the mat but was cushioned by his foam headgear.

Lillian stood, smirking and enjoying for a moment that he was the one flat on the mat for a change and not her. She had practiced that move a hundred times and mentally rehearsed it a hundred more during her strength training—that and a dozen other combo moves Sean taught her.

Still grinning, she took a few steps back to let him stand.

After rehabilitation and physical therapy, she had insisted on more self-defense training. Again, not that she intended to need it, but it seemed it would be valuable if fate was going to continue to thrust her in harm's way.

Sparring was also a great emotional release for her. The Montreal incident did not haunt her the same way Kenya had. She hadn't suffered six months of nightmares and anxiety the way she had after Africa and the attack in Arkansas that immediately followed. Maybe the difference was less bloodshed—though the stakes were higher in Montreal. Maybe the difference was having Sean close. Maybe she was just getting acclimated to the stress the same way she no longer reacted to a medical emergency with more than a ten-point rise in her heart rate. There was no surge of adrenaline as cool, calm, collected rationality prevailed.

With startling speed, Sean was back on his feet and taking the offensive. She blocked his blows—partial strength but still powerful—as she focused on maintaining her balance. When she lost her equilibrium, he could knock her down with the lightest, most-graceful touch—like blowing the seeds of a dandelion, except that she fell to the floor painfully instead of tranquilly floating away. With each strike, he was working himself closer until he grasped an arm, spun her, and clutched her body close to his.

She tried to wriggle free.

"Did I ever tell you how fantastically edible you look in your little spandex outfit?" he purred with a silky, seductive voice into her ear.

Refusing to be distracted, she dropped her weight then sprang up with her left elbow launching toward his face. In anyone else, that maneuver would have broken a nose. But Sean, having taught her that move, recognized it and released his grip to block her elbow.

She sensed her advantage.

With her right hand and arm, she pinned his right arm against her. Bending and leaning forward, she tumbled with the intention of taking him over her right shoulder onto the mat on his back.

But she felt his grip around her tighten, and instead of resisting her over-the-shoulder throw, he launched himself forward and rolled with her. His extra momentum enabled him to continue the roll. The next thing Lillian knew she was on her back, pinned by Sean.

What the—?

She was certain she'd had him this time.

He gave her a wolfish grin as he settled his legs around her waist. He restrained her with one hand while snapping off his headgear with the other. There was another maneuver she was preparing for, but the fight in her deflated at the sight of him. His gleaming smile was framed by a week's worth of rugged stubble. His copper-flecked hazel eyes sparkled. Lean, muscular biceps protruded from his gray T-shirt.

She was panting, as much from the sparring as from seeing him looking devilishly delectable above her.

He must have read the expression on her face because his eyes grew wider as he slid her hands above her head and leaned in for a delightfully succulent kiss.

<<THE END>>

DEAR READER

I hope you enjoyed Whyte Knight. If you enjoyed the book, please take time to leave a review where you purchased the book or at your favorite spots (Facebook, Goodreads, Bookbub, etc). Authors rely on good reviews and word of mouth to gain popularity for our books.

Also, you can sign up for my newsletter at www.cbsamet.com to learn about new releases and bonus material. You can also get access to CIA officer Jenning's dossier and a free novella.

Keep reading to start Gray Horizon, the third Dr. Whyte book and winner of 2019 bronze thriller award (Readers' Favorite Awards).

Sincerely,
CB Samet

OTHER BOOKS BY CB SAMET

The Dr. Whyte Adventure Novels

Black Gold

Whyte Knight

Gray Horizon

The Rider Files Romantic Suspense Novels

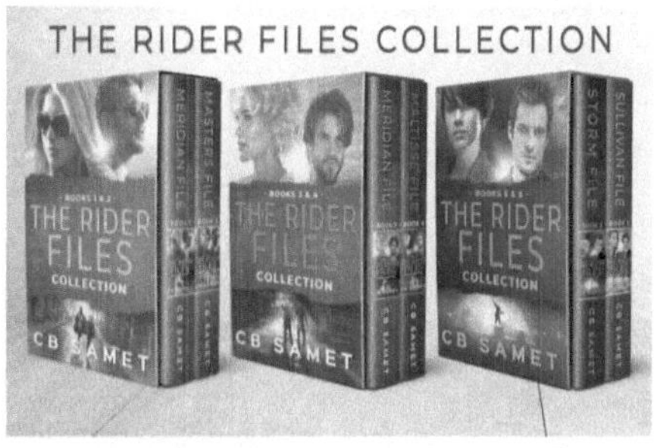

Meridian File / Masters File / Box Set 1

McMillan File / Maltisse File / Box Set 2

Storm File / Sullivan File / Box Set 3

The Avant Champion Epic Fantasy Series

Malakai: An Avant Champion Origin of Malos Story (prequel)

The Avant Champion: Rising

The Avant Champion: Honor

The Avant Champion: Ashes

Brothers' Bond: An Avant Champion Malakai Story

The Avant Champion: Conquest

SAMPLE CHAPTER

Gray Horizon - CHAPTER 1

Lillian heard shouting from across the hallway and looked up from the imaging screen. A red-cheeked, burly man jabbed a finger toward one of her residents in irritation. A bulge in his jacket pocket suggested the presence of a gun. She had seen too much violence in her lifetime to think it could be anything other than a weapon. Too bad the emergency room didn't have metal detectors at the entrance. The slight sway of the man's rotund body indicated some degree of intoxication.

He was trying to force his way to the bedside of a woman who had been brought in earlier after a car accident. She had multiple injuries, old and new, none of which matched a low-impact fender bender.

Lillian's gaze roamed the emergency room to gauge the level of the threat. The bustle of activity was fairly standard for evening traffic. The waiting room was twenty people deep. Resident physicians, respiratory therapists, phlebotomists, and nurses bustled to and fro, while paramedics wheeled in a stretcher with the newest emergency arrival. In one corner, two policemen were helping subdue a psychotic patient until chemical restraints could be implemented.

This was a normal day at the office, except that this woman's inebriated husband might reach for his gun and open fire at any moment.

Lillian leaned over to Mary, one of the nurses. "Please ask security to meet me at bed four. *Discretely*."

Mary looked up from her computer screen and stared at Lillian. Her mouth fell open in alarm. "Bed four. Yes, Dr. Whyte."

The escalating situation couldn't wait for security to finish with the psychotic patient. Lillian needed to intervene, especially since the man was armed. The hair on the back of her neck stood on end as she approached the shouting. She steeled herself for the confrontation.

The young resident looked terrified, but stood his ground to protect his patient.

"Let me see my wife, you damn punk!"

Lillian stepped into his direct view. "Hello. I'm Dr. Whyte. Can I help you with something?"

The man scrutinized her black scrubs and red hair. "You can get this kid out of my way, so I can see my wife," he snarled. He gestured to the closed curtain.

Lillian could smell the schnapps on his breath and see his bloodshot sclera. She positioned herself between her resident and the man.

Although her heart thudded in her chest, she kept her voice calm. "She's resting. If you want to wait in the lobby, we can let you know when visitors are permitted." Her senses were on high alert, watching his every twitch and shift.

"I'm not a goddamn visitor! I'm her husband!"

In a quiet but sharp tone, Lillian said, "Then would you also be the man who broke her wrist, cracked three ribs, and bruised her neck?"

A deep scowl settled on his face causing his bushy eyebrows to nearly touch over the bridge of his beefy nose. His eyes became obsidian. Lillian imagined she was seeing what this man's poor wife had seen time and time again.

Despite sensitivity and leadership training, Lillian's mouth seemed to land her in hot water. She had angered him and was now the object of his wrath. Better her than his wife or her resident.

Events in her Lillian's life over the last decade had propelled her into learning advanced self-defense. She had more training for combat than most people, yet her previous experiences did nothing to dull the adrenaline coursing through her.

The man's knuckles cracked under the force of restrained fury as he balled his fists. "She tell you that?"

Lillian looked him directly in the eyes. "She didn't have to."

The man snapped. He roared and lunged at Lillian.

Time seemed to slow as she watched every motion and took evasive measures. She twisted her torso to the right and dodged him, letting him collide with one of the beams holding the curtains partitioning the room.

He swore and spun around to find her.

Several nurses and emergency room technicians turned to stare. The police were still on the opposite side of the emergency room.

Lillian knew what would come next—the gun. Multiple homicides would be followed by either suicide or the police taking him down when he ran out of bullets. She needed to end the fight before anyone conjured the idiotic idea of coming to her rescue.

The man drove his hand into his pocket and jerked out the gun. The flash of metal glinted in the fluorescent light of the emergency room.

Lillian was already moving closer. She grasped the revolver and launched a knee into the man's upper abdomen. As he bent over with a grunt, she twisted the gun out of his hand.

He took an enraged swing. His tree trunk of an arm barreled toward her. Stepping back, she avoided the blow then kicked at his knee hard enough to shred ligaments.

He unleashed a howl of pain and crumpled to the linoleum floor. If he knew what horrendous germs and bodily fluids lurked on the floor, he might not linger there.

She looked down at the revolver in her hand. It was loaded. She opened the cylinder, swung it out, and dropped the bullets on the counter. With her heart pounding, she laid the gun beside the bullets and stepped back from the counter.

Two police officers scurried over and began restraining the man even as he complained about the assault and the pain in his stomach and leg.

Lillian sighed. Now she had created an extra patient in the already crowded ER. At least nobody got shot.

***

Ivan Kleist splashed water onto his face from the public restroom sink before inspecting his bruised, swollen jaw. He ran his tongue over his chipped molar. He had spit out the bloody tooth fragment during the fight two days ago. If only the German tooth fairy —*Zahnfee*—still paid in gold coins, Ivan wouldn't have to work so hard for fifty thousand Euros.

Verdammt.

He had retrieved the file, no easy feat. But the beating he'd taken would ache for days. Maybe he was getting too old, too slow. Crime had many financial advantages, but sometimes the physical cost seemed steep.

"*Tu va bien?*" Renni asked.

Ivan looked in the mirror at the Frenchman standing behind him. "*Ja.*"

Renni Durand hadn't escaped unscathed either. Ivan wouldn't be surprised if his colleague peed blood for the next week from the punches his flank had sustained. He had a cut on his cheek above his stubbled jaw. One brown iris was encircled with blood.

Renni wiped his face with a damp paper towel. "Ze exchange is in one hour. We've got to move."

As they left the bathroom, Renni lit a Gauloises and took a drag. "Somezing felt off about zis job." A wisp of smoke twisted into the air.

Ivan had no interest in smoking, but at least the smell of the French tobacco was more reminiscent of a cigar than bleached American and Canadian cigarettes. German smokers often smoked American brands unless they enjoyed the German F6. Just like his country to pick a practical name—nothing sexy or luring.

"You say that about every job." Ivan ran a hand through his short, spiked, pale blond hair.

"This one is different."

"You say that too."

"*Zut,*" Renni swore.

"So don't go to the exchange," Ivan offered as they walked the Ring Road away from the Beijing Railway Station. The enticing aroma of chuan'r—roasted meat, charcoal, cumin, and pepper—from street vendors filled the air.

"If I don't go, who has your back?"

Ivan couldn't argue with Renni's logic. They knew little of the individuals who had hired them except that they wanted this flash drive and its contents in mint condition, and they wanted the previous owners of the USB in the grave. The previous owners put forth a stronger fight than expected. They had been surprisingly averse to dying. As a result, Ivan's jaw still ached.

The men they fought had claimed the attack was a double-cross. Ivan and Renni had done the job they'd been hired to do. They were not told of the contents of the USB drive, so they couldn't possibly be double-crossing anyone. The men went to their graves thinking someone had betrayed them.

Perhaps someone had, but Ivan had no way of knowing the details. It wouldn't be the first time he had been hired to eliminate someone previously in cahoots with whomever had hired him. Business was business. If nothing was fundamentally different in this job compared to others, why did he feel the need to be hyper-alert? Now that they had the USB, the job was almost finished. They would make the exchange.

After that, Ivan planned to take the week off and go back home to Germany to recuperate.

Ivan and Renni took the stairs to the third floor of the office building under renovation. The steps creaked under their weight.

Ivan was accustomed to secretive meetings in secretive places. This particular exchange was no different. Except that it *felt* different.

Renni Durand—the cavalier, nicotine-addicted Frenchman—seemed on edge as well. Or was Ivan projecting his own emotions? No matter. They weren't a couple of amateurs. They could outmaneuver any opponent.

Ivan and Renni exited the stairwell on the third floor. Battery-powered LED lanterns dimly lit the room at the end of the hall.

"Are you the cook?" Ivan asked a tall, bearded man sporting a CZ 75.

The sleek, 9mm semiautomatic pistol had been made in the Czech Republic. It was a respectable weapon, but it appeared out of place in the hands of a man whose ridged brow and jutting jaw made him look like he belonged in the Paleolithic era. He needed a club, not a gun. Another man who could have been his twin stood a few feet to the right of him.

The first caveman grunted in amusement. He stepped aside to reveal a petite Asian woman.

"*Annyeong hashimnikka.*" The woman bowed.

Ivan mimicked her bow but was at a loss on how to acknowledge her greeting. He was fluent in German, French, English, Dutch, and Russian, but he knew scant Korean.

"I am the cook," the woman said in English.

Ivan straightened. "I—" he began, but she turned and walked away from him.

—am insignificant, apparently.

This was not his first encounter with arrogance. The people he worked for often thought they were better than him. Ivan knew the truth. The contractor of a thief was no different than the thief himself—or herself. He didn't discriminate as long as he was paid well. And he didn't feel the need to explain the lack of distinction to those who employed him. They could stare down their nose at him as long as he walked away with a bigger bank account.

His gaze followed the cook as she walked to a tiny metal desk with an open laptop.

She extended an open palm. "The package?"

Ivan withdrew the flash drive from his pocket and handed it to the cook. His eyes caught a glimpse of burn scars on her hand. After turning and sitting at the desk, she plugged it into the laptop.

One of the men stepped between Ivan and the cook, blocking his view of the computer screen. He could hear her small fingers as they moved over the keyboard rapidly. She would be opening file after file skimming through document after document long enough to confirm he had provided the stolen information she sought. Ivan had already examined the flash drive and knew what terrible secrets it held, but he kept his expression neutral.

Ivan glanced at his partner Renni, who kept his position, standing back far enough that he was near the exit and could see the cook and her two guards clearly. Ivan had no doubt his partner would ensure their safe escape should the cook intend a double-cross.

The woman nodded in satisfaction. *"Joh-eun."*

Although none of the gunmen had drawn their weapons, a window shattered. Behind Ivan, Renni collapsed with a grunt.

Sniper.

Ivan dove to the floor and rolled. He didn't hear a second sniper shot. Of course the shooter wouldn't want to risk hitting the computer and drive.

With the rustling of fabric, the cook's men drew their guns.

Ivan lurched behind a metal rolling cart with construction supplies as bullets erupted around him. When he drew himself into a tight ball, his joints protested with pain. He positioned his fingers to draw his weapon.

The noise of gunfire and ricocheting bullets filled the room. His ears rang from the deafening roar as his heart, amped up on adrenaline, thudded in his chest. His opponents had the clear advantage. Three against one. Ivan planned to at least put up a good fight.

The hair on his neck stood on end as a trickle of icy sweat ran down his spine. He was accustomed to fear and danger in his work —dark people doing dark deeds—but the contents of the encrypted documents they had stolen for the cook sealed his death warrant. After they had stolen it and before this delivery, Ivan had seen what terrible information was on that flash drive. He had debated the consequences of not making the delivery at all, but that would have certainly made him a target.

Now he understood he had indeed been hired to double-cross the men from whom they had stolen this information. The men he had killed. Just as he would be killed.

When the cook's men had emptied their semiautomatics, Ivan came up shooting.

The cook was already exiting via the stairwell, laptop tucked under one arm. Ivan didn't have much time. Once she was out of harm's way, the sniper could open fire. In fact, when she was out of the building, the whole place could be incinerated if they felt so inclined. He needed to get outside.

He darted across the room. A sniper's bullet grazed his arm.

"*Verdammt*," he growled.

Judging by the timing of fire, he was up against a bolt-action sniper rifle. At least it wasn't an automatic weapon. At fifty, he wasn't as agile and fast as he used to be. He suspected the sniper was positioned in the building adjacent to this one.

One of the cook's guards stayed behind, and Ivan heard him reloading his gun. Ivan faced bullets from two sides. He slid under a vinyl curtain tacked to an unfinished wall, partitioning the room.

Glass rained down as the sniper continued to fire through the windows.

Ivan crawled along the floor, ignoring the shards of glass biting into his bare forearms. He reached a gaping hole in the floor where wires and pipes crisscrossed haphazardly. He squeezed his battered body through the opening, slipping on his own blood before falling into the darkness of the room below him.

Pain shot through his back as he struck a metal beam lying across the floor. He grunted and rolled over, listening for motion as his vision adjusted to the darkness.

The gunfire had ceased, but it was only a matter of time before they found him. His escape routes were limited. The stairwells were not an option; they would be watched. The elevator shaft would be the next logical place for them to lie in wait to execute him. He was too high up to jump without breaking a leg—or worse.

Ivan recalled the construction waste chute on the side of the building. He had spotted it when he and Renni arrived and first inspected the building. Since the chute was on the other side of the building, it would not be visible from the sniper's vantage point.

Gritting his teeth through the pain in his back, Ivan pushed himself to his feet. He wound his way out of the room, down the hall, and toward the rear stairs. As he pressed his face to the glass, he looked outside the building. Streetlights faintly illuminated the forklifts and cranes outside the window. He looked up and noted the chute's opening was two stories above him. It ended in a large, rectangular trash bin. No doubt it would be filled with jagged chunks of concrete, shards of fiberglass, and twisted rebar, because that was the sort of day he was having.

He cringed when the door to the stairwell moaned. Straining to listen over the sound of his own thudding heart and panting breath, he heard no footsteps or voices. He took the stairs two steps at a time up two stories.

He found the chute.

Judging from what he had seen from the stolen drive on the laptop, he would have a permanent target on his back. He needed to go into hiding. He could trust no one, because the bounty the cook would put on his head would be high.

Such a thought made him remember Renni was dead. With a pang of guilt, he softly apologized to his friend. *We should have been more careful.*

Ivan hoped he wasn't such a bastard that he would have ever betrayed Renni. Perhaps he would never know.

His only hope of survival was to hide and change his identity. He had the money and resources for both. Except he couldn't hide.

Based on what he had seen in those files, he couldn't cower and let events unfold. With that thought, he leaped into the chute and hoped to hell it could withstand the weight of an eighty-five kilogram man.

———

Lillian showered and crawled into bed. The adrenaline rush of her ER confrontation had long since worn off. Now she needed rest.

Warm arms enveloped her. The comfort of them eased the tension in her body.

"You're home late," Sean said, scooting close behind her and burying his face in her hair and into her neck.

She had called him to let him know she'd be late, but one hour late turned into three.

"I had to give a statement to the police. And then there was the documentation." The paperwork was never-ending for a physician. Since she had gotten into an altercation, more paperwork presented itself.

"What'd you do this time?"

"Hey." She rolled toward him. "Why would you assume it's my fault?"

He chuckled as he repositioned to keep her close.

She looked into his warm, brown eyes. Small crow's feet crinkled at the edges. She liked to think all of their laughs and fun times together over the years had created those character lines.

"Okay," she conceded, running a hand through his brown hair and along his firm jawline. "Yes. It was my fault. I turned a wife-beater into a patient."

Sean arched an eyebrow at her. "You think a taste of his own medicine will make him repent and turn over a new leaf?"

"No. But he was harassing my resident, and I wasn't going to stand for that."

He pursed his lips. "Is this something we're going to need legal representation for later?"

"No. It's all on video. He attacked me, and then he drew a gun." She tapered the last few words into a quiet tone as she cringed, waiting for Sean's response.

She felt his body tense around her.

"A gun?"

"A little snub-nose Colt."

"Probably a Cobra."

"Which I identified on him early and was prepared for the draw."

Sean sucked in a deep breath, but kept his voice calm. "I didn't give you combat and weapons training so you could pick fights with belligerent wife-beaters. You should let the police and hospital security handle trouble in the ER."

"I would have, but they had their hands full. If I hadn't intervened, I would have been on the other side of the ER when he opened fire on my resident."

Sean squeezed her tight. She could feel the strong and steady thump of his heart. Her cheek rested against his warm neck.

"I would prefer you on the other side of the room when violence erupts."

"That's not who we are."

He didn't reply, but she felt his throat bob in a swallow. She hadn't meant to make the events of Montreal resurface, yet she knew Sean would be thinking of the day she had been shot. The day she nearly died in his arms.

"You're okay?" he asked.

"I'm okay." She nuzzled her nose into his neck.

"Do you want to talk about it?"

She kissed his neck and the stubble along his jaw brushed her cheek. "Done talking."

He massaged a thumb along her back in small circular motions. "You're still tense."

"What does my secret spy suggest I do about that?" She nipped at his ear.

He sucked in a sharp breath as he pressed his firm body against her. "*Former* spy."

"Sure. Whatever you say."

"I suppose I could share my top secret, for-your-body-only techniques for tension reduction."

She wriggled out of her nightgown. "Show me."

———

DEPARTMENT OF DEFENSE
TOP SECRET
NUCLEAR THREAT INVESTIGATION

CASE FILE: 8966B20
Deputy Director: William Austin
Re: Dr. Lillian Whyte and Agent Sean Jennings

TRANSCRIPT:
DEPARTMENT OF DEFENSE INQUIRY

DOD: You've been involved in quite a few violent altercations in the last several years.
DR. WHYTE: Being an emergency room physician isn't for the faint of heart.

DOD: Do most emergency room physicians disarm gunmen?
DR. WHYTE: Not that I'm aware of.

DOD: But you do.
DR. WHYTE: I've had training.

DOD: After Kenya?
DR. WHYTE: Kenya and Montreal.

DOD: Much like those events, you were face-to-face with international criminals again in this most recent incident.
DR. WHYTE: Was there a question in there?

DOD: It is intriguing and confounding that a civilian with no known ties to the criminal underworld would be entangled on three separate events in international crises.
DR. WHYTE: Agreed.

DOD: Would you say there were any abnormal events prior to your trip to Iceland?
DR. WHYTE: None.

DOD: Not even the detonation of a nuclear weapon out to sea by North Korea?
DR. WHYTE: I wouldn't categorize that as abnormal, no.

<< END SAMPLE CHAPTER>>
GET GRAY HORIZON NOW!